WHERE *Grace* GROWS

Secrets of Skyline: Dottie

Written by
TERRI ROSA FOX

First published by Terri Fox Creatives 2026

Edited by Kinzee Baker & Heather Smith

Cover art created and designed by Terri Rosa Fox.

First edition

Dedication

To God, who makes all things new with His abounding grace and mercy.

To anyone who felt they weren’t deserving of such love, remember God calls you *treasured.*

Content Warning

Reader discretion is advised.

This novel explores themes of unwed pregnancy, unwanted male attention, and moments of physical or emotional intimidation.

This book contains G-rated Anti-Italian racial slurs by one character which may be offensive to some readers. The actions, thoughts, and/or beliefs of said character in this book do not portray the thoughts, actions, and/or beliefs of the author.

These elements are essential to the characters' emotional journeys and are depicted with care and discretion.

While all are handled with care and sensitivity, readers who are sensitive to such topics may wish to proceed with awareness.

Disclaimer

Grab the FREE Where Grace Grows Devotional by joining the Joy Bearer Newsletter.

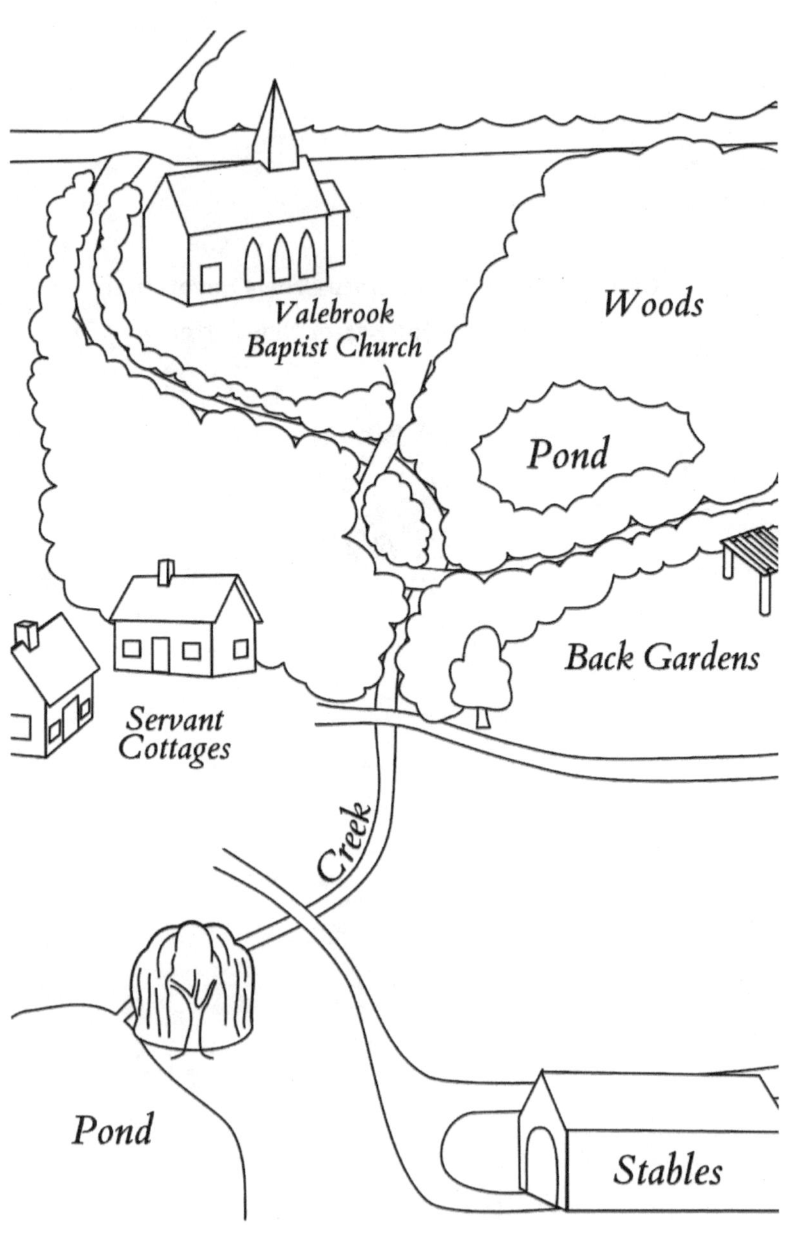
Valebrook
Baptist Church
Woods
Pond
Back Gardens
Servant
Cottages
Creek
Pond
Stables

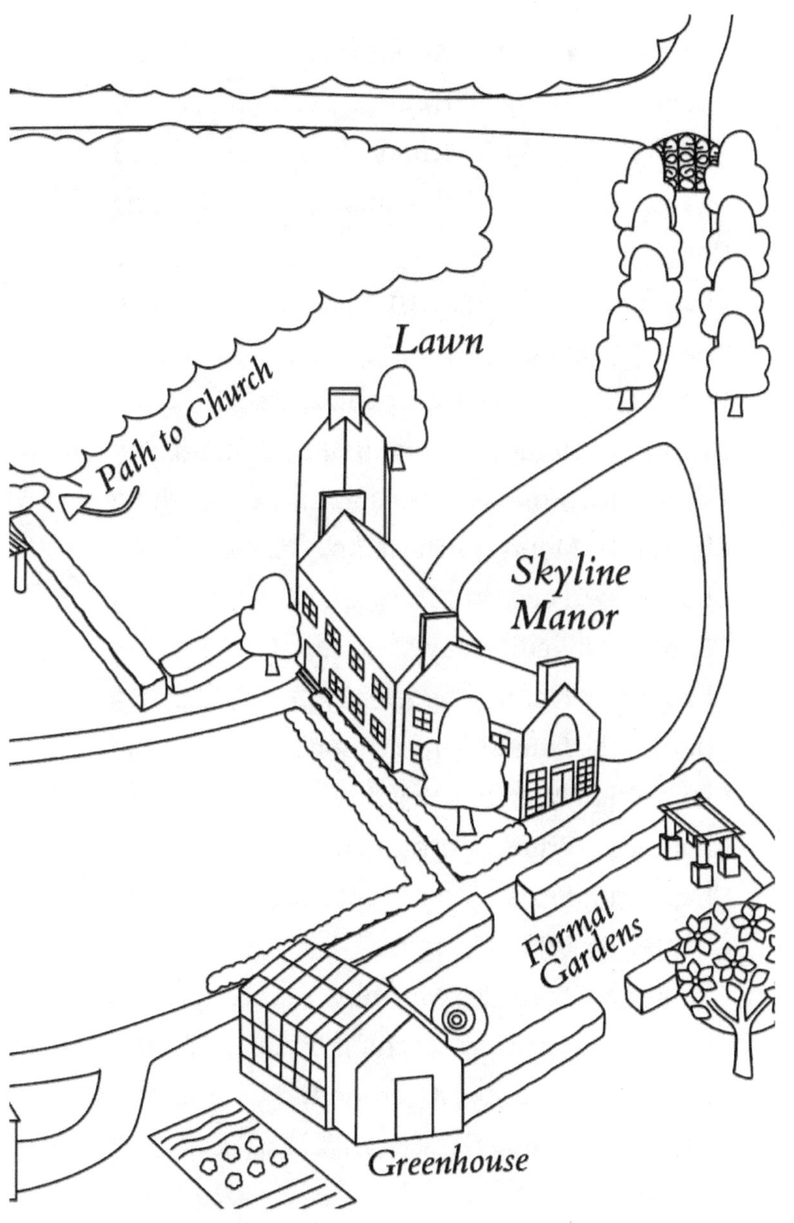
Lawn
Path to Church
Skyline
Manor
Formal
Gardens
Greenhouse

Contents

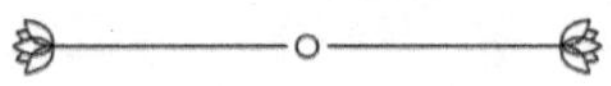

Character Guide

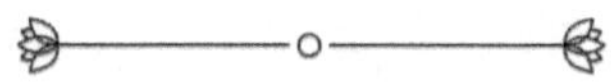

Romano Family
Salvatore "Sal" - 50s - Gardner & Estate Maintenance
Carmela - 50s - Head Cook
Antonio - 20s - Gardener & Maintenance
Vincent - 13 - Student
Anna - 9 - Student

West Family
Leland West - 30s – Retired Detective & Estate Manager
Mae Hopper West - 30s - Parlor Maid
Rose & Violet Hopper - 10 - Twin Daughters

Stratford Family
William Stratford - 60s - Patriarch
Beatrice - 60s - Matriarch
Frederick - 30s - Oldest Son; Head of Household
Philip - 27 - Second Son; Deceased
Daphne - 23 - Youngest Daughter; Heiress

Van Buren Family
Florence - 60s - Widow
Genevieve - 24 - Heiress

Skyline Staff
Eleanor "Nell" Brower - 50s - Head Housekeeper
Walter Griggs - 60s - Butler
Dottie DeGrout - 20 - Parlor Maid/Kitchen Maid
Clara Langdon - 18 - Chambermaid
Katie Douglas - 18 - Kitchen/Scullery Maid
Maria Ireland - 20s - Kitchen/Parlor
Bessie - Teenager - Junior Maid
Timothy Brooks - 20s - Footman
Henry Kelly 20s - Footman
Helen Sindle - 40s - Laundry Maid

Valebrook Community
Thomas Somers - 30s - Pastor
Joseph Somers - 10 - Son
Doctor Winston - 50s - Town Doctor
Charlie Rolston - 20s - Radiator Repair

Italian Words

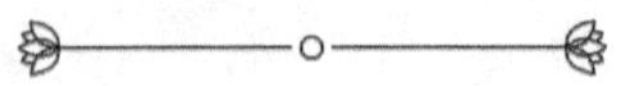

Tesoro: "You're my Treasure"; Sweetheart; Darling

Zeppole: A traditional Italian fried dough balls, like doughnuts, typically served warm, dusted with powdered sugar, and sometimes filled with cream or jelly.

Piccola: My little one

Che disastro!: What a disaster!

Cara: Dear

Stunad: Fool

Furioso: Furious

Padre: Father

Signore Dio: Lord God

Che serpente: What a snake.

Buon Ragazzo: Good boy

Bambinas: Girls

Sorella: Sister

To the praise of the glory of His grace, by which He made us accepted in the Beloved.

In Him we have redemption through His blood, the forgiveness of sins, according to the riches of His grace.

Ephesians 1: 6-7 NKJV

My grace is sufficient for you:

for My strength is made perfect in weakness.

2 Corinthians 12:9 NKJV

Chapter 1: Thursday Morning

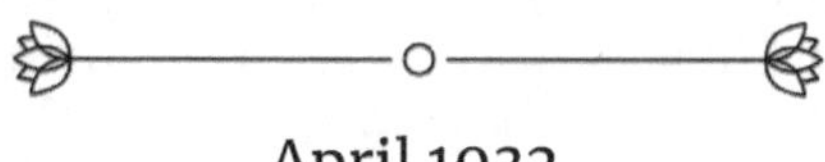

April 1932

Coming down the servant stairs, Dottie's faded shoe hit the last step just as the hall clock chimed six. The clock didn't care that morning should begin when the sun crests the trees, when the fortunate still slept idly in bed. At its appointed hour, the chime rang out all the same, whether Dottie welcomed it or not.

As she scurried into the kitchen, she tied a cotton kerchief around her tawny, copper hair. Tugging the dull cloth snugly against her nape, feeling the soft weave against her fingers.

If only my apron could be this smooth.

"Eh, *Tesoro*, you're late! Start on the onions, we need them for this morning's frittatas!" Mrs. Carmela Romano's voice rang through the kitchen, firm but not unkind. Though she scolded Dottie, a grin reached the Skyline Manor head cook's deep brown eyes. Her flour-dusted apron and the faint aroma of roasted garlic seemed as much a part of her as the care she showed to those around her.

Shaking her head, Dottie wondered if the older woman would ever stop slipping in her Italian words.

Frittatas are just fancy eggs and sausage, nothing more.

"Yes, Mrs. Romano, straight away." She found the items already laid out on the worktable; the hub in which everything in the kitchen revolved around. The worn, smooth oak table, while nicked and dented, still stood solid under the daily tasks set upon it.

Dottie hurried to the porcelain-coated basin in the corner, remembering Mrs. Romano's reminder from her first day. *"We cook with clean hands,* Tesoro. *Always."* Pumping water over a sliver of soap tied with string, Dottie shivered as the icy trickle bit at her skin while she scrubbed.

Returning to the worktable, she slipped past Mrs. Romano, careful not to bump the unpredictable stove with her hip. More than once, a careless nudge had sent the coals blazing, with a rush of heat skimming her apron.

She brushed her bangs from her forehead while chopping the onions, her amber eyes stung with tears. Each move of the knife was in time with the drip from the tap. Mrs. Romano insisted they were paper-thin for the egg dish that would soon sizzle in the skillet. And she strove to live up to the cook's expectations, especially since she was the sole kitchen maid now.

Mrs. Romano had kicked up a fuss over every kitchen maid before Dottie, and she had braced for the same. Yet somehow, the woman gave her more patience than she deserved. Her embrace was always soft, like a well-worn pillow, warm and reassuring. Dottie never understood why she was spared from the cook's harsh judgment, but she was grateful.

But for as welcomed as Mrs. Romano tried to make Dottie feel in the kitchen, welcomed she was not. Since her demotion, some of the help made it their daily mission to remind her just how far she'd fallen.

As Dottie set the onions on the skillet, oil popped and sizzled, leaving a splattering on her apron. Shifting away, she was unaware of the scullery maid directly behind her.

Katie carried a wooden bucket reserved for washing floors. As she came closer, her elbow connected with Dottie's spine. Murky water sloshed over the edge, soaking the kitchen maid's back in a cold chill and sending a splash across the skillet, dousing the onions in a pungent bath.

A curse threatened to escape Dottie's mouth as water squelched in her shoes. Forcing her temper down, she bit her tongue. *It'll do no good to lash out.*

Katie continued walking, tossing a half-hearted, "M'apologies, Dottie. Didn't see you there," without so much as a glance.

Dottie knew snapping at the scullery maid's action would do no good. "No worries, Katie. Accidents happen." But as she scooped the soggy onions off the stove and dumped them into the garbage pail, the look Katie gave told her it was no accident.

Just shy of eighteen, Katie thought she knew everything, despite her trail of mistakes in the kitchen. She'd been bitter ever since Dottie took the role of kitchen maid and she found herself bumped to the lower position. The girl took every opportunity to make Dottie's job more difficult.

Yet, Dottie never spoke a word. Not to her friend Mae, and certainly not to Mrs. Romano. She feared if she complained, she'd lose the only kindness left to her. Keeping her position felt like a saving grace, but she knew better than to believe it could last. Eventually, the Stratfords would throw her out, just like the soiled onions.

As Dottie returned to chopping fresh onions, Maria swept into the kitchen. Dipping her head, the parlor maid whispered to Bessie, a new junior maid, on their way to the servant hall. "My brother told me the breadlines in Silkrow were three blocks long. It's fortunate we have these jobs, not everyone is so lucky."

Focused on the knife lifting and dicing, Dottie agreed. *Fortunate, indeed. If I'm not careful, I'll be in that breadline soon enough.* Still, she kept herself focused on the blade's steady scratch and *shick*, each slice marking its own quiet rhythm.

Maria's voice carried over the sounds of the kitchen. "There she is, the cast off... I'm surprised they'd let her stay." The woman's laughter lingered in the room a beat too long, as if she'd planned the rumor and then watched to see who fed it.

Ever since Maria's promotion out of the kitchen, she never failed to remind Dottie exactly where her place was. Bessie struggled to keep up, her cap askew, giggling as they turned toward the servant hall.

Trying to ignore the jab, Dottie cut through the onion meticulously, watching each layer fall. Gossip moved quicker than steam in this house, and she'd learned the hard way, truth was rarely invited along for the ride.

Then, Maria's newest gossip caught her off guard, causing her grip to falter, the blade nearly catching her fingertip.

"Did you hear? Antonio was unable to fix the water pump yesterday. Took him three hours to get it working. Heard he broke it on purpose!" Bessie gasped as the parlor maid continued. "Something about being upset with

Mr. Leland..." With the servant hall door closed behind them, their voices faded.

Fetching a clean skillet, Dottie glanced at the back door, expecting to see the gardener. A flicker of disappointment passed through her as she mused, "Antonio would never.

If they knew anything, they'd know he respects Mr. Leland. And Mrs. Romano wouldn't take kindly to anyone badmouthing her son."

Her mind wandered while the onions hissed on the skillet. But he has been avoiding everyone lately...

Maybe he's angry. Or maybe it's just me...

She remembered how Mr. Sal used to brag about his son's work ethic and capabilities. Antonio would light up when talking about repairs, taking pride in his work. But last week, he'd barely muttered a word when Mr. Griggs, the butler, asked about the leaky pipe.

Something had shifted in the manor. The air in the halls seemed heavier, as though carrying secrets Dottie wasn't meant to know.

It makes no sense.

Antonio used to smile at her and steal bashful glances, kind words slipping out now and then, tender and unforced. Not like other men, whose compliments carried a motive. Antonio's felt honest. Like he saw something in her beyond her beauty. Something good.

Mrs. Romano called out from her station. "*Mamma mia*, Dottie, don't let the onions caramelize; we only want them to sweat!" Dottie jumped, immediately spooning the onions into a dish.

From the other side of the room, a charming voice, full of confidence and mischief, chimed in. "Mrs. Romano, don't you know the best onions are sweet? Just like Dottie." She turned to find Timothy, the footman, smiling at her. "Morning, Dottie. Didn't think the day could be this good 'til I saw you." His striking blue eyes winked as he passed through the kitchen.

Dottie gave a slow eye roll, but heat still crept up her neck. *Foolish.* For him, it was only a bit of fun, nothing more. But if she wasn't careful, Timothy could make her forget the cost of being noticed. He had a way of making her feel desired, and she'd enjoyed the attention.

Or any other man's, for that matter.

She once floated through the front rooms, polished and pretty, soaking in every glance from men who mattered. Proof she was worth something. Now, she was a shadow below stairs, stripped of the smiles and stares that had once convinced her she was meant for more.

Dottie's expression clouded for a second. Only a few knew her secret, and a secret that would soon reveal itself.

I'm practically ruined. Soon enough no one will want me.

There was no time to linger on such thoughts; breakfast was waiting.

As Dottie sliced bread, her friend's sweet laughter echoed from the servant hall. Glancing up, she spotted Mae in mid-hug with her fiancé, Mr. Leland, the estate manager. And Mae only had eyes for him.

Suddenly, Maria's laughter chimed in from across the room. Making as if keeping a secret, she whispered loudly to Bessie, "I met with him just yesterday, and he wants to meet again this afternoon. I'm so excited!" Dottie wondered who Maria's new beau was, but it made no difference, as long as the woman stopped causing trouble.

Timothy shot Maria a sharp glare, quick and cutting. There was no mistaking how his face morphed into one of sheer annoyance.

But Dottie's attention quickly diverted back to Mae and Mr. Leland. Their wedding was just over a week away, and she was happy for them. Yet, a small pang tightened her chest, a reminder of the devotion she longed to feel herself. She yearned for a man to care for her exactly as she was. She once thought she had it, but she'd learned that love and desire weren't always the same thing.

Just then, Mrs. Brower stepped through the pantry door and calmly cleared her throat. Dottie stifled a giggle as Mae and Mr. Leland awkwardly broke apart. Mae's expression quickly warmed when she spotted Dottie across the room. With a quick kiss to her fiancé, he left the kitchen.

"Good morning, Dear Dottie."

The nickname was something Mae had started a few months back. At first, Dottie bristled at the endearment, but now, she knew Mae meant it and she embraced this newfound friendship. Mae leaned in and whispered, "And how are we feeling today?"

"We're feeling quite fabulous. Spring's here, and happy days ahead." Dottie beamed, but the words felt forced. Sometimes it was hard to believe happiness could come her way.

She'd recently learned of God's love and that He cared for her, but it didn't feel like enough. Not when she felt unworthy, unloved, and unwanted.

Mae studied her, not being fooled by the false smile. "Dottie, days will get better. Have faith. And remember, you can always come to me or Mrs. Brower to talk."

Faith seemed to come so easily to Mae, yet for Dottie, doubts crowded her mind.

With a mischievous glint, she swiped the heel of bread Dottie was slicing, added a slathering of butter and set it on a plate. "Now, before Mrs. Carmela notices, eat! You need more food."

"What's that I hear?" Mrs. Romano rounded on them. "Sneaking bread, Mae? *Piccola*, you know better!" But the wink Mrs. Romano gave was permission enough to indulge in the treat. Dottie giggled as she took a bite, melted butter escaping the side of her mouth.

Mae hugged her shoulders. "I'll see you later." Turning to leave, she paused mid-step. "Oh, and don't forget, I'll still want your help with flowers for next Saturday! You come up with the most beautiful arrangements."

Dottie nodded, swallowing the last piece of bread. "Let's meet tomorrow during break and decide!" Her smile strained. Mae had asked her to be a bridesmaid—*imagine that.*

It would've been lovely to wear a nice dress instead of her drab uniform and flour-dusted apron. But what would people say, seeing her up there in a borrowed dress? With the shame of her past trailing behind her. No, Dottie had declined. "I'd ruin her day just by standing beside her."

"Ruin what, *Tesoro*?" Dottie jumped, the knife nearly slipping from her grasp. She hadn't noticed Mrs. Romano coming up beside her.

"Nothing, Mrs. Romano. Everything's right on task." Expecting her expression betray her feelings, Dottie kept her head low. Mrs. Romano was known for spotting truths no one else could see, and Dottie wasn't sure she was ready for that.

"Mmm, good, good," the older woman patted Dottie's shoulder. "But be sure, nothing's ever ruined. Sometimes slightly bruised." As Mrs. Romano hurried over to the stove, Dottie could hear her muttering, "Even bruised can be used."

The woman confused Dottie sometimes, but she knew Mrs. Romano's kindness was no act. She was warm to Mae and her daughters, never held back from spoiling Dottie with an extra treat, and always had words of wisdom that only an Italian woman could get away with saying with a smile on her face.

Dottie giggled as she thought back to a month before when Mrs. Romano was excited to make Spring Fritters, or as she called them, *Zeppole.* Dottie had been eager to try one of the fried dough treats, covered in powdered sugar. So eager, that she reached for them straight from the sizzling skillet. Mrs. Romano smacked her hand and mumbled, "Take things too quick, and get burned, *Tesoro.* That's the kind of eagerness that'll earn you a blister and a lesson."

In the end, Mrs. Romano gave her an entire batch of the sweet treats. "See what happens when you learn waiting?" She called over her shoulder as if nothing special had happened. "You walk off with the whole batch."

No wonder Mr. Sal always gazed at her hungrily. She could scold and sweet-talk in the same breath! Dottie wished for a love like theirs. But a girl like her didn't get the dress, the altar, or the man.

Best to remember that.

For now, her love would be found in peeling potatoes and whisking eggs to perfection before the parlor maids came in to deliver the Stratford's breakfast.

The day continued in the usual rhythm—pots to scrub, ovens to heat, trays to prepare, until the house grew quiet once more. By nightfall, Dottie's feet ached. The evening air had cooled her bedroom, giving her a reprieve from the constant heat of the kitchen. Her only light was the oil lamp flickering on her dresser, casting dark shadows across the old floor.

A shiver ran through her as her bleary eyes played tricks on the shadows, almost making her think someone was standing in the corner. She shook off the feeling. No one would be in here uninvited. Using her fingers to comb out her braid, Dottie wished for easier days. Her bed frame creaked as she drifted into a fitful sleep, dreaming of things she had no business wanting.

Chapter 2: Friday Morning

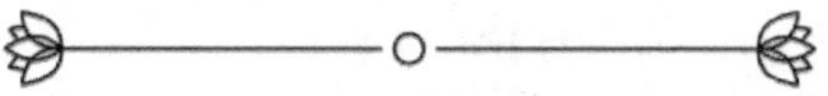

Dottie's lashes fluttered open, waking from habit before the hall clock sounded. White puffs of breath escaped into the air, and a chill racked through her body. Though the blanket was thin, and springs pinched her side, she groaned at the thought of leaving the bed.

April had arrived in Valebrook, and though the flowers were blooming, New Jersey mornings still held a biting cold. Stretching her arms toward the ceiling to loosen her stiff joints, she glared at the offender.

The radiator sat in the corner. Broken. Again. It hissed and sputtered, giving an angry rattle. It didn't care that she was freezing or that she was tired of wearing two pairs of stockings to bed every evening.

Ever since the Crash of '29, keeping radiators running felt like a miracle. Coal cost more than most families could spare, and every furnace seemed to know it.

Easing from her bed, Dottie's feet curled against the chilly floorboards. *Maybe a wood stove would suit us better; there's enough forest nearby to warm the earth twice over.*

Yet Mr. Leland had done wonders updating Skyline Manor's servant quarters in recent months—fresh paint, sealed windows, and cozy rooms. Everything felt a bit warmer and brighter. All except her radiator. He'd already sent for an expert three times.

"Why can't Charlie fix it?" She kicked at the infernal contraption.

Charlie Rolston, the radiator repair man, was handsome enough, with ocean blue eyes that always swept her way when he passed through. Like other men she'd known, he had a way of making her feel desirable.

Pulling her uniform from the dresser, it smelled faintly of soap and the lingering aroma of Mrs. Romano's bread, sweet and buttery. She inhaled deeply, finding a small comfort in the familiar scent.

Her fingers moved fast over the buttons, but it was becoming more difficult to fasten the ones around her midsection. The stiff fabric resisted as she forced each smooth button through its hole. "I need to lay off the treats Mrs. Romano slides my way, or I won't be able to wear this uniform much longer."

She thought back to Charlie's easy smile and unbridled flirtations.

"Mind if I take my time on this job? Feels like a shame to hurry when I'm workin' near someone like you."

Though she told herself he was just teasing, after a month of supposed repairs, her radiator remained stubbornly cold.

Dottie's cheek warmed at the idea of a man wanting to spend time with her, of all people. She knew she shouldn't enjoy his attention, for any man would go running once they knew her secret.

Smoothing her uniform, Dottie never expected at twenty to find herself still scrubbing pots and waiting on others. She gathered her hair into a tight bun, wincing as she twisted the last pin into place. The gesture felt like penance. Grabbing her kerchief, she rushed out her door.

And straight into Katie.

The collision sent Dottie stumbling back against the wall, knocking the breath from her. Her hand pressed firmly against the papered wall, bracing for conflict that always followed the girl.

The scullery maid appeared caught, like she was lurking where she shouldn't be. "G'morning," she mumbled, hurrying off before Dottie could so much as open her mouth. Shoes tapping firmly against the floorboards, she shot a final weary glance in Dottie's direction.

Strange girl.

Dottie shook off the uneasy feeling that Katie left with. Reaching down to get her kerchief, she noticed Katie had dropped a letter, neatly folded and full of words. She couldn't help but wonder what secrets the letter held but knew nosiness would only cause her trouble. "I'll get it to her when I head down. Then I need to tell Mr. Leland about the radiator."

Breakfast was prepared without incident. Fluffy omelets, perfectly cooked sausage, and the sweet rolls rose to perfection. Mrs. Romano sang out while kneading the dough for afternoon bread, puffs of powdery haze billowing into the air. "Thanks be to God for the sunshine today."

Dottie chuckled seeing flour speckled across the older woman's nose and threw a rag at her. "Mrs. Romano, you've missed a few spots here and here." Dottie pointed to her own nose.

"Ah, thank you, *Tesoro,* I can't have my Sal seeing me in such a state when he comes in for lunch later!" She quickly wiped her face and set the dough to rise.

Dottie went back to preparing stock for the evening meal, watching the broth bubble while soft pops released the scent of roasted carrots and herbs into the kitchen. Maria waltzed in. "Oh, Dottie." Letting the name stretch, the parlor maid tossed a piece of half-eaten toast on the worktable.

"Mrs. Stratford insisted the toast be corrected. She stressed it should be lightly browned, not burned to a crisp." Her voice dropped with cold satisfaction as she looked down her nose. Maria was smart, she'd often wait for Mae to be out of earshot or for Mrs. Romano to busy herself before chewing Dottie out. But this time, Mrs. Romano heard.

"Toast?! Oh, no, no." She picked up the offending piece. "We had no toast on the menu today." Mrs. Romano looked at Dottie. "Did you make a mistake, *Tesoro?*"

Katie's scoff sounded behind her, but she refused to turn around as a sinking feeling settled in the pit of her stomach. "No, Mrs. Romano, I made no toast, only sweet rolls and hard rolls today." Someone had slipped the burnt toast onto Mrs. Stratford's tray, *but who?*

Mrs. Romano *tsked*, shaking her head. "Dottie, clean the pots along with Katie. I'll sort this out."

She knew she was in trouble when Mrs. Romano didn't call her "*Tesoro.*" Holding back the pressure that built up behind her eyes, she whispered, "Yes, ma'am." As she brushed past the head cook and kept her head low. "But I didn't ruin breakfast."

The rest of Mrs. Romano's conversation with Maria was muffled as Dottie fought her swirling thoughts.

I know I didn't make toast, so why'd Mrs. Romano side with Maria? Why am I always being kicked to the bottom?

She reached for a large pot in the sink full of sudsy water, and began scrubbing, hoping the action would distract her. Small bubbles clung to her skin, slightly dampening the sleeve of her dress.

But Katie's satisfied smirk said there'd be no escaping the drama. "Funny how sometimes what's meant to be sweet ends up a little... crispier than planned." She shoved Dottie sideways. "And you actually thought Mrs. Romano would choose you over Maria, didn't you?"

Dottie knew she shouldn't stoop to the girl's level, but the girl irritated her. Fingers still wet, she reached into her apron pocket. "You're right, somehow I made a mistake, I forgot to give this to you when we were busy." She held up Katie's letter, now wrinkled and smeared from the water. The letters that once curled now drooped as they bled into each other.

The scullery maid snatched it and tucked it into her pocket. "How dare you!" She stepped closer, knocking the pot from Dottie's hand, causing it to fall with a loud bang. "Why would you have that?"

"You dropped it this morning when we bumped into each other." Dottie's feet slipped from the spilled water, and she grabbed hold of the sink, trying to stay upright. "I'm simply trying to return it!"

"*Mama Mia!* Girls, stop at once!" Mrs. Romano's voice rose above their shouting. "Katie, clean this mess immediately! And Dottie, Mr. Rolston is here to see to your radiator. Find Mr. Leland and inform him."

With the argument interrupted, Dottie glanced at the back door, and sure enough, Charlie was there, with his tousled blonde hair, walking toward her. He stared at her with a hunger that made her want to be kissed, causing her breath to catch.

Her reply was quick. "Yes ma'am!" Taking a step back, she slipped on water, her foot coming out from under her. Just before she hit the tiled floor, Charlie's arm wrapped around her waist.

A breathless "thank you" escaped her lips. Her pulse thrummed, either due to the near fall or from Charlie's nearness, but she'd never know.

Why does it feel so nice to be wrapped in someone's arms?

Realizing herself, Dottie quickly found her footing and forced Charlie's arm from around her waist. "Mr. Rolston, let me escort you to Mr. West." She would never disrespect Mae's fiancé by using his given name in front of outsiders; some things were meant to be kept inside the family.

Family.

"My pleasure, Miss DeGrout. I'll follow you anywhere." Charlie's charming smile found hers as he picked up his tools.

Though she knew he was just being nice, Dottie's cheeks heated at the compliment. She quickly escorted Charlie from the room, ready to escape from Katie's temper and the hurt she felt at Mrs. Romano brushing her off.

It had taken Charlie nearly two hours to fix the radiator. Each time she thought about returning to the kitchen, he had another question, or another comment, keeping her nearby.

On their way back to the kitchen, her mind was occupied with all the work that had been done to the hall, and not by the man walking beside her. The wallpaper was light, and a faint breeze of spring floated through the air. It was a treasure compared to the deteriorating corridors they once were.

When Dottie caught a whiff of something meaty, her stomach rumbled. Her hand quickly rested over it to silence the sound.

"Easy now, if you keep that up, I'll have to start visiting daily just to keep the peace." Charlie pressed his shoulder against hers, glancing her way. "Maybe I'll stay for lunch, if Mrs. Romano'll let me."

Dottie blushed at his invitation, but he wouldn't be coming around much longer. Earlier, Mr. Leland had expressed his frustrations regarding the heater, mumbling, *"We'll just need to replace it."*

"Mr. West, I can fix this, trust me. Give me one more chance, and if not, I'll replace it myself." Charlie's response sounded sincere. And as much as Dottie would miss Charlie's flirtations, she was glad her radiator would be fixed at last. She sighed at the idea of a warm room.

Misinterpreting her sigh, Charlie suddenly squeezed her hand, pausing her musings. His hands were cold, and she resisted the temptation to pull away.

"I'm serious, Dottie. I'd come back every day if it meant I got a chance to see your face." He seemed earnest, but something in Charlie's expression shifted, catching Dottie off-guard.

As they stepped down the servant stairs, she half-expected her heart to flutter, instead an unexpected feeling of dread settled in her middle. Before she could respond to his compliment, Mrs. Romano's warm voice filled the room. "Ah, *Tesoro*, you're finally back! I've kept lunch for you!"

She looked up to find Mr. Sal, Mrs. Romano, Antonio, and Katie eating at the worktable. She couldn't help but notice how closely Katie sat to Antonio, and unbidden, Dottie's jealousy rose.

It was as if the girl knew how it affected Dottie, as she leaned in closer to his side, and cooed, "I saw how lovely a job you did on the boxwoods yesterday, perfectly trimmed like always."

So obviously flirting.

Antonio cleared his throat, easing back from the closeness. His attention landed on Dottie, then darted away the moment their eyes met.

Her fingers curled into her apron at his mixed signals.

Does he want help... or simply to confuse me?

Easing the tension, Mrs. Romano fussed over making space for the newcomers. Dottie shook off her jealousy and agitation, letting the apron slip from her fingers.

Antonio isn't my concern.

But as she took her seat, Charlie by her side, awareness had her attention flicked back to Antonio. His chocolate-brown gaze bore into hers, the same rich hue as the earth he worked each day, and she couldn't turn away. It wasn't like the flirtatious stares from other men. No, his pulled her in and made her feel seen. Protected. As if only he could keep her heart safe.

The fragile shelter of his gaze crumbled when Charlie wrapped his arm around Dottie, leaning in close. "Could you pass me the salt?" His breath reached her ear, and she fought back a shiver.

Glancing back to Antonio, Dottie saw his face cloud over and brow crease as if Charlie was an unwelcomed intruder.

Why's he angry? Has Charlie done something wrong?

Her hand trembled under the pressure of both men watching her with such intensity. And all Dottie wanted was to enjoy a quiet lunch, not navigate the baffling emotions of men.

Distracting herself from Antonio's powerful stare, she fixed a sandwich from leftover hard rolls and corned beef hash. She was glad to see the Stratfords hadn't eaten all the orange slices and canned peaches from breakfast. But before she could add the treat to her plate, Katie snatched the bowl.

"These are fine fruits, aren't they? Would you like some, Antonio?" Her voice dripped with sweetness that made Dottie's chest tight.

What is their relationship anyway?

But Antonio didn't seem to notice Katie's intent. Instead, he remained fixated on Charlie's grip around Dottie, his jaw ticking like a pulse.

Charlie chuckled. "You good there, Antonio?" His arm constricted around her. Though casual to the eye, his grip felt possessive, too deliberate to be accidental. She worried whether the pressure would leave a bruise.

Blinking twice, Antonio pulled his focus back to the table. When he finally noticed Katie holding the bowl toward him, she repeated her question. "Do you want some sweet fruit, Antonio?"

"Ah, no." Shaking his head, a loose wave of hair tumbled down across his forehead. Dottie wasn't sure why, but her hand itched to brush it away.

As if sensing her thoughts, Antonio took the offered bowl and turned toward her. "But I believe Dottie would enjoy some. Yes?"

Confused, Dottie glanced at Katie. The girl fumed in her seat, eyes flashing with aggravation.

Why's Antonio ignoring her?

Everyone waited for her response, and Dottie felt exposed under their expectant stares. "Yes. Thank you, Antonio. I'd like some."

Antonio's hand spanned the entire base of the bowl, leaving Dottie no option but for their fingers to meet. The faint warmth of his skin lingered a heartbeat longer than it should have, differing from the cool ceramic bowl. Tingles danced up her arm at the touch.

But before she had time to note the feeling, Charlie yanked the bowl, thumping it on the table.

"Say, Antonio, I'd love to shadow you this afternoon, learn what you do. Thinking of leaving the radiator business and getting into general maintenance. What do you say?" Charlie's fingers dug into her arm, blocking her body from shifting away. She muffled a whimper with a bite of her sandwich, the sound barely escaping.

If Antonio had appeared irritated before, Dottie watched his expression darken with more fury. "Ah, no. There's no time to teach you this afternoon. We have our hands full with the spring gardens, and Mr. Leland has a task list for updating the Skyline Manor's facade."

Antonio pushed his chair back with a force, banging into the counter behind him, leaving his lunch unfinished.

Putting his hand up in surrender, Charlie left Dottie's shoulder cold. Yet, she could finally relax without his added pressure. "No harm, friend. Just wanted to learn."

"That's no way to treat our neighbor, Antonio!" Mr. Sal stood, extending his hand to Charlie. "We'd be happy for ya help. Come. Find us after you eat."

Walking toward Antonio, Mr. Sal mumbled something about ungrateful children and whacked Antonio on the back of the head. "Let's cool off in the garden, get our hands dirty."

Antonio's gaze found Dottie's once more just before ducking out the back door. For a moment, what appeared to be distress flickered across his face. And she wasn't sure, but possibly a bit of hope too.

Did he feel the tingles as well when our hands met?

"Back to work, girls. The kitchen won't clean itself and dinner needs fixing." Mrs. Romano sounded as weary as she looked worried.

"Yes, ma'am. I'll check the stew and shape the dough." She took off to her tasks while Katie cleared the worktable.

Charlie finished his meal, but still lingered enough to observe Dottie while she worked. "Well, lovely ladies, it was a delight! I'll be seeing you, hopefully real soon!" When he walked out the door, he flashed a cheeky smile to Dottie. And she noticed he didn't hesitate to wink at Katie, too.

Dottie bristled, sometimes he was too forward.

When did I start thinking this way?

Pausing, mid-stir, she was never one to think a man's attention was "too much," yet, here she was feeling slightly sickened by Charlie's. Maybe it was because once he knew her secret, he'd lose interest. No one stuck around long.

Not her mother.

Not Philip.

Not anyone.

Or maybe she was seeing in those around her that attraction and love were completely different.

Isn't someone pining over me worth pursuing? God, I don't understand...

She twisted the wooden spoon nervously while she watched the stew swirl, carrots and onions bobbing idly to the top.

But maybe You do.

Chapter 3: Friday Afternoon

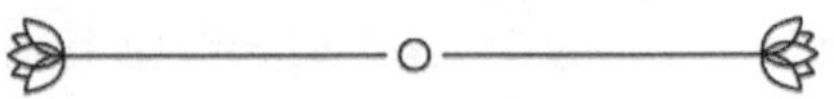

Dottie didn't see Antonio or Charlie the rest of the afternoon. Mae interrupted her work with a short visit, reminding her of their late afternoon meeting. Tea time came with little trouble, and dinner preparations were in full motion with beef stew simmering on the stove. The hardy aroma of onions and salty meat wafted through the air.

Peeking into the oven to observe the bread browning perfectly, Dottie found it fascinating to watch a pile of mush transform into something beautiful and delicious. It was what she hoped for in herself, to become something more. Smiling to herself, Dottie grabbed a knife to chop vegetables and noticed the calluses forming on her palms. They were small, but evidence of hours spent in the kitchen. Reality pressed in, stealing her smile.

Being something more is nothing but a dream.

Timothy swept in bringing a message to Mrs. Romano. But before he left, he passed close to Dottie, and leaned over her shoulder. "Mind your fingers. Be a shame if the prettiest hands in the manor were nicked in place of a carrot."

A laugh slipped out before she could stop it. He'd always been a tease, finding ways to win the attention of a girl. She always tried to hide the way his attention flustered her, but he always saw through it.

She remembered the early days, when he arrived at Skyline, as a timid hallboy without experience. But the moment he stepped into his footman position, the real Timothy appeared.

She threw a sideways glance at the man.

Or maybe he's just as insecure as I am, simply hiding behind a mask of confidence.

The thought caught her off guard. She wasn't used to thinking of men that way—uncertain, a little lost. It made her chest tighten with something like pity, or maybe understanding. Perhaps everyone was just pretending not to struggle.

"You'd better get back to the parlor before Mrs. Stratford worries where her favorite footman went off to." She waved her hand toward the door.

He chuckled. "I have time, Henry's tending the pampered family." Popping a carrot slice in his mouth, he gave a dimpled grin. "And if I rush off now, I'm not sure when I'll get to see your radiant beauty again."

Though she enjoyed his attention, a flutter of apprehension settled in the pit of her stomach. Katie shot Timothy a fleeting, tense look, and Dottie couldn't place why it unsettled her.

It's probably just my imagination.

But even with her chest squeezing with worry, she continued to focus on the vegetables.

Resting his hip on the table, he casually crossed his arms across his chest. "Actually, Mrs. Stratford asked me to fetch her a shawl. Says the brisk wind will make her ill."

Why you and not the parlor maids? But something in his posture told her he'd rather gossip than answer questions.

He leaned in close, dropping his voice to a whisper. "Honestly, the only thing making her ill is the ice in her veins." His lips curled up into a smile, but his eyes lacked the same humor.

Before Dottie could warn him of his errant words, Mrs. Romano swept between them like a barrier. Her knuckles tightened around a rolling pin, as if she was preparing for battle. "Best you get back to your post, Mr. Brooks." She held no kindness or humor in her voice. And there was a hint of something else. A wariness that made the hairs on Dottie's arms rise.

The woman's reaction seemed so different from her usual warmth.

Maybe he's just in the way. Or maybe Mrs. Romano is still angry with me for what happened this morning.

She shook off the worry, her tasks stealing her focus.

As Dottie finished preparing the vegetables for a salad, Miss Edith Sinclair, the upper maid, walked in. She'd been at the manor most of her life and held an air of authority in the way she spoke with the others. "Miss

DeGrout, I've been sent to relieve you of your duties before dinner. I'll be performing your tasks for the time being."

Furrowing her brows, Dottie asked, "Have I done something wrong?" She'd been in trouble enough that day, there was nothing else she could think of.

Miss Sinclair waved her hand and smirked.

Dottie tilted her head, never having seen such an expression on the upper maid's face.

"No, nothing like that, Miss DeGrout. Mrs. Romano and Mrs. Brower, have agreed that you take some time to meet Miss Hopper in the gardens."

Dottie's mouth formed an "o" as she recalled Mae's meeting to discuss wedding flowers. "Let me check with Mrs. Romano first." Turning, she saw the older woman holding a woven basket.

"No need to find me, it's all been arranged. Take this and find Mae in the gardens. Miss Edith's been here long enough to fill your role for a time." Mrs. Romano set the basket on the table and turned Dottie toward the back door. She began untying the kitchen maid's apron. "Your apron is useless among flowers. We'll leave it here."

Dottie feared they were buttering her up, only to toss her away later. It was all too familiar. Staring at the door, she remembered the day before her mother cast her out.

Mrs. DeGrout had been abandoned by her husband, leaving her to care for five children. They stood in the kitchen rolling dough when her mother brushed flour from Dottie's cheeks and peered at her lovingly. "Daughter, I think we'll go on a trip tomorrow. We'll have fun, so wear your best dress." When the next morning arrived, she worked a comb through her tangled hair, smoothed her dress. She polished her shoes, though the scuffs remained.

Gazing at the floor, Dottie saw her shoes no longer held a shine. The black leather was worn and creased.

"Miss DeGrout, are you well?"

Dottie heard the upper maid's words, but they muffled against her memory. She thought she heard the steps creak behind her, only they sounded more like the ones at her mother's house.

Bounding down the old stairs, she found her mother holding a wicker basket, much like the one Mrs. Romano held now. It seemed strangely similar. Rounded handles, frayed in spots, with a yellow ribbon woven around the edges.

The basket knocked against Mrs. DeGrout's leg as they walked, the weave crackling with each step. Her gaze steady with determination.

Dottie soon noticed they weren't traveling to the park. Tempted to correct her mother, she kept silent, knowing it was better to not challenger her mother.

Dottie gripped the table, reliving it all again.

They arrived at an iron gate, large and imposing. A crow cawed in the distance, sending a chill down Dottie's spine. Beyond the gate stood an equally imposing manor, Skyline. Far too grand from anything she knew.

"Mama, what are we doing here?" She knew they didn't belong in this place. Mrs. DeGrout handed Dottie the basket, and her once loving smile became distant and cold.

"You've become a burden, child. I'm taking you to your new home. They'll teach you how to be beneficial and give you a place to live."

Mrs. Romano turned to face her. So unlike her own mother, who wouldn't meet Dottie's frightened eyes.

"Mama, I don't understand. I can be of more help at home, I promise." She reached for her mother's hand, hoping for the warmth she'd known her whole life, but it vanished.

Because no one stays.

Fear took over the memory. Dottie turned to Mrs. Romano with pleading eyes. "Mrs. Romano, I-I'm sorry if I've made too many mistakes." Tears traced her cheeks, big and hot. "I'll do better. Please don't send me away."

Mrs. Romano threw her rag on the table and swept flour off her apron. "You think I'd let them toss you out like scraps?"

It's happening all over again.

Dottie spiraled into a panic, her stomach churning.

"Ah, *Tesoro*, breathe." The older woman inhaled, encouraging Dottie to do the same. Together they slowly exhaled. "Dear *bambina*, you're not being sent away. Mae requested time to work on the flowers. You're simply taking a break."

Dottie stuttered a breath. "But, earlier today, you sent me away when you thought I made the toast!" She was determined to hold back the tears threatening to escape.

"No, *Tesoro,* I sent you to wash the pots because I didn't want Maria to give you more stress. I knew she'd lied. I watch my kitchen, child. You've been my *primo* kitchen maid. I'd never send you away."

For a heartbeat, Dottie forgot how to breathe. She'd heard kind words before, but they usually came with strings attached. This felt... different. Gentle. Dangerous, even. It was easier not to believe them, yet her heart leaned in all the same.

The old cook's arms opened and pulled Dottie into an embrace. It was warm and full of love. "Shh, everything's fine. You're staying right here with me." Her head turned away for a moment. "Miss Edith, please check the bread. It smells ready, and I'd rather not have to begin again."

Pulling back to see the young maid's face, Mrs. Romano brushed a strand of hair from Dottie's temple. "*Tesoro*, oh, *Tesoro.* I need you to remember, you are loved, and you are wanted. Can you do that for me?"

Dottie nodded and blew out a stuttered breath. "I'll try." But she didn't know if she could.

"Good, now, go. Find Mae. She said she'd be waiting near the magnolias." Mrs. Romano handed Dottie the basket and pushed her toward the door.

As Dottie headed out, she could smell the bread and cheese in the basket. One last look behind her, and she saw Mrs. Romano and Miss Sinclair busy preparing dinner. She was grateful for the women. Even with her insecurities, they found ways to make her feel like family and not a burden.

The gravel crunched beneath her shoes, each step leading her deeper into a world of blossoms that felt far away from the clatter of the kitchen. The chill of the morning caressed her cheeks, a reminder that spring was just beginning. Somewhere near the gurgling fountain, a robin let out a sharp chirp, as if to announce the new season's arrival. Her fingers danced over the lilac leaves along the path, pausing to marvel at the small ladybug sunning on a broad leaf.

She frowned at the flower, just for a moment, remembering Mr. Philip. He had given her a bundle of lilacs the year before, whispering sweet-nothings that carried no truth at all.

Her fingers grazed the cufflink at her chest, and her heart ached for a love that wasn't true, and for a man whose life was cut short by a jealous scullery maid. The silver trinket lay heavy against her collarbone, a keepsake she'd worn since Mr. Philip's death, once believing it would keep her close to him. Instead, it only reminded her that she'd never been more than a maid dreaming above her station.

A raspy wheeze sounded behind the lilac bush snapping her back to the present. Her fingers carefully withdrew from the delicate petals. "Hello?" Taking a step forward, she tried listening for a reply, but the sound had all but stopped. "Is someone there?"

The stillness in the air had Dottie back away, her feet urging her to run. She didn't dare look back despite the uncomfortable feeling that someone was watching. The bushes blurred as she ran faster until she turned a corner, and found Mae exactly where Mrs. Romano said, under the blooming magnolia, whose white blossoms were beginning to bloom. The soft petals fluttered in the spring breeze.

She took comfort that her friend was in sight, letting her shoulders relax a moment. Mae's calm presence reminded her of a steady flame, warm and constant, even when all else felt uncertain.

Then Dottie noticed Mae's lids closed and lips moving. Stepping closer, she heard Mae's earnest prayer. "Lord, be with Dottie. Help her see the love You have for her."

The idea was sweet, and though Mae reminded her every day of God's love, she still struggled to believe He could love someone as unwanted as her.

A twig snapped under Dottie's shoe, and Mae glanced her way. "Dear Dottie, come sit with me! And let's see what treats Mrs. Carmela packed in the basket."

Nestling against the magnolia, Dottie tucked her feet beneath her dress and let the mild shade of the tree cover her. She settled the basket between them, savoring the small, peaceful moment.

The garden smelled of fresh dirt and newly budding flowers. Primrose from the cold frame a few feet away drifted through, wrapping Dottie in a comforting embrace, as cherry blossoms danced in the breeze nearby. Sunlight dappled through the branches, spilling warmth across her skin. She'd forgotten that feeling since being stuck in a manor all week.

Both women worked together to unload the basket full of bread, muffins, cheese, and even a few peach pieces. Dottie smiled, lifting a peach to her lips, sweet syrup dripping on her chin.

Mrs. Romano remembered I missed the peaches at lunch after...

She scrunched her nose, trying to figure out why Antonio and Charlie had even argued. There was nothing between her and either man, but maybe they'd had words before.

With a shiver, Dottie couldn't rid herself of the feeling that someone had been lingering in the hedges, watching her. *Surely it wasn't Charlie. Secret lovers, maybe?*

A smile twitched at her lips. With flowers blooming and the boxwoods providing the perfect cover, it really did seem the ideal time for a secret rendezvous. *Perhaps it was Maria and her mysterious beau.*

Mae's sigh pulled Dottie from her thoughts. "It's beautiful out here, isn't it? I'm grateful Miss Genevieve sweet-talked Mr. Frederick into letting us use the garden flowers." With a conspiring smile, she added, "Mr. Stratford would have a fit knowing his son allows the servants to frolic in the gardens."

Giggling, Dottie looked at her newest and now, dearest friend. "It really is lovely." Contentment spread through her chest. "But I'm wondering, how exactly did you convince Mrs. Brower and Mrs. Romano to let me go?"

"Oh, Dear Dottie, those women love you, and everyone, from Mr. Frederick to Mrs. Romano, agreed you needed time away from the frying pan." Mae nudged Dottie with her shoulder. "And honestly, I think Mrs. Romano enjoys doting on you."

Not knowing how to respond, Dottie turned the conversation to flowers, a favorite topic of both women. "So, since you're sitting below the magnolia, are you thinking of those as your statement flower for the bouquet?"

Mae smiled. "You figured me out! Yes, I thought magnolia's would be best." She picked one from a lower branch. "They seem so soft, like they could break at any moment, but they don't. Magnolias persevere in their own graceful way. I'd like to remember that when walking toward
Leland." Handing Dottie the flower, she asked, "What should we set with it?"

Twirling the delicate bloom in her fingers, enjoying the feel of the velvety petals, Dottie surveyed the garden. A faint smell of... "Hyacinth." A slight blush crept across her cheeks. "Sorry, I caught the scent, and the word just popped out."

Standing, Mae walked to the hyacinth beginning to bloom in a nearby bed. "I actually think these would be perfect." Picking one, she walked over and placed it next to the magnolia. "What do you think? These should bloom pink by next week. Do you know what they mean?"

Dottie shook her head.

A flower was a flower, isn't it?

Though she loved arranging them, she never considered their purpose beyond being pretty.

A lot like me, pretty petals with no other purpose... And soon, even that will fade. Her chin wobbled as though the thought might break her.

Mae leaned in, grazing her shoulder. "What were you thinking just now? Where did you go?" She placed another magnolia in Dottie's hand. "Together, these flowers mean 'joy after hardship'. Knowing there will be joy always brings hope." She brushed the tear from Dottie's cheek. "I need you to trust that God's got more, so much more for you."

Dottie sucked in a breath. "I'm trying, I really am." She stared at the delicate flowers, marveling at their fragile beauty. She wanted to feel beautiful too, not the fleeting glances or stolen touches she had once sought, but in a way that mattered.

Somewhere deep in her heart, she longed for someone to see her for who she truly was, not for the mistakes she had made, or the charms she had once wielded, but for who God said she was.

"And what greenery should we add?" Mae examined the area, tapping her chin in thought.

Dottie stood to get a better view of the garden, distancing herself from her worries. "I'll have to think about it. A bouquet feels incomplete without greenery." Glancing around, she wasn't sure.

Before she came up with an idea, she heard shouting from the formal gardens, near the fountain. *"Che disastro!"*

Chapter 4: Friday Afternoon II

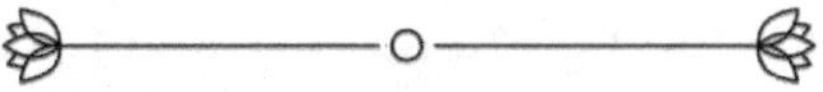

Antonio jabbed the spade into the dirt, loosening the soil that had hardened over winter. The dirt still held the dampness from yesterday's rain, clinging to his gloves while he planted. It felt good to work with his hands, letting out his frustrations.

Charlie had pestered him all afternoon, peppering Antonio and Papà with endless questions. "*Do you plant bulbs in the spring?*" *"Using a trowel instead of a shovel?"*

When he thought the questions were done, the man would just tack on more.

"*Gardening isn't much entertainment, is it?*

He threw the spade into the dirt and yanked off the canvas gloves that rubbed a raw spot between his fingers.

Nuisance.

Just like when Charlie questioned his intelligence.

"Figures an Italian would make it more complicated than necessary." "How do you get work done, talking with your hands all day?"

Antonio was glad when Charlie finally left for his *actual* job. Handling the daily pressure of ongoing maintenance was enough, but the strain of being mocked was something he'd been protected from on the estate.

When his fingers dug into the dirt to break away a "stubborn clump, the calm of the cool soil between his fingers, combined the sweet scent of tulips and damp earth, were the only things that kept him from snapping.

Charlie would never understand the patience it takes to coax life from soil, the quiet joy in seeing it flourish.

Taking an old handkerchief from his pocket, he stood with a groan. Twenty-one was too young for knee pain. But it'd be worth the suffering to see the garden blossom with all God's beautiful creations and colors. To see the butterflies and bees enjoy the provisions. To listen to the babbling fountain and birds chirping in the bowed branches.

He closed his eyes, drinking it all in. The mingling scents of roses, tulips, and freshly turned earth filled his lungs, grounding him to the moment.

Just like life, the garden was unpredictable. Storms came, pests invaded. But just as God held His children in His hands, guiding them and loving them, Antonio would guide and love his plants, helping them through whatever came their way. And his reward was the beauty of it all.

"*Papà,* I've finished with the spade. Do you still need it for that bed?" He dabbed his forehead as perspiration gathered above his brow. Though it was still mild, the April sun beat down while they worked. The only relief was the faint breeze passing by.

"No, I already got the spare and started. If you want, you can carry the petunias over and plant them around the fountain." Papà passed him the trowel. "Be sure to dig a hole that is twice as wide and as deep as the root ball. Don't want petunias resenting us for not taking care."

Antonio rolled his eyes, grabbing the tray from the wheelbarrow. "I know." He'd worked by his Papà's side for years, by now he would've thought he could be trusted with the task. "Handle these petunias gently," Antonio muttered, "or they'll ignore you instead of bloom for you."

Watching a bumblebee burrow into a petunia, he thought about Dottie, and how worn she seemed at lunch, the way she tensed under Charlie's hold, and the way her eyes sought his. Had Charlie not been so close, Antonio would've asked if she was all right.

For weeks, he tried distancing himself from her. Dottie's faith was so new, he didn't want to distract her. Then, with all the garden troubles, he didn't think he could properly care for her. But seeing that man's arm wrapped around her had caused his buried feelings to erupt.

How am I to protect her with him around?

"Annoying pest."

"Did you say pest?" Papà's head popped up from around the fountain. "It's too early for pests. Need me to ready the spray?"

Antonio chuckled, finishing a row of petunias. "No, just thinking of something."

"Ah, I know, I know. You're thinking of *Tesoro.*" The old man winked. "And Mr. Charlie. Sorry, *Tonio,* but the spray won't help. Only honesty and time."

"Hi, *Papà, Tonio!*"

His sister, Anna, ran toward them, her dark braid trailing behind. Mae's daughters, Rose and Violet were close on her tail, scattering pebbles as they ran.

"Ah, *cara*, school is done for the day?" The old gardener stood, and Anna raced into his arms, laughing. She never minded the dirt.

Pulling back, Anna glanced at her friends. "Yes, *Papà*, but if it's okay, can I visit with Miss Mae?"

Antonio's brother, Vincent, meandered into the garden, kicking a pebble. "Oh, no you don't! She's trying to wheedle out of her chores, *Papà*!"

"*Cara*, Mae's working, and your brother's right. What would your Mamma say if she found out?" He patted her head, small strands breaking free from their braid.

Antonio already knew Anna had their Papà wrapped around her fingers, and he'd let her, and Mae's daughters, get away with just about anything.

Rose and Violet flanked Anna, and something squirmed in Rose's outstretched arms. "Oh, Mr. Sal, it won't take long! Our mom's by the magnolia! We wanted to show her and Miss Dottie the toad we found!"

"Miss Dottie?" Everything faded away as Antonio stood, brushing dirt from his hands. He searched the direction of the magnolia but couldn't see past the lined boxwoods.

As he walked toward the tree, he could hear his Papà. "I'm not sure if they'd appreciate the toad, but the toad would probably appreciate the fountain." Antonio chuckled, hearing the girls squeal in delight. They'd always found some mischief, but it made life a little more exciting.

Excitement.

Just seeing Dottie had Antonio's heart pounding as he took the path toward the cold frame. He longed to see her smile. Not the one she thought men enjoyed, but the one that made her eyes turn into golden orbs.

She'd been so broken after Mr. Philip's death, and something deep inside called him to rescue her.

But I'm nothing more than the gardener's son.

Antonio's steps faltered; Timothy and Charlie were far better in station and appearance. And yet, Antonio couldn't stop himself; he wanted, no, needed to safeguard her. He'd seen the way Timothy and Charlie ogled her, wanting her without caring for her.

His pace quickened with determination, until his boot connected with something hard and immovable. The destruction that laid before him sent a chill up his spine.

"*Che disastro!*"

Freshly pruned boxwoods were uprooted, splayed across the path, and resting over the newly bloomed tulips. His jaw tightened when he noticed the tool marks—crisp, practiced strikes, not the blunder of a passerby. He glanced up as if trying to spot the shadow that had done this.

Running his hand through his hair, Antonio bent over the first bush. "How? When?" He yanked on it, hoping it hadn't fully destroyed the tulips beneath. "No, no, this can't be happening."

Papà called out from the fountain. "What disaster, *Tonio?*"

"It's ruined! I need your help!" His voice shook with the effort of moving the offending shrub.

Taking stock of the chaos. It was as if someone had used a shovel to uproot them.

But why?

Footsteps approached, crunching the gravel below with quick steps. He expected to see his family, but instead he saw the most precious person, with copper hair falling from its pins, delicate freckles hinting across her fair cheeks, and concerned amber eyes. His pulse raced at the sight. Dottie was the smallest reprieve to his otherwise unfortunate day.

"Antonio? What's wrong?" Dottie rushed toward him, focused only on him, completely ignoring the trouble along the path. But before he could warn her, her shoe caught on an upturned root. Panic filled her eyes as she began falling forward, palms outstretched.

Something deep inside Antonio startled him awake, sending him into action. "Dottie, grab my hand!" He threw out his arm, snagging her around the waist before she tumbled into the boxwood. His footing slipped with the momentum, propelling them backward.

Cradling her against his chest, his only concern was blocking her fall with his body. Her breath brushed his collar, quick and warm, sending his pulse galloping.

They crashed onto the path, dust clouds forming around them. Antonio's head thudded against the gravel with stars dancing behind his closed lids. He didn't dare move. The pulsing in his skull wouldn't allow it, and neither would the thundering in his chest.

With Dottie wrapped tightly in his hold, her hands clutching his shirt, nothing else mattered. He'd always dreamed of holding her so close, to feel the rise and fall of her breaths; he just never expected their first true embrace to be in a heap on the garden grounds.

He felt Dottie's heartbeat, strong and wild against his chest, as he absentmindedly caressed her soft hair. It smelled of bread and magnolias. Sparks flew up his arm as the silky strands slipped through his rough fingers, and he fought the urge to tuck her closer under his chin.

Shifting to peek at her face, Antonio groaned from his pounding head and gravel digging into his spine. Even with his spotty vision, he didn't miss her flushed cheeks when she tilted up to look at him.

He refused to believe her flush came from being so near. No, it had to be the stumble.

Foolish Antonio—always hoping for more.

And, yet he didn't let go. Her gaze dropped to his lips, and his heart stuttered. Without meaning to, his attention instinctively drifted to her lips, so soft and kissable.

If she only knew what this did to me.

"Are you all right, Antonio?" Dottie's voice was nearly breathless.

When he didn't answer, she pressed against his chest, rising to search his face. Her hair tumbled from its pins like a sunset waterfall, and he reached up to tuck a piece behind her ear.

She didn't recoil from his touch. If anything, she leaned in closer. His hope soared that maybe, *just maybe*, she'd let him care for her.

The warmth of her palm leached through his shirt. Afraid to let go, Antonio's grip remained firmly at her waist, up until he realized several people stood over them, staring. Heat prickled up his neck when he realized he'd held her longer than appropriate.

Why am I acting like a stunad?

Antonio finally released his grasp. And her gaze seemed almost wistful from the lost contact, so he settled his hand over hers, which still rested on his chest. Tingles spread up his arm and straight to his heart. "I'll be fine," he whispered.

And he would because she didn't pull away from his calloused and clumsy touch, and he had every intention of memorizing the feeling.

"Would someone care to explain what's going on here?" Mr. Leland's voice forced Dottie to jump back, pulling her hand from Antonio's. Even with his toughened palms, she instantly missed the steadiness of his touch. The scent of freshly turned soil mingled with blooming flowers clung to him, and she had found herself breathing it in unconsciously.

She didn't know what possessed her to lean in and almost kiss him, but the undeniable truth was, she felt she belonged in Antonio's embrace, only there was she safe.

Hoping he hadn't noticed her faltering, Dottie turned away to hide a blush. "I'm not sure, Mr. Leland. I heard Antonio yelling and found him in this mess!"

Mr. Leland quirked a brow. "You're telling me you found him on the ground between uprooted boxwoods and crumpled tulips?"

Dusting her dress as she stood, Dottie addressed the estate manager in utmost seriousness. "No, sir, he was on the ground because I toppled him."

Wait, that didn't come out right...

Dottie went to correct her miswording, "Wait, that's..."

From the corner of her eye, she caught Mae's amused look. And Dottie inwardly groaned.

I'll never hear the end of this...

"Miss DeGrout." Mr. Leland interrupted. If his brows could go any higher, they would've. "There are much more suitable ways to express your affection than destroying the hard work of the man you wish to woo."

Dottie's ears tingled at the accusation. It's not at all what she intended to say, but then again, Antonio was a handsome and good man. Any woman would be a fool not to pursue him.

Any woman without a tainted past.

"No... that's not..." But her explanation was cut short when Mae elbowed Mr. Leland in the side, resulting in a grunt.

He laughed. "I'm simply joshing you, Miss DeGrout." Mr. Leland moved past her to help Antonio stand, Mae coming to her side.

"Are you sure you're all right? That was quite a fall." Mae tucked Dottie close beneath her arm.

"We are perfectly fine, Mae." She put on her biggest smile, but it was all a lie. Not only did Dottie's heart crave to be near Antonio again, but the fall caused her stomach to cramp. But she wouldn't say anything, because Mae worried over her enough as it was.

Mr. Leland clapped Antonio on the back and addressed the group. "If everyone can pitch in, we might be able to save a few of the tulips. Miss Dottie, could you please get extra gloves from the shed? Sal, Antonio, let's start with the least damaged area."

Dottie hurried to the shed, finding the gloves quickly. But when she exited, Charlie came from behind the shed carrying a shovel. His unexpected arrival made her jump, stomach tightening with surprise. "Charlie, what are you doing over here? Weren't you helping Antonio and Mr. Sal? They've got an absolute mess."

Charlie scratched his stubbled chin. "Actually, I was over by the pond, trying to get a few wildflowers." He gave a sheepish grin. "I thought if I planted them around the fountain, they'd make it look enchanting. But I mistakenly shoveled too close to the roots." Clumps of dirt clung to the shovel's blade, and mud spotted his pant hems.

Dottie had a feeling he was telling a half-truth. She knew, unless Mr. Sal or the Stratfords approved, there'd be no changing the planned gardens, but she wasn't going to be the one to tell him. "Well, how about you come help with the boxwoods?"

"Actually, I can't. I need to get back to work. I've dawdled long enough here today." Charlie took her hands, causing the gloves to drop.

His were still cold, and something in the way he seized hers made her feel unsafe, not like when she was with Antonio. Backing up, she removed his hold and retrieved the gloves. "Well, best get too! They're waiting on me! See you around."

Charlie grinned. "Till tomorrow, then, Dottie." His voice was smooth, almost kind, but his eyes didn't match.

She didn't stop to ask why he'd see her the next day. And honestly, as much as she enjoyed his attention and flirting, something inside told her to be careful, to keep a distance from the man. Quickly turning on her heels, Dottie hurried toward the path.

Just before the turn, she checked over her shoulder. Charlie's unflinching gaze lingered, sparking an unease in Dottie's core. It was the same feeling she had while at the lilac bush.

Why does it feel like he's up to something?

Antonio's hands burned while trying to lift the second large shrub. Adjusting his grip, branches scraped at his arms and leaves fluttered through the air. He was grateful Mr. Leland showed up when he did, otherwise, he wasn't too sure he'd be able to move the boxwoods with Papà alone. Mae and Dottie, along with the girls, were quickly picking through the tulips for any survivors, repacking their dirt and watering as needed.

It bothered Antonio, that someone had purposefully shoveled out the boxwoods. But how they did it so quickly, he didn't understand. It would've taken hours to uproot them all, not minutes. He lifted his head, letting the breeze cool his brow.

Unless someone worked overnight loosening the roots and waited until today to push them over...

"And then the silly fool said—Good heavens! What is happening here?"

The shrillness of Mrs. Stratford's voice rang through Antonio's still throbbing head. He turned to see the older woman with Mrs. Van Buren, a long-time guest, and strolling behind, speaking in hushed tones, was Miss Daphne Stratford and Miss Genevieve Van Buren, wearing wide-brimmed straw hats, though the sun wasn't quite hot enough for it.

He watched Mrs. Stratford run over to Mr. Leland. "What is the meaning of this mess in *my* garden?" She waved her hand down the path. "How are my guests and I supposed to enjoy spring if we cannot get through? Are my gardeners that inept?" With each question, her voice rose another octave.

If he wasn't watching, Antonio would've missed the smirk on Mr. Leland's face. But Antonio didn't find it amusing at all. He took pride in how well maintained he kept the estate, able to handle anything that needed planting or fixing. This disaster was a mark against him and his handiwork. Behind the older Stratford, Antonio noticed concern etched across Miss Genevieve's face.

She'll certainly be telling Mr. Frederick about this.

"Mrs. Stratford, please be calm, we are checking into the incident. And as you can see, we are working diligently to correct the situation. Your garden is in great hands." Mr. Leland gestured toward Antonio.

With the praise, Antonio stood a bit taller, grateful for Mr. Leland's support. "*Si'*, Mrs. Stratford, we'll have the garden even better than before." He wouldn't let this ruin everything.

"*Hmph*, honestly, Mr. West, it might be time to hire more capable hands." Mrs. Stratford looked down her nose at Antonio, even though she had to crane her neck to glower.

Each word sank like a stone into Antonio's pride, yet he forced himself to stand tall. He knew Mr. Leland wouldn't make a rash decision based on Mrs. Stratford's hysterics. Yet part of him still braced for it. One wrong word to Mrs. Stratford, and she'd cut at his competence. Just to remind him of his place.

"Mr. West, Mr. Romano," Mrs. Stratford stared down Papà, "This is simply unacceptable! I demand this be fixed no later than tomorrow morning, as I'll need immediate use of my garden."

Both men responded in unison with a nod. "Yes, Ma'am." The women turned and walked back toward the lawn and orchard. All the while, Mrs. Stratford lamented about her incompetent servants.

Trying to feel at ease now that the woman was gone, Antonio snuck a glance at Dottie, who huddled near Mae, almost hidden. What he saw in her reaction had his chest constrict.

Pity.

The pride he had felt after Mr. Leland's praise was swept away with the breeze and replaced with the sinking feeling that he'd failed.

I'm not enough.

"Mae, I might need to go lie down." Dottie nervously pushed her hair behind her ear. "Do you think Mrs. Romano will mind? It's so close to dinner." She seemed ready to bolt, as if being anywhere near him caused her great suffering.

"I'll speak to Mrs. Carmela. She'll understand. Go rest." Mae hugged her tight and whispered something Antonio couldn't hear. Tears rimmed Dottie's lashes.

His body pulled him a step toward her, wanting to fix whatever he'd done wrong, but Dottie rushed away with her head hung low and arms wrapped around her waist.

"Antonio, we better get to work or Mrs. Stratford will find me tomorrow and give me more grief." Mr. Leland patted him on the back. "And don't worry about her fussing, she tells me to replace someone at least twice a day, and I haven't yet." He winked and nudged Antonio in the shoulder. "Let's move this boxwood."

Lord, help me make sense of this.

He meant the boxwoods. But deep down, he knew there was more beneath the soil than roots.

With one more look over his shoulder, Antonio watched Dottie leave, and with her, his hope.

Chapter 5: Friday Evening

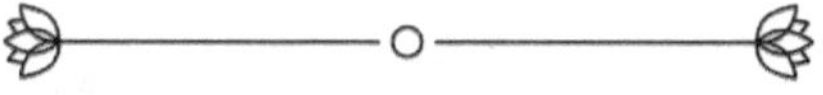

The air brimmed with spiced cinnamon apples blended with the savory pull of gravy as Dottie came down the old servant stairs after her rest. And supper was in full swing. It seemed Mrs. Romano prepared both the family's meal and servant meal without her assistance.

Though Dottie was grateful for the break and her stomach was no longer ached, the worry of being scolded by Mrs. Romano wormed its way in.

She passed through the pantry, stocked from shelf to shelf with canned vegetables and all manner of goods needed to run a kitchen. When she reached the servant hall, Dottie hesitated, listening to the laughter and stories of the others just beyond the door. She used to sweep through the room, *but now...*

Steps away was the supply closet, full of secrets, linens, and the sharp scent of mothballs. Quiet. Safe from the calculating eyes of her peers in the other room. It had been her hideaway when she needed a sanctuary before everything changed.

Touching the heavy cufflink hanging on the chain around her chest, she wanted to smile, but a bittersweet feeling settled in her heart.

Right now, I could disappear.

She'd be forgotten in an instant. Cold spread through her body, and the idea of slipping away felt dangerously tempting.

A faint draft prickled the back of her neck, though no door had opened. A shadow slowly formed over hers, the edges still blurred. The cufflink bit into her palm while her chest heaved in anticipation.

I didn't hear footsteps...

"Why are you hiding out here?"

The sudden whisper had Dottie grabbing at her heart.

"That happy to see me?" Mae stifled a chuckle as Dottie turned wide-eyed at her friend.

"You frightened me, Mae! My heart jumped so high it almost flew clear out of me." She took her friend's arm, grounding herself, her pulse still teeming through her veins. Leave it to Mae to show up exactly when Dottie needed her.

Resting her hand on Dottie's shoulder, Mae watched her friend carefully. "Didn't mean to startle you. But I saw you hiding out here and couldn't help teasing you a bit." Moving closer, her dress brushed against Dottie's, her eyes searching for some hint as to why she was waiting in the pantry.

Dottie shifted, eager to steer the conversation from the weight pressing in. It would do no good to have Mae fuss over her anymore. Painting on a silly grin, Dottie asked, "Why are you so late to dinner? Were you sneaking kisses with Mr. Leland?"

Mae's cheeks pinked. "No, I'd never. That's completely inappropriate while on the estate."

"Please, me and everyone else spied you just yesterday coming from the morning meeting." She leaned in, so her voice wouldn't carry. "And when finding a man who loves like he loves you, nothing's wrong with a little affection." She gave Mae a coy smile.

Mae's whole face turned as red as an apple. "And, with that, I think I hear Mrs. Carmela calling, let's get our food." Mae tugged her toward the servant hall, and Dottie's laughter threatened to spill over.

When Mae suddenly stopped short, Dottie collided into her back. Rubbing her nose, she fussed at her friend. "Next time, give me a warning. My nose is bruised!"

Turning around, the parlor maid tweaked Dottie's nose with a smile. "I forgot; I have to meet Helen. We're taking dinner together in the laundry."

Dottie pulled back, confused. "Helen, the laundry maid? What do you have to see her for?" Mae always ate in the servant hall, and at Mr. Frederick's insistence, her twins had been joining in the meal too.

Why would she leave with Helen?

Mae grabbed Dottie's arm once more, coaxing her to walk. "Yes. Did you know, before she came here, she was a renowned seamstress in Silkrow? But just like me and you, her life took a turn, and she ended up here. I've asked for her help with my wedding dress."

"Do you have to rush off or can you stay for a bit?" Dottie's voice wobbled. She'd grown used to Mae being near.

"Dottie, look at me." Mae's palms framed Dottie's face. "You'll be fine. Mrs. Brower, Mrs. Carmela, and Edith are all in there. You're safe."

She inhaled and nodded. She'd just have to fake being brave. "Let's go. Mrs. Romano's gravy smells heavenly, and I'm going to need whatever she has the cinnamon apples in."

Bracing herself, she squeezed Mae's hand as the door swung open. The warm sunshine spilled through the back window, lighting the room in an orange glow. It was full of people and food. Dishes clinked, voices hummed, and the savory smell of gravy covered meatloaf washed over her. The familiar noises wrapped around her like a worn blanket, reminding her that despite everything, this place still held a piece of home.

A chair scraped along the floor as Mrs. Romano stood. "Ah, *Piccola, Tesoro!* Come. Eat." Mrs. Romano scooted past her husband, giving his chair a bump with her hip. "You know, if you ate less, you'd give more room for people to walk by!"

"Ah, *Amore Mio,* but if I ate less, you'd complain that I hate your cooking! And as you can see, eating is an expression of my love!" He gave his belly a good shake. Everyone laughed as Mr. Sal dramatically ate a forkful of meatloaf.

But Dottie wasn't watching, her gaze naturally gravitated toward Antonio, who seemed more interested in his boiled potatoes than his parents' antics. She wondered if he was still mulling over the boxwoods. True, Mrs. Stratford's rebuke was harsh, but Mr. Leland vouched for him. She wondered why he still seemed so downcast.

Probably just tired from the day.

Mrs. Romano blocked her view of the handsome Italian. "I missed you this afternoon!"

Too distracted by her thoughts, Dottie failed to notice the woman's wide smile, and braced for the scolding. But instead, the head cook scooped her into a hug, her dress brushed softly against Dottie's skin.

She'd never had such an affectionate hug from her own mother, and the action nearly broke her as she thought back to the year before her mother forced her out.

Dottie came home, cheerful as the sun was bright. "Mama! Mrs. Parsons said I did exceptionally well on my recitation today!"

She found her mother hanging laundry beside the house, diapers and children's clothes filling the rows. The siding was chipped and fading. Where flowers once bloomed, weeds stood. Rusted tools rested against the lopsided shed. But none of that mattered, because to Dottie, it was home.

The woman's weary eyes glanced up, barely acknowledging her daughter, only to turn back to her work.

"Mama, listen!" She stood tall and took a deep breath as the fresh smell of soap filled her lungs. "Jeremiah 29:11 'For I know the plans I have for you, saith the Lord, plans to prosper you and not to harm you, to give you a future and a hope.'"

But her mother didn't smile, didn't cheer for her. Instead, Mrs. DeGrout picked up another sheet and muttered, "Prosper, my foot. The only prospering I see are from those uppity folks from Silkrow."

The excited little girl didn't understand, confused by her mother's cold reply.

A whisper tugged her back to the servant hall. "*Tesoro!* Why are you crying?"

Tears slipped down Dottie's cheeks, heart cracking. Why hadn't she seen her mother's bitterness sooner? Even she seemed to understand Dottie was destined for nothing. Looking into the crease-lined eyes of the cook, she saw no bitterness, just tenderness. Her heart ached for a mother to look at her in such a way.

"Come now, let's fix you a plate. And you will sit beside me." Mrs. Romano spoke tenderly as she wrapped her arm around Dottie. "We'll talk later about your tears. Right now, food will fix most things." The woman gently steered her to the seat next to her own.

Turning, the head cook let out a huff. "And Mae, Helen left with her meal ten minutes ago. She'll think you've forgotten her!"

"I'll get going straight away." Mae quickly filled her plate. Before walking out the door, she squeezed Dottie's hand. “I’ll come see you later.” And she was gone, leaving Dottie alone in her embarrassment.

As she spooned gravy on her plate, her knuckle grazed the large hand beside her, reminding her just how close her seat was to Antonio. The spot tingled at the contact.

“So, Antonio,” Maria chirped, breaking the quiet connection between them. “I heard you had a little mishap today.” Her smile was hidden behind her cup, but to Dottie it felt threatening.

Antonio tensed. “*Si’*, yes. Mr. Leland and I plan to find out how it happened. But *Papà*’ and I were glad for Mr. Leland, Miss Mae and Miss Dottie’s help.” His glance down at Dottie carried an unspoken thanks.

She shrugged her shoulders, not wanting to seem too excited for his praise. “I just got gloves and helped with flowers. It wasn’t much, but glad I could help.”

Barking a laugh, Maria set down her cup. “Well, she probably needed the work anyway. Seems you’re getting a bit of shape.” She scanned Dottie appraisingly, while Katie snickered from across the table.

Dottie’s vision blurred as everyone turned their focus her way. All she wanted was to escape while they assessed her appearance.

But instead, she berated herself. *I used to be just like them. A quick taunt, proud to be noticed.*

The taste in her mouth bit with regret. She’d known her words had hurt others in the past, but never realized how cutting they truly were, how much torment she’d inflicted on others...

“Well, I’ve always enjoyed women with a bit of curve to them.”

Katie coughed into her napkin, but quickly masked her expression at Timothy’s brazen comment. Maria’s smile dimmed, her jaw tightening for the briefest moment as her eyes cut toward the scullery maid. And a heaviness settled over the room that Dottie couldn't avoid.

The bold footman sent her a suggestive grin. Just when he was about to speak again, Mrs. Brower suddenly knock-ed over a pitcher of water, dispelling the oppressiveness of his attention. “Clumsy hands of mine. Miss Sinclair, do help.”

Edith stood to assist in wiping away the water, while her voice gave no room for argument. "We'll not tolerate remarks regarding women's forms during mealtime, or any other time." She gave a pointed glare to Timothy. "If we hear it again, there will be punishment. Now eat quietly or find something nice to speak about."

Timothy lifted his fork in mock submission, but Dottie heard his muttered insult clearly. "The hag's a nag."

Dottie's eyes widened at his blatant rudeness.

Edith acted as if she didn't hear the slight, but Dottie saw hurt flicker across the upper maid's face. It struck Dottie then how strength sometimes looked like silence, how a brave heart could bear insult without a word. With a final rebuke, Edith took the soiled napkins to a bucket near the door. "And questions about helping, Miss Ireland? I seemed to recall you went missing this afternoon when you should have been serving tea to the Strafords."

Maria stammered. "I—I was with..." It wasn't lost on Dottie that Maria flicked a glance toward Timothy.

Or maybe she's looking for an escape.

Mrs. Brower interrupted with her hand raised, halting the parlor maid's excuses. "We will meet tomorrow to discuss this further."

Dottie's fingers clutched the napkin in her lap, as the conversation turned to other things. Its coarse stitching poking into her palm.

Henry made a joke about which was more uncomfortble, pinafores or bowties. Then, surprisingly, Clara, the chambermaid, piped in with her small voice. "Try hauling hot water up and down the stairs every day, then we can speak about what's uncomfortable."

Uncomfortable.

Just like how Dottie felt sitting in the wooden chair, its back too straight to relax. She willed her hands to move, to pick up her fork and eat, but the tension wouldn't release. She wished to join in the conversation, laughing like she used to...

A rough hand enveloped hers, stopping her thoughts. The warmth radiating from Antonio's caress eased her anxiety, and Dottie couldn't ignore the spark that danced beneath his touch.

Silently, she reveled in the support of his touch. Then she noticed him peek down at her for a moment, providing an encouraging tilt of his lips that made her breath hitch. With a gentle squeeze, he released his hold and quickly focused on a question from across the table.

Dottie's thumb grazed the space where his hand had just been, missing the comfort it brought.

"*Tesoro*, please pass me the bread," Mrs. Romano leaned over, pointing to the basket. Dottie could swear that the older woman's eyes held something knowing.

I'm sure she saw Antonio take my hand.

She thought of Antonio's kindness, how caring he seemed to be. And the old feeling of wanting to be seen as more rose up. She wanted him to pine after her like other men had.

Dottie leaned unnecessarily close, her shoulder nudging him. His bicep flexed against her arm. Tipping her face upward, she noticed just how near her lips were to his jaw. Allowing her breath to feather against his collar, she murmured, "Excuse me, Antonio."

She watched him swallow, and the action excited her. But somewhere deep down, knowing how shameless she flirted made her heart heavy.

Why can't I behave?

Dottie *knew* what she was doing was bold, and scandalous, yet the need for men to pay her attention drove her to it. But shame along with the reminder that she was unworthy always followed.

Antonio shifted uncomfortably and angled away. His earlier warmth was replaced with something icy and distant, as he kept his attention trained on the wall across the room.

He's slipping away, and I'm the one who pushed him.

Regret instantly settled over her as she picked up the basket and turned to Mrs. Romano. "Here—here you are, Mrs. Romano. It smells delicious."

The cook cleared her throat. "Well, of course it does. You're the one who baked it, Dottie." Turning away, Mrs. Romano fussed over Mr. Sal's plate that was apparently missing any form of greens, adding more string beans to his plate.

She'd overstepped, and the whole table knew it. Ashamed, she focused on the forkful of meatloaf, ready to savor what wonders Mrs. Romano had done to the meal. But Antonio abruptly stood, his chair knocking into hers. The meat fell onto her potatoes with a thud.

"*Papà'*, I forgot to close up the greenhouse. I'll finish that now. *Mamma*, I'll see you at home."

"*Tonio*, it can wait, finish your food. It's not like the seedlings will grow legs and walk out!" Mr. Sal picked up his plate. "Stay. Eat. Your Mamma might pop you if you snub her meal."

"No, I need to leave. Now." Antonio's gaze met with Dottie for a moment, but he frowned and excused himself from the room without another word.

I really did mess up.

With his seat empty, the warmth she had felt faded into a cold dread. Refusing to acknowledge the glare Katie shot her way, Dottie attempted to focus on her meal, but the food had lost its flavor.

Soon after, everyone finished their meals and left to complete their evening tasks. Dottie stayed to clean the servant hall. She'd just stacked soiled plates in her arms when Mrs. Romano walked back in.

"Put those down, *Tesoro.* We need to talk." The woman pulled up two chairs to face each other, humming softly while waiting for Dottie to sit.

Fingering her apron hem, an ache inside rose, spilling through her defenses, while she told Mrs. Romano everything from her past, about her mother and Mr. Philip, to her current fears. But she left out the biggest piece of all.

The less people who know, the better.

"Oh, *Tesoro.* Such pain, such a burden. We will pray." She pulled Dottie into one of her wonderfully cozy hugs, and Dottie savored the feeling of unmerited kindness.

"Dear Father, Dottie is a precious treasure, made by You and for You. Help her see, Lord, Your love for her. Remind her that she can come to you with her weariness and burdens. That you can give her rest. She needs rest, Father. Amen."

Dottie's hold relaxed as Mrs. Romano leaned back, searching Dottie's face. "Now, let's clean the kitchen and finish for the day."

Inhaling, Dottie smiled, a small weight lifting from her heart, as if God was reminding her that she wasn't alone. For the first time that day, she believed she didn't have to carry the pain alone.

If I had a mother like her, would I have turned out differently?

"Yes, let's go, for the dishes won't clean themselves."

Chapter 6: Saturday Morning

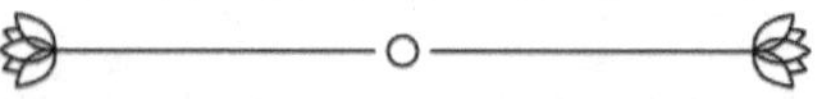

Between Mrs. Stratford's threats, the garden fiasco, and thoughts of Dottie's alluring closeness the evening before, Antonio hadn't slept well. He was sure he kept his parents awake with his constant tossing and turning.

In the pre-dawn darkness, his boots shuffled up the path. A nip in the air had him pull his coat tighter around his body. He had promised Papà he'd wait until just before sunrise, but Antonio didn't trust the work would get finished in time.

Though a lantern swung at his side, Antonio's feet moved by habit. The world muted beneath his steps. His only company was the sound of his shoes, the fountain's faint babbling in the distance, and his thoughts. A dewy heaviness lingered in the morning air.

Who would have been malicious enough to ruin the hedges? And to what purpose?

He'd turned it over in his mind all evening and into the morning. The only person he could figure was Charlie, with his interest in Antonio's job and obvious interest in Dottie.

His jaw ticked. Something about the man felt crooked. Antonio muttered into the cool air, "Didn't he ask about the best way to remove dead bushes?"

The lantern's faint light cast the magnolia in ghostly shadows, and Antonio's thoughts turned to Dottie.

Sitting near her during dinner was torture. When she brushed against him, he fought everything in him to not wrap her in his arms. All Antonio had to do was lower his head and their lips would've touched. It took all his restraint to not focus on her lips. Lips he'd imagined kissing since... *when*?

Stumbling over a root, Antonio caught himself before falling into a bush. "I'll need to fix that." The misstep tugged up a memory. The day Dottie arrived on the estate. He'd just turned fifteen, pulled from school to work that year. She appeared younger than her fourteen years, with clothes a size too large, tattered and worn.

Entering the back entrance, Dottie had tripped over a step. Her mother turned a sharp eye on her. Antonio never got the image of her shoulders curling into themselves, as if bracing for a scolding. It was in that moment that he'd wanted to keep her safe, the way an older brother should.

The branches rustled above in the cold breeze, carrying with it a faint scent of lavender; Mamma always had the plant hanging in the manor's pantry. Pulling his collar tighter, he inhaled the familiar aroma.

Within five years, Dottie had climbed from scullery to parlor maid on sheer ambition. The once timid girl had grown into a confident woman, and Antonio's protectiveness eased. But after last year's promotion, she seemed altered, her light had wavered.

There was a stirring in the air and Antonio stared into the darkness, watching shadows flicker ahead. *Nothing.* He stepped closer to the garden shed, listening. The sound of rushed footsteps carried in the distance. His fingers twitched around the lantern handle.

Someone's out here.

As he waited, the sound moved further away until there was silence again. He shook out his shoulders. Whoever it was, they were long gone, and he needed to get to work.

With his next step, the crunch below his boot wasn't just gravel. He swung the lantern to find light reflecting off shards of glass, spread around the footpath.

At first, it was just a few small pieces; then he noticed larger chunks strewn across the ground. Lifting the lantern higher to the shed, Antonio hoped it was just a single shattered window. Instead, both front windows and the door had been busted out.

The odd silence that followed pressed against his ears. Had the intruder really gone, or were they hiding in the shadows?

"Oh, *Papà* will be *furioso*," Antonio whispered, dragging his hands through his hair. Incidents like this had gone on since winter, and it seemed every mishap landed at his feet. Papà had taught Antonio to take pride in his work.

But lately, his heart just wasn't in it, battered by the constant issues.

He reached for the doorknob but jerked back. Splintered wood around the lock jabbed his finger, causing a cut to form. Adrenaline prickled across his skin, with fear that the inside was just as destroyed. Throwing the door open, he let it slam against the wall. Once he scanned the cramp-ed space, his shoulders sagged in relief. "Everything's in its place."

As he reached for a nearby bucket, a paper shifted under his boot. Lifting it to the lantern, he read the words: "*To My Sweetheart.*" The handwriting unrecognizable as the letters had smeared.

Who'd leave their love letter here?

He shoved it in his back pocket to read later.

Grabbing the bucket and a pair of worn gloves, he set to work collecting the shards. Jagged edges glittered in the lantern light. "This will take some time, but hopefully, I can clean it before *Papà* or anyone else arrives." Each piece clinked softly as they landed in the bucket, echoing the pressure mounting inside him.

His thoughts drifted, unbidden, back to Dottie. A year ago, she'd been hiding in the supply closet, when Mamma sent him to fix a loose floorboard. The light was dim, but he could still see her red-rimmed eyes as she huddled in a corner. Putting his tools down, Antonio tucked her into the crook of his arm and whispered a prayer. Her hair had brushed his jaw, and something in his chest shifted, like his world was thrown off axis. He knew, then, that he didn't see her as a little sister, but as something more.

Moments had ticked by until someone called after her. Without a second glance, she was out the door, chin up and ready to face the world as if she had never cried. He never discovered the reason for her sorrow.

Perhaps that was why he clung so fiercely to the things he could fix, since he couldn't fix her pain. Antonio loved his job, but with accusations spreading that he was sabotaging his own work, he felt less than capable.

Rubbing the burning in his chest, he scooped up more shards, wishing problems were just as simple to sweep away. "Father. *Padre.* My heart is breaking. For every step I take, it feels as if someone pushes me five steps back."

He stared into the sky watching dawn approach, lightening to shades of navy and purple. "I'm frightened that this'll all be taken from me. That I'll be torn from the people I love." Lifting another shard and watching the lantern light catch its edges, Antonio raised the last of his prayer. "Help me, *Signore Dio.* Help me honor You with the gifts You've placed in my hands."

Dottie had never been an early riser, but something pulled her—called her to the gardens. Nightmares of an unhappy future had broken her sleep. Images of Mr. Philip, Antonio, and maids mocking at her had drifted into her dreams.

Her fingers skimmed the fountain's icy water, dim in the twilight. The cold prickled her skin, making her wish for mittens. She drew in the scent of marigold and tulips, with a hint of magnolia floating on the April morning air. Snuggling into her heavy coat, she looked toward the magnolia tree, remembering her short-lived picnic with Mae. Her lips quirked up in a small smile.

Joy after hardship. "Maybe those nightmares won't come true."

On a neighboring farm, a rooster crowed, signaling the start of the day. "Lord, if You're listening, and I'm sure You are. Help me. I don't really know what to say, or what to ask for, but somehow, I know You can help."

A bat swooped past her head, silencing her from her prayer. Hearing a low murmuring near the garden shed, she inched closer, not wanting to startle the person, nor make herself known. Her pupils widened, scanning the darkness for a hint of movement.

And then she spotted him. *Antonio.* Barely visible, but his low baritone voice rumbled and coursed through her veins. Tiny goosebumps pricked along her arms. Something about him pulled her closer. Her foot slid forward before she realized herself. Then everything in her cooled.

Maybe I should just keep walking.

She couldn't shake the image of his back departing, strained and unyielding, from dinner the night before and she ached to right her wrongs.

"I'm frightened..." His voice pleaded into the darkness.

He's praying.

Never had she heard him pour out his heart to God. It felt so intimate, like she was intruding on something she shouldn't be hearing.

"...that this'll all be taken from me. That I'll be torn from the people I love..."

Dottie halted her footsteps.

Did I hear him right? Even Antonio fears of abandonment?

She'd always seen him as strong, protective, afraid of nothing. Peeking over the hedge, she noticed the glass sprawled across the ground, and her gasp echoed through the dark morning.

"Is someone there?"

Dottie heard him shift and walk closer. Tightening her coat, she peeked over the bushes once more. "It's just me." Masking her anxiety, she forced her voice into a cheerful cadence.

His steps slowed and Dottie couldn't help but marvel at how even in the dusk light of morning, he was more handsome than any other man.

Where'd that thought come from?

A shiver went up her neck. She'd seen him almost daily for six years, and though Dottie always found him attractive, she'd thought other men were just as handsome too. But not now, it was only him.

As he drew closer, her pulse quickened. With his gaze holding hers, she saw more than kindness—something warm and deliberate, enough to make her breath catch. "G-good morning, Antonio." Her palms nervously rubbed against her apron.

Why am I stuttering?

"Good morning, *Tesoro.*"

Delight swelled in her core; he'd never called her that before. Even when Mrs. Romano said it, it felt like doting on a child. But with Antonio, the way '*Tesoro*' fell from his lips, those full, kissable lips, felt so intimate, like the name was his, and his alone.

Antonio's hand came up, and, for a moment, Dottie wondered if he wanted to touch her, but he caught himself, securing his hand in his pocket. It surprised her. Other men would've taken the chance. Antonio's restraint was a welcomed change.

Dottie kept her head low, not wanting her surprise to show. "I haven't slept well. And I've been trying to pray. But it's so new to me, I'm not sure if I'm doing it right."

She stepped closer, and Antonio mirrored her, like maintaining the distance wasn't possible. "Why are you out so early?"

Rubbing the back of his neck, Antonio glanced past her. "I'd planned to finish with the boxwoods this morning before *Papà* woke. But then," he motioned to the mess behind him, "I found the windows shattered."

First the boxwoods, now the windows?

Dottie's lungs tightened seeing the defeat in Antonio's eyes. Her arms itched to comfort him.

But before she could, he moved closer again, his chest inches away from her, but he didn't touch her. He bent low and softly spoke into her ear. "Prayers are never wrong if they're spoken from your heart. God hears no matter how jumbled they are." His breath danced across her neck as he backed away.

I shouldn't want this. I've told myself to stop chasing these fleeting feelings.

But she knew this wasn't a passing feeling. She wasn't chasing Antonio or seeking out his affection.

It just felt...true.

Something deep within her leaned toward him, uninvited, her shoe catching on her hem. The situation was strangely familiar.

He must think I'm a klutz.

Antonio's arm caught her securely around the waist, steadying her. For a moment, it felt like an embrace, intimate and warm. His presence steadied her, even as it set her off balance.

As she righted herself, the smell of flowers and dirt on his shirt invaded her senses, bringing her comfort. There was safety in his arms, and her desire to stay there was strong. Instinctively, she nuzzled into his hold, the fabric of his coat scratching against her cheek.

Antonio froze, unmoving, until his chest rose with a shaky inhale, but he didn't let go.

Dottie feared she'd overstepped again. That is, until he pulled her closer. His free hand braced at the curve of her upper back, as he burrowed his face into her hair.

"A-Antonio?" Dottie tried angling away to see his face, but his grip tightened around her waist, as if she'd take flight with the early morning breeze.

What's happening?

Dottie's mind swirled with confusion from how he treated her the day before and how he acted now. Whatever it was, she allowed herself to sink into his embrace, letting the predawn activity to wake around them.

The moment broke when Mr. Sal's voice rang out through the garden. "*Tonio*, I told you to wait for me!"

Straightening, Antonio cleared his throat and backed away, his hands finding their home in his back pockets once more.

Dottie tried catching her bearings, everything she thought was muddled. Peering at the sky, she noticed it had changed to blues and pinks.

"Oh, goodness, I'm going to be late!" She started toward the manor, but turned, and darted back to Antonio. "Thank you for catching me, and, well, for everything else!"

Standing on her tiptoes, she pecked him on the cheek. His beard brushed roughly against her lips as his breath hitched. Her feet carried her swiftly toward the manor. There was hope for a better day ahead.

The servant door slammed into Dottie's back as the clock struck six. She closed her eyes and rested her head against the wood, trying to calm her fluttering nerves.

Why'd I do that? He'll think I'm flirting again.

But then again, he had matched her embrace and Dottie wondered what it all meant.

"Ah, *Tesoro*, where'd you come from?" Mrs. Romano passed her a kerchief. "Did you run here? Your face is flushed."

Thinking of Antonio's embrace, Dottie's stomach dipped. She wouldn't dare tell Mrs. Romano she'd been hugging on her son in the gardens. How would the woman react?

She imagined Mrs. Romano waving a rolling pin in the air, scolding a quivering Dottie. "*You wicked girl, my Tonio deserves better.*" A giggle bubbled up from her throat, and she caught it with a cough.

Mrs. Romano would never.

"Sorry, Mrs. Romano, I was out walking this morning, clearing my thoughts and time ran away from me." Tightening her kerchief around her hair, Dottie headed to the worktable.

The air in the room brimmed with tension; the normal chatter hushed. Even pots were silent without their usual clanging. And everything seemed to be waiting.

Mrs. Romano came to her side, handing her a bowl of fruit. "Pay extra attention to today. Mrs. Stratford is madder than a hornet in a jar. We won't want any missteps."

"Yes, ma'am." Sensing someone watching, Dottie glanced toward the sink. With every harsh swipe of the rag, Katie's glare darted toward Dottie, her eyes slitted with resentment.

It's the same attitude I used to give Mae.

Dottie's chest tightened with sadness for a girl who seemed just as lost as she was.

"Don't pay her any mind." Mrs. Romano blocked Dottie's view. "Drama's her bread and butter—take it away, and she'd starve. And if she or Maria cause any, keep your head low and let me handle it."

With a nod, Mrs. Romano ambled to the stove and Dottie was left with her thoughts and cutting fruit for breakfast.

Slices of fruit scattered on the plate, reminding her of the shattered glass.

Who could've broken the windows?

The way Antonio's face fell, Dottie knew with everything in her that he wasn't causing the destruction.

"Saw you getting cozy with Antonio this morning." Katie's whisper dripped with resentment. "Be careful, Mrs. Romano won't take kindly to a girl like you being close to her son." The basket of soaps and sharp-smelling solutions wobbled in the young maid's arms.

When did she see us?

Heat pooled in Dottie's stomach, and she impulsively placed a hand over it. "What do you mean by that?"

"He's got better options than you." Katie smirked at Dottie's belly, and Dottie quickly retracted her touch. "So, stop flirting with all the men. The good ones don't keep girls like you."

With a satisfied smirk, Katie walked away, but not before knocking the bowl of freshly cut fruit onto the floor. The bang resounded through the kitchen.

Dottie stood frozen, waiting for Mrs. Stratford to bust through the door. But of course, the woman would still be in bed at that early hour. But that didn't keep Dottie's pulse from racing.

Mrs. Romano lifted her head from the oven. "Girls, what is going on? Katie, get back to your station and empty the bucket! Dottie, clean up the fruit and fetch more from the root cellar."

The morning meeting was just letting out when Dottie opened the trapdoor in the pantry. People scooted past her to get on with their tasks, faces crestfallen and serious.

Except Timothy.

The dimple in his cheek deepened as his eyes roved over her. "Well, my morning just got a little better. Need help in the root cellar?"

Dottie knew that expression, the one he saved for unsuspecting girls when he wanted their attention. Something she had always enjoyed; the thrill of men seeking her, the heady sweetness of being wanted.

But this time it unsettled her.

I don't want that anymore.

"I'm all right. Just fetching a few fruits."

His gaze lingered longer than necessary as she began to descend the steps, as rush of cool air greeted her from below. "No, I think I'll come anyway."

She watched his newly shined shoes take the first few steps, and a sense of dread settled in her stomach knowing how badly this could end.

I wish he'd just leave. I shouldn't be alone with a man.

The room was dark, with only a dingy window letting a small shaft of light in. Shelves stood in perfect order, lined with jars and cans, while bins of vegetables waited underneath. The scent of fruits, mixed with dirt and mildew bit at her nose; the cold chill prickling her skin.

"Are you cold?" Timothy stood behind her, his hands slowly rubbing her arms. "You know, we've never really had a moment alone."

Flustered and uncomfortable with his advances, Dottie stepped away, trying to put space between them. "I'm fine. Really."

From above, she heard Mrs. Romano call out. "Dottie, you need to quicken your steps!"

Flicking her gaze to Timothy, she noticed he was inching closer. "You really need to go. Don't want Mr. Griggs catching you slacking off again." She edged away, the jars behind her clinking on the shelves.

As he came to stand directly in front of her, he fiddled with a jar just above her head. Dottie froze, blood pumping, not with desire, but with the sudden, sharp awareness that she was trapped in the dim, enclosed space with him.

With a glance at her lips, he grinned. "Just one kiss? I've always wondered what it'd be like." His fingers brushed at her jaw.

It's the moment dreams were made for, a secret space and an attractive man, but something in Dottie told her it was wrong. That the wrong man stood before her, and this man had no right touching her.

She tried to think of a way out. The shelf dug into her spine, and she could only think to knock a few jars over. But she hesitated, fearing it would create more problems for Mrs. Romano.

With a sigh, Dottie yielded. "Just one. And then you leave." Trying to make light of it, she rolled her eyes and forced her face to appear bored. She didn't want a kiss from Timothy.

Dear Lord. Please help.

The prayer nearly escaped her, but she clenched her lips, stopping the words.

"Dottie, are you down here?" Mae's voice broke through the fear. The cellar steps creaked as she moved down them.

Timothy immediately stepped across the room and picked up a couple of oranges. And Dottie turned to select a jar of peaches, her hand quaking with the action.

Thank you, God.

"There you are. Oh, Timothy, you're here too." Mae's voice sounded warm, but Dottie still picked up a touch of strain. "That's great. Mr. Griggs is searching for you."

Timothy raised his chin, barely acknowledging the parlor maid. "Dottie, I'll just leave these on the work-table, we'll finish our conversation another time."

"Ok." Dottie's voice was just above a whisper, the jar in her grasp shook.

As soon as Timothy left the root cellar, Dottie's legs gave way as she dropped to the floor.

Mae's arms wrapped tightly around her. "Did he threaten you?"

Shaking her head, Dottie huffed. "No, but he followed me down here, asking for a kiss." She let out a dark chuckle. "I didn't know how to escape. I didn't want his kiss." Plucking the hem of her dress, she refused to meet Mae's eyes.

"I'm proud of you."

The kitchen maid looked up, bewildered at her friend's approval. "Proud?"

"Yes. Very. You had the opportunity to do what you used to, to seek validation in a man's attention, but you held back. Your heart changed." She stilled Dottie's fidgeting fingers. "And that, my Dear Dottie, is the Holy Spirit guiding."

Tucking a stray lock behind Dottie's ear, Mae grinned. "Now, let's grab these peaches and return upstairs before Mrs. Carmela thinks we've wandered away."

Dottie wiped wetness from her lashes. "Thank you, Mae. Thank you for showing up when you did and for being a light when I needed it."

The rest of Saturday slipped past in hushed movements and downcast glances. Even the typical laughter in the servants' hall felt stifled, as if one wrong word might summon Mrs. Stratford's wrath. As Dottie worked through her tasks, she wondered if Antonio finished fixing the boxwoods, if his shoulders still carried the weight she'd seen that morning.

Placing the last dish on the shelf to dry, she prayed someone would come to his rescue.

Mr. Frederick is a kind man; if he wouldn't toss me out, he wouldn't toss out Antonio for something that wasn't his fault.

She turned down the lantern and made her way up the servant stairs, the wooden steps creaking under her tired feet while the rest of the house settled into silence. A peace wrapped around her as her fingers skimmed the smooth wooden banister. "Dear God, thank You for sending Mae today. Please show Antonio he won't be torn from the people he loves. Amen."

Tomorrow will be better.

Chapter 7: Sunday Morning

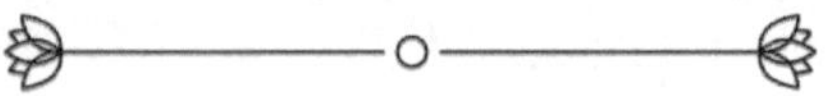

Dottie slipped into her only non-work dress, faded green and worn, the edges had frayed months ago. The fabric thinned in places, but thankfully still glided smoothy down her back.

It won't be fitting much longer. Clara had offered one of her extras, but Dottie didn't want to become a burden to the girl.

Hastily fixing her hair in a simple plait, wandering wisps framed her face. Dottie sighed, catching her reflection in the window. "It'll have to do."

Sunday mornings were quickly becoming her favorite time of the week. When Mr. Frederick assumed control of the household from his father, he laid down strict instructions that all servants were to have Sunday mornings off, save for a few early morning chores.

Mae once mentioned that he hoped everyone would attend church, though Dottie noticed many servants spent the time on other pursuits.

Descending the servant stairs, she ran headlong into Timothy, who just come through the back door. "I know you're excited to greet me, but maybe with a little less force." Clutching his chest, his breath came out ragged.

I've got to stop knocking into people.

"At this point, I should just wear a warning bell. Knocking into people is quicky becoming a favorite pastime." Taking a step back, Dottie was struck by Timothy's casual attire.

No longer in his dark tailcoat, he wore simple, gray trousers and a pressed button-up shirt; his leather shoes shined despite a bit of mud.

Dottie frowned at his shoes. She recalled just the day before they had a new shine. Yet, the caked-on mud seemed fresh, as if he'd just come in from a rainstorm. *It hasn't rained since Tuesday.* Her stomach tightened. Where had he been?

When he took a sudden step closer, Dottie remembered his forwardness in the root cellar. She raised her hands and backed up a few paces, putting the worktable between them. "Sorry, rushing off to Mae's before we go to church." She coughed, trying to dislodge the fear of being near him. "You're more than welcome to come, we nearly take up two whole rows."

Timothy waved her off. "Nah, I'd rather spend my time elsewhere. Thanks anyway." He glanced back at the door. "But I think your other *beau* is waiting to walk with you." His jaw ticked and Dottie had the feeling he wanted to say more, as an uncomfortable silence settled between them.

Before she could slip away, Maria ambled into the kitchen, prattling with Bessie and Katie. "I waited near the gate for ages," Maria said too brightly, smoothing her dress. "Thought Timothy might enjoy a walk this mornin—" Catching sight of the man she just spoke of, her smile faltered, the edges brittle.

Dottie held her breath, waiting for the barrage of insults. Her fingers found the edge of her sleeve, twisting the fabric until it pinched her wrist.

Cutting her eyes to Dottie, she let out a snicker. "But I suppose he had *better* company." Her chin lifted with mock-dignity as she shot Timothy a scowl. When she refocused on Dottie, her expression felt like it could cut Dottie down to nothing.

"Off to church? Think God has time for someone like you?" The others giggled beside her. Bessie resembled a gaggle of geese with her twittering, but Katie's lsounded forced.

Dottie wanted to argue at the jab, but the guilt from her past kept her silent. She fiddled the cufflink around her neck, a reminder of old mistakes. "I—Mae asked me to come, so I'm going." Her chin lifted.

Mae has told me before; God is greater than all my fears.

She knew it was true, yet her fear had her frozen to her spot. The heat from the kitchen felt almost suffocating, pressing in around her.

Timothy came around the worktable to stand beside her, his hands clenched like he planned to defend her. However, his mouth remained closed, seconds ticking by.

"What, Timothy? Going to ride in on your noble stead and defend her? We all know you're a shameless flirt, just like her." Maria's voice trembled just slightly, almost vulnerable. But Dottie wouldn't look up, keeping her focus on a cracked tile beneath her shoe.

Lord, I need to escape.

The prayer felt empty, like searching for water when the well was dry.

"Oh, there you are, Dottie."

The quietest voice brought Dottie immediate relief. She hadn't noticed Clara coming into the room. And though the chambermaid always appeared timid, she'd never hesitated to speak up when necessary.

Clara inched past the other women, gently snatching Dottie's wrist. She kept her head low, directing Dottie with a hushed voice, her fingers trembling ever so slightly. "We'll be late if we don't hurry." As Clara pulled her to-ward the door, Dottie felt Timothy's fingers linger against her arm, something in the grip made her skin crawl.

Leaning in, Clara whispered, "Don't pay them any mind. You belong with us." She whisked her out the back door without another look back.

Departing the dim kitchen, Dottie squinted against the bright sun. The warmth spread over her, easing tension that she didn't realize she carried.

Sunlight spilled over the garden path, warming the grass beneath her shoes. A gentle breeze lifted a strand of hair across her face, and she closed her eyes for a brief second. Relief felt like this: quiet, soft, and unpressured.

Surprise filled Dottie's mind at how such a quiet girl could so boldly step into the quarrel. Peeking at Clara, she smiled. "Thank you for saving me back there. If you hadn't shown up, my only option was to faint dramatically and hope they believed me."

Clara winked mischievously as she adjusted her flowered hat. "You're not the fainting type, more of a fighter." Shrugging, she added, "And that's what we do. God called us to love, care, and shoulder each other's burdens. I'm willing to help whenever I'm able..."

"G'morning Dottie."

Dottie jolted to a stop. This wasn't the voice of the man she expected.

Charlie. So that's who Timothy's talking about.

She slowly turned to see him lazily leaning against the wall, arms crossed, and wearing his Sunday best. Though still neatly pressed, like Timothy's clothes, Charlie's shirt had clearly been mended and he wore his work boots.

Catching herself perusing him, she quickly glanced away. Clara's arms clenched Dottie's tightly, as if unsettled by the man. Dottie assumed it was simply because he startled them, but the look of apprehension on the chambermaid's face wouldn't dissolve. "What brings you here on a Sunday morning? No radiator kicking up a fuss today."

He ignored the girl, choosing instead to openly ogle Dottie a little too long. Her old self would have swooned, but now she inwardly groaned. Something about the intensity of his attention made her skin crawl.

"Came to walk you to church." Charlie took her free arm, slipping it through his. Everything in her fought to pull away, but his gaze told her there'd be consequences if she did.

Clara quietly piped up, her sweet face masking what her deep blue eyes appeared to be saying. *Run.* "That'd be wonderful, Charlie. The more, the merrier."

"Actually, we need to go by Mae's first. We all walk to church together." Dottie hoped this would dissuade him. To her dismay, he only smiled.

"That's all well and good, but I don't want to share you." The sharp edge of his stare made her shiver, giving him a dangerous air.

Thankfully, Anna, Rose, and Violet came scampering up the path, all speaking at once. "Dottie, guess what!?" "We found something real nice in the gardens yesterday." "Right where some of the boxwoods were removed." "It's *so* pretty, Dottie."

She couldn't keep up with all the chatter, and despite her unease, she giggled at their delight. "Calm down. So, what exactly did you find?" She hoped by indulging the girls, they wouldn't notice the terror she felt.

"This!" they said in unison as Anna held up a beautiful silver comb.

Dottie stammered, "That's... that's mine. But how in the world did it get in the gardens?" It was the only gift her mother had ever given her. Mrs. DeGrout would praise Dottie's copper hair. *"It's a rare and beautiful gem, your hair. So, I wanted to add something to it."* Dottie recalled wearing it the day she came to the estate.

Who would have taken it?

Charlie stiffened beside her. "That's a lovely comb, why don't we place it in Dottie's hair." Snatching it from the girls, he placed it right above her ear with more force than necessary. The teeth scraped along her scalp, causing her to flinch.

"I'm glad you got it back, Dottie!" Anna didn't seem one bit phased by Charlie's behavior. The young girl grabbed Dottie's hand in hers and pulled her forward. "Let's get to church!"

Mr. Frederick and Miss Genevieve had taken to walking to church with the servants every Sunday. He'd attempted to convince his parents to attend, but the elder Stratfords always feigned migraines.

From Mrs. Brower, Mae and her girls, Mr. Leland, and the whole Romano family, Dottie knew this was where she belonged. They'd taken her into their fold as another part of their makeshift family. Even Clara had begun to join them.

Walking down the gravel road, Dottie smiled at the vivid scene before her. Wild violets and spring beauties clung to the edge of the wooded path. A long, white butterfly skittered from one early bloom to another. Near the opening to the road, sunlight streamed down, illuminating a dogwood just begging to bud. The girls giggled up ahead, collecting wild violets and dandelions. And best yet, she was away from the oppressive manor.

Charlie had been pulled aside by Mr. Sal to discuss the radiator when they first set off. And she was grateful she could walk in peace, her steps her own.

Mae sighed beside her. "I wish Edith would come with us." She looked up, like throwing a prayer to the sky.

Then, with a smirk, Mae pointed to Miss Genevieve. "They've been talking an awful lot lately."

Since Miss Genevieve had been staying at Skyline Manor, the household ran more smoothly, and the help felt a sense of ease. The Van Burens had been long-term guests, and gossip whispered that Miss Genevieve and Mr. Frederick would one day wed.

It might be considered a scandal; Miss Genevieve marrying her once-betrothed's brother so soon, but perhaps the heart doesn't wait for propriety. Everyone knew Miss Genevieve never loved Mr. Philip, simply a business deal. But then again, what did she truly know of timing, especially after Mr. Philip's death?

Something pricked at Dottie's chest as she fingered the cufflink.

Would Mr. Philip have accepted me if he knew?

The memory of the man's lifeless body, murdered out of jealousy, still gnawed at her heart. She knew he never really loved her, but she had once... hoped.

A breathy laugh slipped from her, sharp and brief. Mae turned to Dottie. "And what's so funny?"

Not wanting to rehash the past, Dottie pointed. "Frogs, the first weapon in every little girl's arsenal." The girls were running around the group, giggling. A bullfrog's legs dangling from Rose's outstretched hands while she chased Vincent. "And Vincent looks a little less than thrilled."

Mae shook her head. "Nothing strikes fear in a boy like a determined girl with a frog."

Antonio walked along on the far side of the group, rolling his eyes at something Mr. Sal said. But every so often, his gaze drifted her way, his expression softening when their eyes met.

Her breath tangled, thinking back to how comfortable she was in his embrace, the feeling of being wanted without earning it, of being accepted as she was.

Banter and laughter filled the cool spring air as they drew nearer the old church, the only Baptist church in walking distance, and the pride of the mountain town it was named after, Valebrook.

Over the years, the glass windows had grown slightly cloudy, but the sun beamed through as brightly as the smiles of the faithful who entered. Neighbors greeted each other, children ran about, and little old ladies sat in the corner solving all the world's problems. Perfume, fresh dirt, and aftershave mingled together in the small church, while people filed in shoulder to shoulder for worship.

Miss Betsy had already started her organ prelude when the Skyline Estate brood filed into their usual pews, the old wood creaking under their weight. Dottie happily sat tucked between Mae and Clara, allowing her to focus on the sermon, and not the men at the other end of the row.

Pastor Somers stepped up to the pulpit. "Beloved, it is a joy to worship with you today! Let's bow our heads and give thanks." When his prayer ended, amens resounded through the chapel.

Opening his worn, leather Bible, the pastor cleared his throat. "Today we will be reading out of Genesis. A servant, no, worse, a slave, named Hagar, with no authority over herself, was forced into a dehumanizing experience."

Dottie peeked around the room; many were servants to someone.

How do they feel about this?

The rest were just regular farmers or small-town business owners. She wondered about Mr. Frederick. Would he be smug, hearing servants spoken about as mere things? The pew squeaked as she peeked around Mae. What Dottie saw proved that the man was pure gold. Instead of arrogance, Mr. Frederick's expression held sympathy.

"She let scorn get in the way, was rejected and abandoned." He scanned the congregation, and Dottie shifted under the weight of his words. The silence felt thick, only broken up by someone sneezing in the back.

"Bless you," Pastor Somers joked. The crowded room lit up with laughter. Holding up his hand to quiet the room, Pastor Somers continued. "But God heard her affliction. Even with God's command to submit and His reassurance that He heard her, Hagar's life was still not easy. Sarah despised her, even though the situation was of Sarah's own making."

Dottie grazed her fingers along the cufflink, the metal was cold beneath her fingers.

My own making.

Pastor Somers inhaled, and she forced herself to focus on his words. "We have all had times when our choices come back to hurt us, and we despise them, reject them, but they are ours. Our only hope is to listen to the Holy Spirit and use those things in our lives to glorify our Father in Heaven."

"Have you been rejected? Abandoned?"

I will not cry.

Clenching her jaw, Dottie willed her tears away. From Dottie's left, Clara leaned in, giving a comforting weight with her shoulder, and from her right, Mae squeezed her hand, spreading warmth to her heart. She knew these women would not abandon her.

Pastor Somers read from Genesis. "And she called the name of the LORD that spoke unto her, 'Thou God seest me': for she said, 'Have I also here looked after him that seeth me?' God sees you in your burdens. He hasn't left you. Have faith like Hagar, trusting that the God who saw her will also see you."

As the sermon ended, Miss Betsy's crooked fingers glided smoothly over the keys. The room sang in harmony, "Jesus, lover of my soul, let me to thy bosom fly..."

Jesus. Loves. My. Soul.

Not her body, but *her.*

With her thoughts muddled, she only caught snippets of the song. "Leave me not alone, still support and comfort me... grace to cover all my sin; let the healing streams abound; make and keep me pure within..."

Dottie's heart broke within her.

Lord, I want that. I want Your support and comfort, Your grace for things I don't deserve. I need no other but You.

When the song ended, others milled around saying goodbyes. But Dottie's focus was on a stream of light cutting through the dust, encircling the wooden cross in a soft glow. She didn't notice the space emptying until the silent, steady breathing of someone beside her was all that remained.

"*Amore*. That's what you're seeing."

Glancing up, she half-expected Antonio to be staring at her adoringly. Wasn't that what all the romance serials taught her? Men look longingly at the woman they loved when uttering those types of words? But Antonio wasn't watching her at all; he was solidly focused on the Cross, eyes misty with emotion.

He drew in a breath. "Christ suffered for sins He never committed. Taking on mine, yours, and all the world's. God allowed Him to bear the weight of those sins, and He willingly walked into it. That's love."

Finally, looking down at Dottie, his smile widened. There was no motive, no expectation, just joy. "You felt it today, didn't you? Jesus's love. It hit you right here." He rubbed his chest.

"I think I did." As the words tumbled out, Dottie knew it was true. "I don't understand it all, but you're right. Something hit me, fast and hard, right in my heart." She allowed her tears to release for the first time that day.

Antonio stood by her side. He didn't touch her, didn't speak, just reliably stayed as she let herself begin to heal.

When her last sniff echoed in the quiet church, Antonio briefly put his arm around her shoulder and gave a light squeeze. It was no romantic gesture, yet goosebumps erupted across Dottie's skin. "Rumors are going to start if we don't get going."

Angling his head toward the door, he released her, but the goosebumps remained in full effect. "The sun's calling, the weather's perfect, and I'm pretty sure *Mamma* has a picnic feast waiting on us."

As Antonio strode out the room, Dottie stayed, allowing the moment to fill her soul as she smiled at the cross. "Thank You, Love."

Chapter 8: Sunday Afternoon

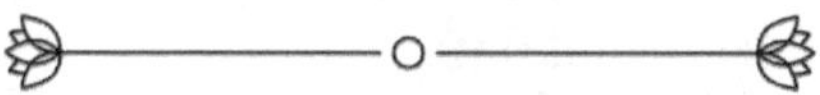

When Antonio had walked back into the chapel to find Dottie, a shaft of light poured from the window, reflecting off her copper hair. It sparkled like a fiery babbling brook, entrancing him for a moment, and his pulse quickened at the beautiful sight. It wasn't just how the light danced around her, but how she looked so longingly at the Cross.

The faint smell of old hymnals hung around them. As he stepped into the pew and witnessed the peace radiating from Dottie's face, relaxed and completely in awe, he knew she'd met Jesus there. He had forced down the impulse to shout for joy and pull her into a hug. So instead, he waited quietly for her to be ready.

Just standing beside her had Antonio's body humming with excitement. Her life would be forever changed. And more-so, Antonio understood that now he was allowed to love her, pursue her, and completely cherish her.

Descending the church steps, each creaking under his weight, his lips twitched into a beaming smile. Sunlight scattered across the yard, highlighting the bright green grass. Lofty clouds floated lazily across the sky. It all seemed so wonderful.

Antonio held back a song, knowing all too well if someone heard, they'd laugh. It wasn't that he had a terrible voice. It was just so deep, people often said it was the kind of bass that could shake the floorboards and scare off demons.

"What has you smilin' like a Cheshire cat? Had some alone time with that sweet thing in there?"

Antonio's high spirits immediately chilled. Charlie stood directly behind him; his menacing aura making the hairs on Antonio's neck rise. He briefly looked toward the path noting that the entire Skyline group was out of sight. No one remained in the church yard.

I swore I saw him take off with Papà.

The man stood so close; his heavy breath ruffled Antonio's hair, triggering a sense of alarm.

But he refused to cower to a man who used dominance to overpower people. He wouldn't give Charlie the privilege of ruining God's special day.

"Actually, I had to fetch my hat. Dottie's praying, she should be done soon." He gestured toward the faded doors. With his heart hammering in his chest, Antonio hoped the man wouldn't catch the lie.

Lord, forgive me for being misleading.

Stepping into his space, Charlie scoffed. "She's not the praying type." The man growled, grabbing Antonio's collar, the fabric roughly cutting into his neck.

This fella's cracked. What made Charlie switch at the drop of a coin? Antonio didn't understand, but he did know this man was too dangerous to be around Dottie.

The faintest tilt of Charlie's head carried a threat, as sweat beaded on his brow. "You need to back off. That one's mine. So, keep your eyes off."

Trying to turn away from Charlie's foul breath, Antonio felt something slick on his cheek. Disgust filled his stomach when he realized spit snaked down his skin.

Charlie sneered, his voice dripping with disdain. "She deserves a proper man, not some tawny immigrant who can barely pass for white."

Antonio had witnessed prejudice toward Italians before. Mamma shortchanged at the market, Papà trying to find work outside the community, other children at the school giggling at their accents or darker skin. But never had someone outright been hostile for his heritage.

"Little pasta boy needs to go back over the ocean. I can pay your steerage if you don't have enough." Charlie's grip tightened, his knuckles turning white with the effort.

Antonio heard enough. He wouldn't fight, but he wouldn't allow anyone, especially someone as rotten as Charlie, to speak down to him. This man had no idea what it took for the Romano family to come to America, the sacrifices, the work, and the faith in God's plan.

Grabbing Charlie's hands, Antonio yanked them from his collar and then drew to his full height, stepping inches away from Charlie's face. "I don't think you want to go there, Mr. Rolston. My family, and I don't just mean my blood-kin, don't take kindly to people speaking ill about us."

Taking a few strides back, Antonio wiped off the spit and hoped that would be the end of it. But as his arm came down, a fist came flying. Before he had time to duck, there was a loud crack as he was slammed to the ground, his cheek burned. Dry dust billowed into his face and small pebbles dug into his hand, causing it to sting.

"You've been warned, *Mr. Macaroni.* You'll be off that estate soon enough, and then I'll come swooping in to take your place and at Dottie's side. Stay down where you belong." Giving a swift kick to Antonio's thigh, Charlie took off in the opposite direction of the manor.

Antonio's face throbbed. Placing his forearms on his bent knees, he wrestled with all that had transpired. All the happiness and excitement from just a few moments ago was knocked right out of him and replaced with uncertainty.

He plans to replace me? No wonder he'd been asking so many questions. Doubt crept in like it always did. Antonio dragged his hands over his face and grimaced when his palm met his injury.

He's right.

Shaking his head, Antonio believed he didn't deserve Dottie. But neither did Charlie Rolston.

Yet in the stillness, Antonio felt a quiet whisper of God's presence steadying him, a reminder that he wasn't alone in this struggle.

Lord, if not me, find someone who can protect her properly, love her properly...

His breath slowed, the spring air cooling his hot cheek, as the burden lifted from his heart.

Dottie gasped, interrupting his prayer. "What happened to you?"

He hadn't even noticed her leaving the church. Embarrassed that he sat in the dirt and likely looked unsightly, Antonio thought of the first thing he could. "I thought I could fly, then gravity reminded me... I'm just a man." He thought of saying, "*Just an Italian gardener,*" but held back. It was bad enough she found him on the ground, she didn't need to hear him complain like a child, too. He groaned as he stood, brushing the dust from his clothes.

"I hate to break it to you," Dottie grimaced, her hand reaching for his face. Antonio's breath stilled, and the space between them crackled. Her feathered touch reached his cheek, slowly dancing across his skin. "But this looks a lot worse than gravity's doing." Dottie's voice was just above a whisper as Antonio leaned into her touch.

Even though she had the morning off, she still smelled of fresh baked bread, like it was a permanent part of her. His eyes locked on hers, open and expectant. Slowly, he dipped his chin, but the added pressure to his fast-forming bruise made him wince. Dottie quickly drew back her hand and he instantly missed the contact.

Her pink lips drew into a frown.

Maybe a kiss could turn her mouth into a smile. Would her cheeks flush?

His thumb twitched with a desire to trace the edge of her bottom lip.

Stop thinking this way. Much too dangerous.

Pulling him from his errant thoughts, Dottie stepped closer. "It seems more like you met with a fist. Who did this to you?" She nervously glanced around the empty lawn. Except for a few sparrows roosting on a nearby branch, the area was deserted with no sign of trouble.

Antonio willed her to look back at him. It was the same feeling he had in the garden. Drawn to her as though being without her would drain the world of color. He wanted to protect her, not just from Charlie, but from himself. And he knew they shouldn't be alone; everyone was expecting them to return for lunch, though Antonio's heart craved having this moment just to themselves.

Rubbing his hand across his neck, he took a few steps back. "It was just a little pebble, easily missed. Let's get going. Mae will kick me clear to Silkrow if you don't get a chance to eat before we need to report back to work."

They walked in comfortable silence back to the manor, passing glances like a game of toss, but to Dottie's dismay,

Antonio always kept a few feet between them. She scolded herself for hurting his already injured cheek, the blues and purples spreading down past his beard.

She knew he was lying; it was no fall, and the only person who was around and bold enough to throw a punch was Charlie. She had heard them arguing, how Charlie provoked Antonio. She should have stepped out to help, but the way Charlie had acted terrified her. And she couldn't risk him hitting her as well.

When they finally arrived in the back gardens, a spot Mrs. Stratford didn't frequent, the blankets were already laid out, baskets open, laughter lifting into the air. The unmistakable smell of crushed wild onions mingled with fresh oatmeal cookies which were tucked away in Mrs. Romano's basket. Small platters of sliced meat and rolls waited for the next hungry stomach.

Dottie was sure the girls had found another creature to terrorize Vincent with. Rose's spirited laugh echoed off the nearby trees while she chased the boy. Looking closer, it appeared to be a poor spring peeper. Its frantic squeaks piercing the air.

"Did you hear old Mrs. Cornwell snoring in the back? She probably woke up all those souls in the graveyard." Mr. Sal laughed louder at his own joke than anyone else. Glancing up, he winked at Antonio. "Well, it's about time you showed up *Tonio*, I was about to eat all of *Mamma's* Taylor Ham!"

Antonio shifted uncomfortably and stepped away from Dottie, leaving her feeling exposed. She noticed him rub the back of his neck again, fingertips grazing the edges of his hair, and she wondered if the strands were as soft as they looked.

I did it again. God. Why can't I behave? Handsome man, someone sweet, and I immediately go there.

She blushed, and quickly found a seat next to Clara. Smiling, she handed Dottie an apple, shiny, red and without blemish. They brushed shoulders and Clara whispered, "I'm glad you got here when you did. Between Mr. Sal's stories and the two lovebirds oblivious to anyone else, I was getting a bit lonely."

Dottie giggled. "I can see that." She peeked over at Mae and Mr. Leland, with their heads bowed low together, speaking in hushed tones, fingers entwined. Mae always carried warmth, even on the tough days, but now, pure happiness radiated from her whenever she was with Mr. Leland.

Will I ever find that?

Sighing at their romantic scene, Dottie bit into the sweet apple. She wiped the juice from her chin, only to find Antonio watching her; his lips twitched in amusement before he snapped his attention back to Mr. Sal like he'd never looked her way and her face warmed.

He saw that, didn't he? So embarrassing.

Trying to be discreet, she shifted her focus around the gardens, casually wiping any remaining juice from her lips.

With the gardener only yards away and impossible to ignore, Dottie turned her attention to her friend. "By the way, where's Mr. Frederick and Miss Genevieve?"

Clara smiled. "They had *business* to discuss and headed back to the manor early." Dottie didn't miss the emphasis on business. "Mmhmm," she hummed with a playful grin.

"Well, girls, break's over. We all know Mrs. Stratford's current attitude. She'll not appreciate a late tea time." Mrs. Romano put the plates back into the basket and allowed Mr. Sal to help her stand.

Everyone worked together to pack away the picnic. The girls and Vincent said their goodbyes and ran off to the cottages.

Stepping onto the path toward the manor, a screeching sound, much louder than a spring peeper's, resounded through the gardens. It was followed by Mrs. Stratford's shrill scream, sending shivers down Dottie's spine. It was far too similar to the sound the woman made when she found her son dead just months ago. She could still see him lying on the floor in his study.

Bile threatened to rise up and Dottie clutched her stomach, her chest heaved in panic. Rushing to her side, Mae placed a careful hand on her back. "Are you well?"

"I'll be fine." She inhaled deeply. "Just old memories." Nothing else needed to be said, Mae understood the ongoing healing from that day.

The rest of the party ran ahead, leaving them alone. Mae's brows furrowed in concern. "Do we need to go in?"

"No, no. Let's go check on what happened. They might need help." Straightening, she squeezed her friend's hand. "I'm fine now." Mae didn't appear convinced, but with a slight nod, she took Dottie's arm.

Cutting through the garden, the women arrived to see the fountain had toppled over, cracked down the middle. Water gushed from the broken pipe, spraying in every direction like an umbrella, while a frantic Mrs. Stratford laid on the ground screaming.

Antonio, Mr. Sal, and Mr. Leland worked to pull the cast-iron bowl off Mrs. Stratford's dress, ignoring the errant water drenching them. Flecks of the cold spray scattered on Dottie's arm, sending chills through her body. She wrapped her arms across her chest to fend off a shiver.

"This is a one-of-a-kind gown from Paris!" Her face flushed with rage. The woman wore a frock of printed chiffon, the fabric scattered with small pink roses. A row of buttons ran down the front, while the sheer flutter sleeves stirred with every movement. It was the sort of day dress Dottie wished to own, delicate and tasteful. "If there's a single tear, I'm docking EVERYONE's pay!"

She jabbed her finger at Antonio. "And *you!* The way your father speaks, you're a protégé! So why do you allow these things to keep happening to my beautiful home?!" Mrs. Stratford's voice rose an octave. "This is the LAST straw; I'll make sure my son kicks you and your whole family out!"

I shouldn't speak ill of my employer, but that wretched woman needs a lashing. None of this is Antonio's fault.

Dottie's fingernails dug into her elbow.

As Mrs. Stratford smacked his arm, Antonio's fingers slipped, and a loud rip silenced the woman. All the color drained from Antonio's face.

Backing away, he left the fountain bowl on the ground as Mrs. Stratford's dress ripped clean from the hem to her knee. Her eyes darted at her gown, then to the young gardener, and in a split second, she launched herself at him, screeching like a banshee.

It was the second time Dottie found him in the dirt that day, but this time, his collar was torn and there was a gash along his other cheek. It pained her to see him in such a state. *If only I could make things easier for him.*

Mr. Sal and Mr. Leland quickly pulled the irate Mrs. Stratford off Antonio. As she opened her mouth, no doubt to berate Antonio again, Timothy ran up, out of breath and carrying a shawl. "Mrs. Stratford, I'm sorry I'm late, but it took some time to find your favorite shawl."

"Took some time? Boy, I asked you over twenty minutes ago to retrieve it! And I told you I left it in the morning room!" Her voice grew another decibel as she stomped toward the footman.

Thankfully, Miss Daphne redirected her mother's attention toward the manor, something about updating the terrace. Timothy trailed behind, but not before he peeked back to the fountain.

Was that... a smirk?

Honestly, Dottie couldn't understand why he'd be happy about the misfortune. The footman knew all too well that once Mrs. Stratford was upset, the entire day was spent treading carefully.

Mr. Leland helped Antonio to stand, then whispered something into his ear. When Mr. Leland pointed to the toppled fountain, Dottie followed his hand.

She tipped her head sideways as she inspected the ornament. The fountain base seemed off. Dottie might not be an expert, but she knew for something heavy like the fountain, screws were necessary to keep it in place. And they were missing.

Glancing back toward the men, Dottie watched Antonio shrink further into himself with each passing second. There's no way Mr. Leland would think it was his fault. Antonio had been with her ever since before church, and Mr. Leland knew it.

Antonio peered at her between locks of drenched hair. His expression was one of defeat and she wanted to console him. But when their eyes met, he turned away.

Am I being rejected when nothing's even begun?

At last, Mr. Leland left to soothe Mrs. Stratford, giving Mae a quick peck on the forehead before he departed.

Dottie expected Antonio to start working again, but instead he took slow steps toward his family cottage, each stride heavier than the last. Her heart raced at the thought of not getting to speak with him.

I'll not let him dodge me!

Before she thought better of it, her feet started towards him, quickening to catch up.

With an outstretched arm, she tugged his sleeve, willing him to stop. Refusing to glance her way, Antonio shrugged off her touch. "There's nothing you need from me, Dottie. Please. Go."

The gravely words speared her heart. Fighting back the pain, Dottie snapped out her next words. "I'll not be ignored!" The words shocked even herself as they tumbled from her lip and suddenly things became clear.

I get it now. All this time I've cowered and not spoken up for myself.

She grabbed his sleeve again, the fabric slippery against her finger, but her grip wouldn't be shaken off this time. "Turn around."

This time, Antonio submitted to her demand. The wet fabric of his shirt clung to his body as water dripped from his head, hair plastered along his temple. The bruise had deepened into dark purples, almost black, and blood trickled down his beard from the cut on the other cheek. The man that stood before her appeared beat down.

Dottie breathed, "Oh, Antonio!"

Nothing else mattered. Her fingers lifted and brushed his damp hair off his forehead. They trembled as they traveled to his jaw, the beard scratchy below her fingers. Then, of their own accord, they lightly grazed his neck. Dottie watched his mouth part under the touch.

Kissable.

"Dottie, I'm ashamed for you to see me like this." His eyes squeezed closed, and his muscles tense beneath her palm. "Please don't tease me with your attention. I'm trouble. I'm one bad day away from being jobless."

She remembered his morning prayer and realized then that he wasn't rejecting her. He felt a similar type of pain she had. That deep felt unworthiness that weasels its way in, making one believe the Enemy spoke truth.

"Hear me, Antonio, I know none of those things were your fault." Slowly, she pulled him down so their foreheads met. His skin was cool against hers. "Antonio." His name was a breath on her lips. "Look at me."

For a moment he pinched his lids tighter, then finally relaxed, peeking one eye open then the other. His brows furrowed as he watched her. Her fingers ached to ease the crease formed there.

"I know you don't know all my story, but I'm pretty certain you know most of it."

He nodded against her temple while his hands settled on her waist, the warmth of it seeping through fabric and into her bones.

"God created us in such magnificent ways. Mae and your mother have reminded me over and over, that I'm..." she hesitated, a smile trembling on her lips, "fearfully and wonderfully made. And so are you, Antonio." Her grip around his jaw deepened as she tugged him more firmly towards her. "Remember, we are— "

"Tesoro."

A mere whisper, he spoke it like a wish, full of hopes and longing. A single word, but the meaning behind it was something Dottie had always dreamed of.

Their gazes held as a sudden wave of longing pulling her closer. Something inside her told her he was the one.

God, please let me have it right this time.

"Tesoro."

Antonio's palm grazed her neck as his calloused thumb lifted her jaw. For a moment, they stood frozen, breaths mingling.

Dottie lashes fluttered closed as they drew nearer. He smelled of rainwater, with just the faintest trace of cherry blossom from the garden.

Light footsteps sounded behind her. She'd grown to recognize Mae's tread. But she forbade the moment to end, refused to leave this special space where it was just her and Antonio.

With a tender kiss to her forehead, his trim beard tickling her nose, Antonio released her. She waited there, suspended in time, until his footsteps faded away.

Taking her forearm, Mae gently guided her back to the manor. "Dear Dottie. Mrs. Romano's searching for you." Reaching over, the parlor maid wiped a tear from Dottie's jaw, giving her a sisterly smile. "He's a good one, you know." She nodded down the path where Antonio had just been.

Dottie exhaled. "I know." She tugged at her dress, the seam digging into her stomach. "But do you think he'd still be good if he knew... everything?"

Pulling her into a hug, Mae responded as Dottie had hoped. "Even more than good. If he knew everything, he'd be great." Dottie smiled, letting God's quiet whisper of reassurance settle in her heart—that love, faith, and grace often show up in the messy, broken moments. She could trust Him in that.

Chapter 9: Sunday Afternoon II

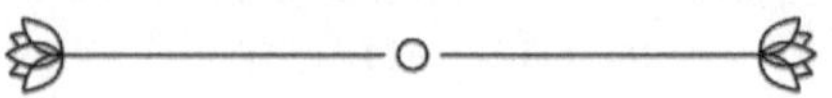

Finally arriving back in the kitchen, Dottie tightened her apron as best she could. A stray drop of water clung to her brow, and as she brushed it away, her chest swelled at the memory of Antonio's tender kiss. She wanted to hold it close, just a little longer.

The swish of Mrs. Romano's skirt pulled her from the moment as a sweet, yeasty scent drifted through the room. The cook moved briskly from the pantry, stove, and worktable in quick succession, gathering the items she needed. Checking the sink, Dottie realized that Katie was missing.

The grandfather chimed down the corridor, reminding Dottie it was almost tea time. She swiftly moved to the pantry, picking up the Stratfords' favorite tea trays, and called over her shoulder. "So sorry I ran behind, Mrs. Romano. Is everything all right?"

"That daft girl, running off like she did. And leaving her mess for me!" Mrs. Romano passed by, handing Dottie a batch of scones to add to the tray.

Katie was known for trying out her own recipes, then randomly disappearing. There was a similar scene just a few weeks before. Every muffin tin had been dirtied and nearly half the servants spent the next two days frequenting the privy, after Katie mistook prunes for raisins. Dottie's nose wrinkled at the memory.

Mrs. Romano paused and rested a hand on Dottie's shoulder. "*Tesoro,* I was worried about you earlier, when you doubled over. Are you feeling better?"

"I'm much... much better." *Amazing, in fact.* Her neck heated where she could still feel Antonio's touch.

"Mmmm, yes, I think you are, *Tesoro.*" Mrs. Romano's expression was one of a woman who knew more than she let on. "But we'll have a talk about that later."

She nodded toward the hall door, noting the servants rushing through with their tasks. No chattering from the parlor maids or laughter from the footmen.

While plating the buttery scones with perfectly spaced raisins, one would think her reddened cheeks were from the kitchen heat, but she knew the flush was from thoughts of her near kiss with Antonio.

I think it was almost a kiss.

What would Mae say about such a moment? Probably that the Lord's timing was a thing of beauty, even when hearts rushed ahead. Dottie laughed softly at herself. If she'd learned anything from her experiences, it was that real love waited—it didn't demand, it *invited.*

I've been going about it all wrong, haven't I?

Giving the porcelain teacups a final adjustment, she let a faint giggle erupt. And quickly stifled it before anyone noticed.

Will do no good to draw more attention.

As she finished, Henry walked in, speaking in hushed tones. "She was like a bull charging in, her dress torn, mud on her face. Thought I'd grab a red tablecloth to step into the ring. I tried not to laugh, but she caught my snicker...".

Dottie realized Timothy followed behind the lanky footman. Seeing him gave her a pause, conviction overflowing in her heart.

Just yesterday I said yes to a kiss...

And now a chance for real love was just steps away, out in the gardens. Her hand slipped, causing a teacup to clink against another.

"Oh, hey Dottie!" Henry waved, none the wiser to her battling thoughts.

"H-hi, Henry... Timothy." She didn't want to encourage his flirting, not with her growing feelings for Antonio, but she didn't want to be branded as rude.

Her hands shuffled the tray, adjusting the scones, anything to appear busier than she was.

Please, let him keep walking.

But he didn't. Timothy hesitated, then took a step toward her like he intended to speak, his charming dimple on display.

"No time to dally. Mr. Griggs will have Helen hang you by your toes on the clotheslines if we don't hurry back. It's bad enough you keep disappearing all the time." Henry pushed into his shoulder, urging him to move on.

Dottie let out the breath she had been holding.

Disappearing?

He's always been the picture of a proper footman, attentive, punctual, and handsome. She was surprised to hear that he'd been in trouble.

How many maids has he flirted with?

From experience, she knew it was all too common. Then she recalled Maria's comment from the morning. It felt so long ago.

Mrs. Romano snuck up beside her, and Dottie jolted, disrupting the carefully placed cups. "Be wary, *Tesoro.*" Her voice deepened with the warning. "*Che serpente...*"

Dottie's skin prickled. Yes, he was a flirt, but serpent felt a bit harsh.

Maybe she knows something I don't.

The older woman peered out the back window, her mouth breaking out into a smile. "Ah, there's *Tonio*. Such a good boy, *buon ragazzo,* he works so hard to make us proud."

Shaking her head at Mrs. Romano's blatant meddling, Dottie wiped down the table. "Timothy's just a tease. And you *should* be proud of Antonio. He'd a dedicated worker. And has a dedicated faith to match."

Trying to appear uninterested, Dottie carried an empty plate to the sink; not because she wanted a clear view out the window. No, she was being a good kitchen maid. Simply clearing the workspace of unnecessary clutter.

It wasn't her fault the window just happened to be there. Dottie smiled as she watched him clear the path of low branches. He mused his dark hair, still damp, strands shimmering in the sun. His shirt did nothing to hide his strong biceps as he raised his shears, the cloth straining across his shoulders.

But Mrs. Romano's wrong about one thing. He's no boy.

A rush of something light and dizzy swept through her. She stood there, almost in a trance, until she realized she was gawking at the man and swiftly went back to the worktable.

Humming came through the hall door. A song Dottie didn't recognize, and she grinned. Mae's songs were beautiful and always had a purpose.

As her friend entered the room, she asked, "What song is that?"

Mae winked, quietly singing, "Can I doubt His love for me, when I trace that love's design? By the cross of Calvary. I am His and He is mine."

Dottie let her lashes fall, allowing the words to push through her healing heart. "I am His, and He is mine...."

Oh, such joy to know I am God's!

She believed it now. God had been with her through the hardest times, even when she refused to see it.

Turning, she found Mrs. Romano watching with a wide grin. "It's true, we can't doubt His love, not with the Cross before us."

With her attention back to the oven, Mrs. Romano checked the cinnamon swirl bread for the next morning's breakfast. Sweet warmth danced throughout the kitchen. "Finish cleaning up the worktable. Pork and scones—two good things, but not meant for the same plate."

The back door creaked open. Katie peeked past the crack and slinked through. Dottie almost ousted her as her silent steps moved toward the servant stairs, but Mrs. Romano's soft chide cut in.

"I see you!"

How Mrs. Romano saw the girl without turning around, Dottie couldn't understand.

It must be a mother's instinct.

"And I saw the mess you left me! You'll oversee the evening clean up," Mrs. Romano turned, wielding a spatula like a baton. "And all by yourself, too!"

Katie knew not to cross Mrs. Romano, but the glare she hurled at the cook said she considered the idea. "Yes, ma'am. I'll change and be back straight away." She bit out the reply.

The scullery maid wore a new gingham dress, her hair flawlessly curled, and a fresh amount of lipstick on her face. As she moved toward the steps, her dress swished as if it was meant to be seen.

Who's she trying to impress?

Immediately Dottie recalled the other day.

Katie likes Antonio. And she'd gone to visit him.

Something foul swirled in Dottie's core. Though what she felt for Mr. Philip was not true love, she'd felt this before. Jealousy, ugly and hot. But this felt different. The jealousy she held for Mr. Philip was possessive, a threat to her perceived standing. But for Antonio, it was measured with affection, a desire to protect his heart.

"..., *Tesoro,* can you hear me?" Mrs. Romano stood by her side, her face full of concern.

Dottie had no idea how long she'd stood there, nor why the jealousy felt so powerful. Blinking, she peered up at the cook. "So sorry, I let my mind wander. Worktable is cleaned, what's next?"

"Come help me with dinner; the clock's ticking impatiently! I'll fetch the ingredients from the pantry."

Meeting at the stove, the two stood shoulder to shoulder. In time with one another, one would grab the salt, another the seasonings, one would stir, and the other would flip. Even the bite of the kettle heating on the range added its note to the rhythm. Soon the meaty scent of sizzling pork rose through the room, interlaced with buttery potatoes, promising something delectable.

When Katie finally returned to the kitchen, she was tasked to scrub not just the floor, but every counter, window, and cabinet door.

"You'll learn to better respect my kitchen by scrubbing. I should never find it covered in flour, pans, and chaos ever again. You clean what you dirty."

Mrs. Romano was on a roll. Dottie had seen her angry before but never beyond a harsh word and better expectations. But this time her face was as red as a ripe tomato, as if something more than a messy kitchen was upsetting her.

The woman picked up a cleaning rag and handed it to Katie, still bickered. "And why on earth did you have coffee grounds out? You've never drank it before."

Already scrubbing, Katie's head shot up from her crouched position. "Coffee grounds!?"

"Yes. Coffee grounds. Didn't you check the tin lid before taking it from the pantry? And you used so much of it, I'll have to place another order soon."

"Oh, no," Katie groaned. She dragged her hand down her face, forgetting the rag between her fingers. Only realizing a moment too late as sudsy water trailed down her nose.

Dottie felt a twinge of pity for the girl. For all her trouble, Katie was still naive and learning.

Just like me.

Dottie huffed a laugh. Who was she to help someone when she couldn't even help herself? But something pricked in her chest. She always wondered how Mae had been so patient with all her antics. But now she understood, it was the Holy Spirit guiding.

Nodding to only the invisible force prodding her, Dottie needed to help the scullery maid.

"Katie, would you like some help with the cleaning? Dinner's nearly done. And I know it'll take the whole night to finish everything."

Katie scoffed. "Help me? You realize I loathe you, right?"

Dottie managed a smile despite the sting. It made no matter what Katie thought; she was going to help. "Doesn't matter, I'm here, and I'm able." Picking up a nearby rag, she set to washing down cabinet doors. Mrs. Romano silently allowed the two girls to work. Anytime she caught the cook's eyes, they seemed to soften with motherly affection.

Maybe I'm doing something right.

With the bottom cabinets finished, Dottie paused, admiring their white surfaces gleaming brighter than they had in months; the water streaks catching the light from the window.

Moving to wash the upper cabinets, Dottie struggled to reach the top edges. Glancing around, she spotted her solution.

Soap stung her hands, and she rubbed her palms against her apron before gripping the wooden chair back. "Please don't wobble," she whispered. Though a bit rickety, it still held up during their lunch breaks, so she believed it could support her even now.

The chair groaned as she climbed on, wobbling a bit when her arm extended above her head.

Please don't fall.

With the last cabinet wiped clean, Katie shoved past, muttering, "Always in the way." The force knocked everything off balance.

Letting out a panicked yelp, her only thought was to brace herself by turning onto her shoulder and wrapping her arms securely around her middle. The air whooshed out from her lungs.

The crack of wood against tile echoed loudly, like a single note announcing danger. The chair clattered to the ground one way as Dottie landed with a thud the opposite direction. Her cheek stung at the impact, yet the tiles' coolness provided a small sense of relief.

For a moment, she closed her eyes, allowing her pulse to calm. And then she felt it. Something wet trickled at her temple. The metallic scent nipped at her nose. Sounds around her muffled. Then everything went dark.

"*Tesoro... Tesoro...*" Someone was calling her, but by the wrong name. *I'm not Treasure...*

She tried opening her lids, but the bright light assaulted her eyes. Shifting her body, a groan escaped her lips.

"Stay down, *Tesoro.* You've hit your head. Doctor Wilson will be here soon."

There was murmuring in the corner of the room. Even with the pounding in her skull, Katie's whispers still reached Dottie's ears.

"Antonio was so rugged today, bearing a bruise and a gash. I asked if he wanted me to patch him up, but he refused and said he'd already taken care of it." Worry filled her voice. "I worked so hard on those brownies, but I think I ruined them."

Dottie wanted to laugh, but her head drummed too fiercely.

So, she made brownies with coffee grounds?

The scullery maid sighed. "I hope he read the letter..." Katie's voice faded as Dottie's mind blurred again.

When she woke again, her muscles ached but Dottie was grateful to be off the kitchen floor. A thin quilt felt cool across her legs, while the bed springs found places to jab her back. Slowly taking in her surroundings, she recognized her own room.

Despite the spring air filtering through the window, a sharp, medicinal smell filled the small room. Afternoon light poured through her window, giving her more reason to grimace.

"I'm so glad you're awake." Mae sat on the edge of the bed holding a bowl and rag.

Anything more than a faint tilt of her lips had her head ache. "Why do we always end up in this position?" She thought back to just a few months ago. She'd been so ill and depressed, she truly believed nothing would pull her from the darkness. But then there was Mae, not giving up, staying diligently by her side just like now, pushing Dottie into the light.

"It'll be your turn one day. For now, I'm here to help."

A movement by the door caught Dottie's attention. "It's all right. Just me." Miss Genevieve stepped out from the shadows. "The doctor just left. He stitched your temple and said, with a little rest, you'll be fine."

Dottie threw a questioning glance at Mae. "Ev-everything's all right?"

Nodding, Mae set the bowl down and leaned in with a whisper. "He said all is well."

Blinking away a tear, she noticed Miss Genevieve approach the bed. "Dottie, I want to give you something. But I'm not sure what it is yet." Her smile made the edges of her eyes crinkle.

"No, I don't thi—"

Mae grasped Dottie's hand. "I have an idea." The parlor maid's eyes glinted with her typical mischievousness, unsettling Dottie. The one that said she knew better but would proceed with her plan anyway.

She's up to something.

Dottie wasn't used to undeserved kindness, and she struggled with how Mae has always cared for her.

Giving a conspirator smile to Miss Genevieve, Mae stepped away. The two women quietly conversed in the corner.

Dottie lifted her head, just enough to eavesdrop, but their voices were too hushed to hear clearly.

"That is of course with your cooperation, Genevieve."

Did I hear right?

Mae called Miss Genevieve by her given name without formalities.

What exactly is their relationship? She squirmed in her bed, hoping to find a comfortable position. Her muscles screamed at the movement.

This question would have to wait for another day.

Letting out a moan, Dottie laid her head back against her pillow.

Abandoning her conspiring, Mae helped Dottie adjust, the springs creaked in protest. "You need more rest. I'll be sure no one disturbs you."

"Thank you, Mae..." her voice drifted as she drifted back to sleep.

Chapter 10: Monday Morning

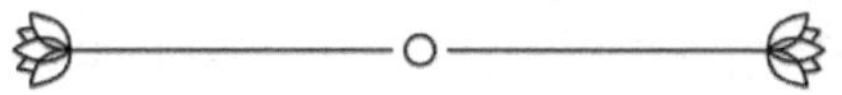

Antonio yanked a weed from the vegetable garden, its roots quickly giving way from the loosened soil. The morning was just beginning as the sun filtered through the trees, dew glistening off the bright new leaves. A few birds nested in a nearby tree, cooing in contentment, while the crickets provided a symphony of chirps. Mist rose from the wood line, creating an almost ethereal scene. Pausing for a moment, Antonio watched a robin forage, hopping closer to the garden in search of breakfast.

On top of his usual duties, he now had to fix the fountain. Time in the stillness before his list of duties piled on was the solace he needed.

He felt God's peace most clearly here, between the furrows and creatures—where work felt like worship.

With a groan, he remembered the embarrassment from the afternoon before.

Yesterday's afternoon flashed in his memory. After the fountain disaster, Antonio had headed home to change, needing time to recoup. From the yelling, the messes, and emotions that Dottie stirred in his heart. He was grateful for a rare moment of silence, with his folks working and his siblings running around, causing mischief somewhere.

As soon as he had peeled the soaked shirt from his arms, someone had knocked on the door. Assuming it was Mr. Leland, come to follow up on their conversation, Antonio opened the door without thought.

Katie had gasped but refused to avert her gaze, her gaze roaming his bare chest. A muscle jumped in his jaw as he fought to step back from her open perusal.

Antonio's stomach clenched at the memory, staring at the dirt beneath his glove, so like her plated offering.

She hadn't said a word, simply thrusted a covered dish toward him and sprinted away. The smell of burnt coffee mixed with pungent perfume trailed behind her. Antonio kept a steady expression as she threw girlish glances over her shoulder.

The girl had followed him around the past few months, and her repeated advances were burdensome. He had tried politely declining Katie's gestures, but she either refused to take the hint or naively believed he faked disinterest.

"Those were terrible brownies." He shuddered, pulling up another stubborn weed, the dirt's coolness seeped through his gloves. "I'll have to be more direct." He didn't want to be unkind, but her persistence grated his nerves.

He rubbed his forehead with the back of his glove and threw the weed into his bucket with more force than necessary. Mamma had warned him of Katie's open harassment toward Dottie.

Just like the tangle of weeds in his hand, sin crept in the same way—choking out the good. Anger bubbled as he recalled Mamma saying, *"I'm just so relieved Dottie protected—protected herself the way she did when she fell from the chair."*

Protection I couldn't give.

He wanted to eliminate every remnant of selfishness, every trace of pride that made him believe he needed to be Dottie's savior instead of trusting God to be hers.

Lifting his eyes up, he caught the light dappling through the branches. Its faint warmth filled him with the reminder that God had everything under control. Maybe that was the lesson he needed to learn. Not to work so hard to fix everything, but to trust that God could.

"Lord, thank You for keeping Dottie safe. Keep her in Your hands."

Antonio stretched, letting tension drain from his shoulders. God wasn't surprised, and He was in control. All Antonio needed to do was... *let go...* A slow breath slipped from his lips, taking his concerns with it.

In the distance, Antonio heard several feet dashing along the path. "Love you, *Tonio!*" Anna squealed as she ran past, with Rosy and Violet, carrying their school things. Without stopping, she called over her shoulder, "Oh, and you have dirt on your forehead!"

"Love you too, *sorella*." He brushed at his face, laughing. "Don't bring any surprises home!" He was certain the last part fell on deaf ears.

"And neither do I." Vincent walked by kicking a stick toward the brush.

Antonio gave his brother an impish laugh. "Do you remember when you gave *Mamma* a used handkerchief one birthday? Quite surprising."

"Oh, shut it." The boy grinned like a rascal, kicked a pebble at his brother, and ran ahead. "See you, *Tonio!*"

With a chuckle, Antonio focused back on weeds that still needed tending.

Maybe I should get her a gift. It'd be fine, something to cheer her up.

"*Tonio*, I knew I'd find you here." Papà clapped Antonio's back and gave his shoulder a gentle squeeze. "Toiling away and never resting. *Bambino*, you need to accept God's gift of rest."

Plucking another weed, Antonio refused to recognize Papà's admonishment.

He doesn't understand, I can't stop until I prove I'm worthy. Until I'm enough.

Papà pulled on Antonio's shoulder. "Come, we have something more important to do."

Leaning back on his heels, Antonio rested his elbows on his knees and pinched the bridge of his nose. "More important than work?" It was frustrating how the man rarely took anything seriously, yet still managed to do his job flawlessly.

The old gardener chuckled, his face reddening with amusement. "The right woman's always more important."

I guess I'll have to humor the old man.

Antonio knew once Papà had his mind set, there was no going back. Antonio stood, brushing mud from his knees. "And who might be the right woman, *Papà*? Katie? Did you see the brownies she brought? Even the hogs turned away."

"No, not that *bambina*. She's not the one for you." Papà let out a belt of laughter. With eyes turned to the sky like a prayer, the man muttered under his breath. "Stupid boy doesn't know what's good for him."

Maybe I don't.

Antonio held out his arms in defeat. "All right, you win. Lead the way, *Papà*." He'd have to wait for the man's answer on who was the *right woman.* And based on the overcast sky, weeding would be put off for another day.

When they reached the formal gardens, Papà rubbed his chin and turned in a slow circle. "So, tell me, what's good for a headache?"

How does this man always know what I'm thinking?

Antonio smirked. The old man knew exactly who his right one was. He pushed down the embarrassment that his affection for Dottie was so transparent because he couldn't deny it.

A water drop landed on his swollen cheek, immediately cooling the bruise. Glancing up, Antonio hadn't noticed the sky darkening. Soon, droplets fell in a steady rhythm.

Papà tipped his flat cap back, squinting at the sky with eyes still full of mischief. "Looks like we'll be working indoors today!"

Antonio couldn't hold back his laugh. "We better hurry! And I know exactly what to pick."

I hope she likes them.

Rain pounded against the window, waking Dottie up from a fitful sleep. Dreams of falling and never rising again plagued her mind throughout the night.

I'm glad it was just a dream.

A spring pressed deeply into her shoulder blade. Stretching the sore muscle, she decided it was time to ask Mr. Leland for a new mattress. Hers had turned into a bed of nails, each spring finding its way into her back.

Something light and sweet floated through the air, ridding the room of the astringent smell of medicine. Carefully turning, Dottie spotted a simple glass vase on her dresser, filled with a few hyacinths, bruised sprigs of rosemary and a tucking of wild violets. She brightened at the offering. A small bowl with water and mixed with wild violets, sat beside it.

Probably Mae or maybe one of the girls, no one else would take that time.

It reminded her of Mae and Mrs. Brower's cottage, always warm, and smelling sweet. A place she found peace in, even with the twins' constant chattering. Her lips tugged into a smile imagining the quaint living area, warm and full of light and laughter.

Dottie gingerly pushed herself to a sitting position, she couldn't stay in bed all day. Her head swam with the motion. She gripped her bedframe; the coarse blanket needled her fingers.

I can get up.

Shifting to rise, nausea threatened to overtake her. Cringing, Dottie scooted back onto the bed, focusing all her attention on the downpour outside. She prayed the steady pelting against the window would divert her attention from her gurgling middle.

Carefully, she reached up; her hair was matted along her temple. Accidentally grazing the wound, she winced. "It feels like a mountain ridge." Her groan matched the distant thunder rolling through the valley. "Maybe no one will notice with my hair parted differently."

Not like that matters, anyway.

A giggle rumbled in her throat. "Rounded, wounded, and graceless. What a mess I'm in." She shook her head until the throbbing returned.

In the past, these things would've aggravated her. Her whole life had revolved around her beauty and allure. But now, sitting in simple servant quarters, with a shoddy bed, damaged temple, and... well, she was more content than she'd been in years.

"What's changed?" She looked back at the window; the storm was letting up and the sunlight splintered through the clouds.

God's grace.

Her eyes danced. "Thank you, Lord."

She'd heard it so many times, but this time it was *hers*. Grace wasn't something she'd earned. It had come uninvited, like the rain washing over the garden outside her window, where something new began to grow. She gazed at the flowers once more.

Just maybe I can begin again too.

Laying her head back, Dottie listened to the light drip of rain droplets rolling off the roof and hitting her sill. The soft melody enticed her lids to slowly drift close.

The sound of heavy footsteps echoed down the corridor. Each step sending a wave of warnings up her spine.

"Dottie!" Timothy shot into her room, his voice booming in her ears, causing the pounding to return. The door rattled on its hinges.

Clara rushed up behind him, panting. "Timothy, I'll have to fetch Mr. Griggs, you can't be in a woman's room." The chambermaid's soft voice brooked no argument, but Timothy's focus was solely on Dottie as he kneeled before her bed.

She tried scooting back until the wall pressed hard against her spine. Trusting Clara wouldn't abandon her, Dottie allowed herself the slightest bit of relief. Yet the intensity in the footman's stare made her nerves raw.

Why's he so close?

"Oh, Dottie, your beautiful face is ruined." Timothy reached up as if to caress a fallen hair from her jaw. Before his fingers reached her, Dottie flinched away, hoping the space behind the wall could swallow her up.

Clara's firm whisper could barely be heard over Dottie's hammering pulse. "Timothy… I think you should step back." The girl leaned halfway out the door yet continued to keep a wary eye on Timothy the entire time.

Ignoring the girl, he tilted further into Dottie's personal space. She fumbled for her pillow, hoping it would shield her from the footman.

He hasn't even asked how I'm feeling…

Timothy continued to utter, "Your face, your poor face…" beneath his breath, all the while he gazed only at her injury. His obsession with her appearance was unsettling, and Dottie clutched the pillow tighter.

God, please make him leave.

Pastor Somers's message came to mind; how God hadn't forgotten.

You'll not leave me, Lord. Thank you for reminding me.

Like a breeze in the air, her tight chest broke free, and fear gave way to assurance. She didn't have to cower like some child anymore.

"Timothy, I'm still unwell and need rest." Her throat was dry when she tried to speak. "We can talk later. I need you to leave."

Pulling back, Timothy's features hardened. Huffing, he stood and ran a hand through his perfectly styled hair. "You're probably right, but that girl," he growled, "she hurt you!"

Dottie blinked, surprised by the outburst. "Surely, it was an accident."

Timothy paced her cramped room. "But it wasn't. Don't you understand, she's conniving. And don't trust Maria either, she's just as wretched!" He approached her again.

Could it be true?

Dottie searched for all the memories. Sure, the girls were cruel, but not enough to intentionally harm someone. "No, they're just young and jealous."

Clara spoke up, bolder than before, edging toward Timothy. "Timothy—time to go. Now."

As she looked toward her friend, Dottie saw a flash of a familiar uniform drift by the door, a uniform too nice to be someone from the kitchens. *Maria?*

Dottie wasn't sure, but from the quick exchange it seemed the woman was glaring. The look lingered just long enough to raise the hairs on Dottie's neck.

"Timothy." Clara hissed, her patience fading.

As he backed away, Dottie's fists slowly relaxed, but remained securely wrapped around the pillow.

For a moment, Timothy stood rooted in place, his eye roaming her from hair to foot. Finally, with an inhale, he took another step back. "It'll heal. The doctor did well with the stitches." Frowning, Timothy glanced at the dresser. "So, you like these?" His chin jutted toward the vase of flowers, jaw ticking.

"Yes, they're lovely."

"I agree," he sought her face again, "but only as lovely as you are." There was no smile, just a chilling stare.

Dottie's stomach clenched under the intensity.

Did Timothy give those to me?

She wondered if he was upset that she hadn't known. Wanting to ease any irritation, she complimented the thoughtful sender.

"Whoever brought them was extremely considerate. They helped relieve my headache and were a welcomed sight when I woke."

Timothy grinned. "Good. Good. Glad you like them." He turned and rushed toward the door, almost knocking into Clara. Stopping mid-step, he opened his mouth to speak just as Mr. Griggs voice bellowed down the hall. "The clock waits for no man, Mr. Brooks, though you appear intent on testing it."

"I gotta go." He produced his classic dimpled smile and rushed out the room.

Dottie let out a sigh and dipped her chin, releasing the tension from her neck. Even when the door closed, the echo of Timothy's voice clung to the room like stale air. She hated that fear still had power over her.

"Thank you, Clara." She rasped, as she forced the trembling from her voice.

"I've said it before, and I'll say it again. It brings me joy to help others when the Holy Spirit calls me to do so. He'll not leave you, and if He leads me, neither will I. Now, lay down and rest. You're not well enough to work. Miss Edith's stepping in to cover for you."

Doing as the young woman ordered, Dottie found herself sliding down, resting her head on her crumpled pillow. She breathed in the fresh hyacinth as Clara brought the blanket up around her chin.

"The flowers are lovely, aren't they? Funny, he would've brought them to me. He doesn't seem the flower type..." Dottie murmured as she drifted to sleep, but she didn't miss Clara's next words.

"No, Timothy wasn't the one. Someone more worthy brought them."

Worthy?

There was only one man, aside from Jesus, who Dottie could define as worthy.

Antonio.

She smiled softly, her last thought was his beard against her cheek, rough yet soft, holding her as he spoke her name, "*Tesoro.*"

Chapter 11: Monday Afternoon

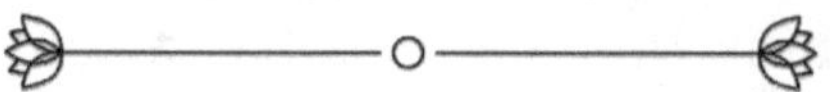

Dottie's lashes fluttered open to Mae sitting quietly on a nearby stool. "You've given me quite a scare, Dear Dottie. But I'm glad you're awake." Mae dipped a cloth into the bowl of violet-infused water, droplets lightly splashed as she wrung out the excess. She draped it carefully over Dottie's forehead. The coolness and light flowery smell eased Dottie's tense brow.

Lifting her arms toward the ceiling in a stretch, Dottie wondered how long she'd slept. "Mae, what time is it?"

Through the window, Dottie could tell the sky was still overcast, drizzle still pinging against the glass. But based on how the shadows stretched across her floor, it was already well past noon. She worried her lip.

At this rate, Mrs. Romano's going to fuss at my frequent absences.

Pulling her from her thoughts, Mae replied, "It's just before two. Mrs. Romano and Edith are working hard to get tea time ready."

"Two?!" Dottie shot up, damp rag flopping to her lap. Immediately regretting the hasty motion, she grabbed her head to steady it. "I've got to get to the kitchen."

With a faint chuckle, Mae pushed her down to the pillow. "Hold on and let's start over. I need you to *slowly,"* she stretched the word, "sit up and see how you feel."

Dottie shot her friend a look. "I'm not a child."

"True, but you're stubborn like one."

Rolling her eyes, Dottie couldn't help but smile. "Fine."

Mae knows me far too well.

Easing her way to sitting, she shifted her legs over the bed. "I'm not so woozy."

"Good. Now, try standing."

Gripping the edge, Dottie shifted her weight. For a moment, the room tilted, then righted itself.

Mae steadied her. "Now, how do we feel?"

Placing her hand over her stomach, Dottie drew in a breath. "We're fine." She brightened and peeked at Mae. "Yes, we're all right."

"Good. We'll return to the kitchen? And I'll stay until you're settled." Mae pulled the work dress from the dresser. "I think Mrs. Carmela has a spot set up at the worktable. No unnecessary moving and no more climbing on chairs, Dr. Winston's orders." Mae nudged her shoulder. "And why risk a tumble when God made tall men for such things?"

Giggles erupted from both women. But Dottie quickly sobered. "What about Katie?"

"Oh no, she's not nearly tall enough."

Even though she smiled, Dottie shot her friend a pointed look. "You know what I mean."

Grabbing her shoulders, Mae peered into Dottie's face. "Don't worry, she's working laundry with Helen, and that woman doesn't tolerate attitude." Righting herself, Mae inhaled deeply. "So, breath. Everything's fine."

Dottie nodded, afraid her throat wouldn't release a thank you without crying.

Mae helped Dottie ease into her work dress. But as Dottie went to fasten the buttons, the once taunt fabric was looser. Fingering the side seam, she felt additional inserts had been added, along with laces. Turning to Mae, her eyes misted. "Did..."

Mae interrupted. "While you rested, Miss Genevieve and I had Helen make some adjustments. How does it feel?"

Dottie thought back over the past few months with Mae by her side. Wiping at her wet lashes, she met her friend's eyes. "Perfect. Thank you," she whispered, lifting a prayer.

And thank you, God, for sending me people who remind me of Your constant love. I wouldn't have survived without them.

Just as Mae said, Mrs. Romano had set up a station at the worktable, complete with everything she needed and a comfortable chair.

"Miss Edith, please make sure the tea pot gets to Dottie before the parlor maids arrive." Mrs. Romano's usually boisterous commands had lowered to restrained requests. The woman knew better than to order about the strong-willed upper maid.

A wrinkle formed between Dottie's brows. "Mrs. Romano, why isn't the new maid Bessie helping?"

"Oh, heavens no, she'd be just as much trouble as Katie, and I'll have no more of that in my kitchen." Mrs. Romano flicked a towel her way, "Now, back to work, we've got a feast to prepare for tonight!"

The ladies worked in pleasant silence, only speaking when needed. The chamomile's sweet apple-y smell filled the room as it simmered, giving Dottie a memory of an apple orchard.

Her father had pulled an apple from a branch and placed it in her outstretched hands. "See this apple, child? Roll it in your hands; check for any bruises." Her hands fumbled but followed her father's instruction. "It's perfect, Daddy."

She fingered the china set before her. Just like the apple. *Everything's perfect.*

"Good. That's what people want. Perfect apples." He had lifted one from the ground; bruises oozed with yellow mush, and a rotten smell wafted before her.

"Now, see this one?" Dottie's hands recoiled as he handed it to her, and it rolled to the ground.

Dottie heard a door creak open while Mrs. Romano murmured something to Edith. Not noticing the kitchen around her, she traced her finger along the tray's edge, a slight nick jabbing her skin sharply.

"That apple's rejected. It's ruined, no longer beautiful. No longer usable. People don't want those." He had crouched low, looking in her eyes. His sun-wrinkled hand brushed a stray hair from her brow. "Be a beautiful apple, Dottie, and people'll want you. Once you're ruined, you'll be tossed away."

I don't want to be rejected for being less perfect.

She gave a quick sniff. No use crying over something she couldn't change now.

"Tesoro." Mrs. Romano's soft voice pulled at the memory. "Are the tea trays about done? I heard the chime; Mae should be here soon."

"Yes, Mrs. Romano, everything's perfectly in place." She shook her head. Her father's words clung to her all these years, molding her into the woman she'd become. But maybe he had it all wrong. Dottie was a rotten apple, and yet, every day she found God calling for her, ignoring her tattered choices, showing her every day that He loved her no matter what. "You-Are-the-God-Who-Sees."

She inhaled, watching the steam curl from the teapot when the smell of machine oil and stale smoke replaced the chamomile's aroma, but before she could register it, a gravelly voice spoke into her ear.

"What's that Dottie?"

An uninvited shiver ran up her spine. Turning, she found Charlie directly behind her. Both Edith and Mrs. Romano were no longer in the kitchen, and she was now alone with Charlie. Images of him punching Antonio filled her mind.

"Oh, you startled me, Charlie!" Holding her hand to her chest, Dottie tried to calm her racing heart. She didn't want to let on that she was afraid.

Find a safe place.

She scrambled off the chair and eased away from the imposing man. "Are you here to fix something?" She slowly rounded the worktable, praying someone would walk in.

His eyes sparkled as he followed her. "I came to see you. Heard you had an accident." He gestured to her injured forehead. "I wanted to make sure you were well."

Dottie's foot caught on the table's leg, but before she tripped, Charlie grabbed her wrist. "Honestly, Dottie, I wanted to talk to you about something important." His words sounded sincere, but his expression didn't match.

Her skin burned beneath his meaty fingers as he dragged her through the pantry and into the servant hall. Shelves blurred past her. Everything felt tilted as she stepped past the threshold.

The sun casted long shadows across the long dining table, worn from years of use. The fireplace, extinguished since the morning chill, still smoldering on the far wall. Yet, everything appeared foggy.

God, protect me.

When she tried jerking her arm away, he tightened his grip, refusing to release her. "Now, Dottie, do make this easier. I came all this way to talk to you." His tone carried a clipped, condescending edge that made her stomach tighten. The same she remembered from her childhood scoldings, but she'd not let him treat her like a child.

"If Mr. Leland or Mr. Frederick find you here without reason, you'll get in trouble." Finally yanking her wrist free, searing pain shot up her arm. Red marks quickly bloomed on her skin. "Say what you need to and go. I don't want trouble."

Charlie's mocking laugh bounced off the empty room's wall. "Trouble? Me? No, Mrs. Stratford likes me. But you, miss, have been troubling my mind for weeks."

Dottie's throat bobbed as she backed away. His sudden change in attitude unsettled her.

"In fact, I'm certain I'm in love with you." He flashed his most handsome smile.

It's the one phrase she'd always wished to hear. But coming from Charlie, it didn't make her heart flutter. She knew what he felt was not love but infatuation.

A stillness wrapped around her, God was with her, granting her a bravery she'd never known. With chin raised, she challenged his declaration.

"Charlie, it's not love. You barely know me."

By now, Dottie had walked herself into a corner near the fireplace, with no escape. If his attitude flipped, she'd be trapped.

If I can just get to the other side of the table...

She slowly inched away from the wall.

"No, I do know you, Dottie. You're beautiful, full of life, your hair shines like an autumn day..."

His love is only skin deep.

Reaching the table, her fingers grazed the wall behind her, hoping to find the door frame.

But Charlie was no fool. As she reached the knob, his arm blocked it shut, his breath dancing across her brow. "Tut, tut. Now don't go doing that..." Her stomach rolled as his hand gingerly brushed against her jaw. Though the Lord's presence didn't erase her discomfort, it gave her strength to speak past her fear.

"I—I need some space, Charlie." Her chin quivered, her plea just above a whisper. "Please..."

❀ ❀ ❀

The sweet mixture of spices from oregano to cinnamon reminded Antonio of Mamma's small cottage kitchen. The pantry, like most of the estate, needed constant repair. Placing down his tools, he removed jars stacked on a broken shelf. The smooth wood creaked beneath his fingers, speaking of years of hard work.

He paused when he heard shuffling in the servant hall and cocked his head, a tuft of hair fell across his brow.

Mamma's been nagging me to trim this up.

"No woman wants a sheepdog as a husband, Tonio'. *I'll snip your hair in your sleep if you're not careful."*

Antonio's lip quirked up as he moved closer to the door. It wasn't mealtime, so the room should have been empty. He heard murmurs and a floorboard creak.

He tried to edge the door open, but it wouldn't budge. Something was blocking it. Resting his ear on the smooth oak, Charlie's voice cooed through the cracks. His stomach knotted, knowing they were directed at Dottie.

A secret rendezvous?

If she was choosing Charlie, Antonio would step out of the way. He had no claim over her. But he had hoped her feelings had changed. His heart caught mid-beat, disappointment cracking around the edges. As he was about to step away, Dottie's voice broke through, faint like a whisp.

"I—I need some space, Charlie."

Antonio heard the distressed plea for help. And after the punch to the face, Antonio couldn't trust Charlie not to hurt her.

Squeezing the doorknob, he attempted to stay calm. The rusted hinges groaned as he shoved his body into the door, forcefully moving whatever blocked it.

"God, give me courage," he whispered as he stepped between the two, trusting the Lord to steady him. One glance at Dottie's quivering form told Antonio everything he needed to know.

"Why are you here?" Charlie glared at Antonio. "I told you to back down!"

Watching the vein in Charlie's neck throb, Antonio pushed Dottie behind him. She huddled close, gripping his shirt. His pulse surged, warning him that this could end poorly, but he refused to let the bullying continue.

Face to face with a man who threatened everything that he held dear, Antonio swallowed down the bitter words he knew he shouldn't say. The idea of this man intimidating her ignited a surge of rage in his chest.

"Mrs. Stratford might like you, but Mr. Frederick doesn't take to people who bully others." He glanced back at Dottie as she gripped his shirt, her trembling form providing him the courage to continue. "If this is what you call love, I'm sure Dottie wants nothing to do with it."

"What's it to you what some maid wants?" Charlie drew up to Antonio, bumping his chest. The man's shadow loomed over, and his clothes reeked like he'd forgotten to bathe.

Antonio knew he'd have to lay out his heart to protect her. Taking a breath, he stood to his full height, his eyes nearly level with Charlie's brow. "You heard her; she clearly said she needed space, and you'd do well to respect that." Dottie put her small hand in his, giving him strength to push forward. "Because she matters to—"

"Oh!"

His declaration was interrupted by a basket thudding on the floorboards. Katie bent low, hastily gather the freshly laundered napkins that tumbled across the floor. A gripe passed through her lips, "Why's it always gotta be Dottie?"

Drawing Antonio's attention back to the situation, Charlie's broad form knocked into his chest. His gruff voice rumbled in Antonio's ear. "We'll talk about this another time." With one final word of warning, Charlie retreated out the door. "And we're not done either, Dottie."

Quiet sniffles morphed into sobs. Turning, Antonio tugged Dottie into a gentle hug and slowly rubbed her back, sparks pulsing through his fingertips with each touch. "It's fine. Everything's all right." He kept his voice calm, trying to not only soothe the woman in his arms, but also himself.

Dottie peeked up from beneath her lashes, an endearing little glance, and shook her head. "No, Antonio, it's not all right." Her voice wobbled, taking his jaw in her palm. "And I'm not sure that it'll ever be." Dottie stepped away, letting her hand slip from his face.

The warmth it left felt like a tether, leading him to follow. Antonio reached her just before she left the servant hall. Holding her middle, she closed herself off.

She knows she's safe with me; I could feel it.

Katie slammed the basket on the table, the sound ricocheted off the walls. For the first time Antonio realized the girl was still in the room. "Dottie, Dottie, Dottie... I don't understand why *every* man on the estate is so charmed by *Dottie*! Just because of her pretty face?" The young maid gave an assessing eye toward Dottie.

Antonio's jaw ticked. The need to protect Dottie' from the unwanted probing coursed through his veins.

"Well, she's not so pretty anymore, is she? Putting on weight and now with that gash on her head." She shrugged in disbelief. "Why would anyone want her?" Disgust dripped from each word of Katie's tirade. With each word she stepped closer to a nervous Dottie.

How could she say such things?

Flashes of Katie harming Dottie rushed through Antonio's mind. "Katie, that's enough." As he reached toward her to pull her away, she yelled, "Don't touch me!"

Antonio's gut tightened as her elbow was on a direct path toward Dottie's face. Snatching Dottie's waist, he pulled her out of the way.

For just a moment, everything felt right. With one arm around her waist and the other around her shoulders, Dottie was where she belonged, in his arms again. And this time he didn't hesitate to brush a light kiss to the top of her hair.

Dottie's body shook as he held her firmly, his pulse still racing from her near injury. Only when her trembling eased did Antonio allow himself to relax.

Katie's expression flitted from shock, to hurt, and landed on frustration. "Bah! I'm done with this!" Her shoes squeaked as she rushed from the room, slamming the door with a bang, her basket forgotten on the table.

Dottie flinched in his embrace. But he didn't dare move, much less speak. Her head fit perfectly against his chest. The only sounds were small inhales of breath while adrenaline tapered off. As his fingers skittered down her arm, she sucked in a breath and drew back.

Antonio wanted anything to pull her in again. But her pale face and the way she slunk against the wall made it clear she wouldn't accept his affection.

I'm an idiot. She's minutes from being harassed, and I'm over here practically flirting.

Still, he needed to know she was unharmed. Lowering himself to her level, he met her eyes. "Are you hurt?" He gently bopped her nose.

With a tentative smile, Dottie brushed him away. "I'm right as rain. Well, not really. But what about you? I thought he'd all but knock your teeth out." Her laugh was stiff as she tightened the hold around her knees. "And then, how'd you get to enjoy your Mamma's great cooking?"

He saw the slight tremble of her hands and felt his frustration bubble.

Forgive me, Father. I told You I'd trust You in this. That I'd let go. But seeing Dottie like this is just too much. I'm not sure I can avoid getting involved.

Moments ticked by and Antonio felt the distance between them growing. She searched his face until her lips finally parted. "Listen, Antonio, I appreciate your help, but maybe next time just stay out of it." Her voice faded into a whisper.

Antonio's jaw tightened. There's no way he could watch someone mistreat her.

She wants me to stay out of it? That won't be happening.

"Dottie, the man was harassing you! And you want me to stand down?" His arm flung out in frustration, and she flinched.

She's scared.

Pacing back, he shoved his hands into his pockets and softened his reply. "Dottie, I'll never be able to stand by, doing nothing and knowing you'll be hurt.

"But you have to, Antonio. I'm not—" Looking up, a tear tracked down her cheek. He wanted to wipe it away, but he kept his hands securely in his pockets.

Dottie licked her lips as she hesitated, withdrawing further into herself. "I'm not worth your care. So, please. Please stop."

He'd heard enough. There was no point convincing her that she deserved to be treated better. "Fine. You'd rather I sit back and let you get taken advantage of?" He ran his fingers through his hair. "Fine."

Without a second look, Antonio left the servant hall. Left Dottie. And left his heart behind. With the pantry shelf forgotten, the garden called to him.

"But I'll not stand by and watch, Tesoro."

Chapter 12: Tuesday

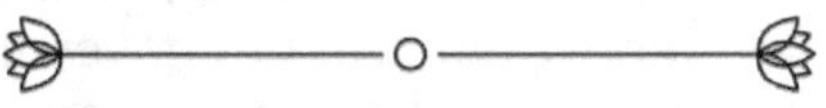

Adjusting her kerchief, Dottie nibbled her lip. She didn't understand what had made Antonio so upset. He skipped dinner. Mrs. Romano made an excuse that he was unwell, but Dottie knew the truth. He was avoiding her again.

Can't he tell I'm trying to protect him from Charlie? From myself?

And yet, she didn't want to push him away. Every time Antonio came near, something would pull her in. Every brush of his beard left her heart aching to stay close. And he kissed her...

...well, kissed my head.

It had felt more intimate than any stolen kiss she had shared in the past.

Dottie sighed as she tightened her dress laces, grinning that her clothes now fit properly. Once her shoes were on, she sped down the corridor, only noticing midway that the familiar thud against her chest was absent. Reaching up, she found the cufflink missing from around her neck.

"I must have left it on the dresser." Pressing her hand against the empty space, she smiled. "I think I can go without it today." She'd not gone without it for months, but something inside said she could face the day without it.

Fresh bread wafted up the stairwell, greeting Dottie before the sounds did. The smell of greasy bacon had her mouth watering.

Reaching the final step, she found Mae leaning on her elbows at the worktable, sipping a cup of tea, while Edith and Mrs. Romano bustled about fixing breakfast. Bacon sizzled on the stove while a large stockpot bubbled on the back burner.

"You're here!" Mae's face brightened, straightening in her seat. The air felt unsettled, like Dottie was about to walk into battle.

Maybe I need my necklace after all.

She glanced up the stair until she distinctly heard Mrs. Romano grumbling at the stove. "The girl's bumped her head and forgotten the time we start work, and how to let a man properly love her." She *tsked* under her breath.

Edith let out a snort but tried to cover it with a cough as she finished stacking freshly washed pots. Dottie would have missed it if Mae hadn't cut a disapproving glare at the two women.

Clearing her throat, Mae patted the seat next to her and slid an extra cup in front of it. The chair creaked as she sat.

I've got to watch what I eat.

Mae pushed a plate of steaming bacon and a buttered biscuit in front of her.

Casting a sideways glance at her friend, Dottie thought, *this woman can't be trusted. Always in my head and doing the exact opposite of what I want.*

She'd just have to hold off and enjoy the tea; she had enough self-control to do that. Wrapping her fingers around the teacup, the swirl of minty steam rose to greet her, warmth radiated through her body. With a flitting glance at Mrs. Romano, Dottie turned to Mae. "So, is this gossip hour or are you about to interrogate me? Because you all are making me a bit nervous."

"Nothing that serious." Mae nudged the breakfast closer, the crisp bacon threatening Dottie's resolve. "We're just having a little talk."

Dottie took a long sip. A *little talk* sounded more dangerous than an interrogation. She kept her head low, focused on the swirling steam from her cup.

"So, want to tell me about yesterday?" Mae peered over her cup. "And not the short version, I need the detailed, moment-by-moment version."

With a sharp inhale, Dottie glanced around the room. "Here? Now?"

"No time like the present, *Tesoro.* Get to talkin'." Mrs. Romano's muffled command meant, even busy checking bread, she had every intention of listening in.

Dottie hesitated as she blinked back tears. She didn't want to tell them; it was too hard. But Mae's encouraging smile told her she could trust these women. With a shaky breath, she unloaded the events from the moment Charlie arrived to when Antonio walked out.

At the end, Mae pulled back Dottie's dress sleeve and gasped. "He did this to you?" The bruises had deepened overnight, leaving a trail of finger impressions along Dottie's wrist.

"It's not so bad, they'll heal fast." She quickly tugged her sleeve down; her father's words ringing in her ears.

Once you're ruined, you'll be tossed away.

She tucked her chin against her chest, focusing on the now lukewarm tea. The bruise throbbed faintly, a cruel reminder that Charlie hadn't truly gone, not from the estate, and not from her thoughts.

"You're wrong. This isn't just bad, it's unacceptable. I'll talk to Leland. He'll not let that man back on the estate." Mae gently lifted Dottie's chin. "Now, for the other matter. Why'd you tell Antonio that you're not worth his care?"

Dottie's face heated.

No doubt Antonio told Mr. Sal. And that man won't keep secrets from his wife.

From behind, she heard Mrs. Romano grunt. The woman was going to hold a grudge if Dottie wasn't careful. Leaned in, she lowered her voice so only Mae could hear. "This is probably not the place to discuss it. You know my situation."

"What's this whispering?" Mrs. Romano's voice was just behind Dottie's ear, tickling the strands that had fallen loose from her kerchief.

"N-nothing."

Mae took her hand and squeezed. "There's no need to be afraid, Dear Dottie. They already know."

They know?

Dottie's hands felt clammy; pulling them away from Mae's, she carefully dried them on a rag left on the table.

Glancing from Mae, to Mrs. Romano to Edith, Dottie's face felt like fire. "But—but how?"

Mrs. Romano gave a full bellied laugh. "Oh, *Tesoro*, you can't hide it from ones who've been there before. Well, not Edith, but she's old enough to know."

Dottie felt exposed as she pressed her palms to her eyes, trying to keep the tears at bay. "Then you know why I'm not worthy?" Hot tears ran down her cheeks. Mrs. Romano pulled Dottie close and smoothed a hand over her hair. Through broken sobs she released her worries. "He'll not want me. He's far too good."

"Oh, *cara*," the older woman cooed softly, "if the right man loves you, he'll not care." She cradled Dottie's cheeks in her hands, and her features softened with amusement. The fine grit of flour on the woman's palms scratched at Dottie's skin. "Give *Tonio* the chance to love you. I can see it, *amore'*." Mrs. Romano glanced out the window. "Just as I can see God's ever-loving care for you every day, I can see *Tonio's* as well."

Dottie's chest tightened at the memory of his hand enclosing hers the day before—warm, steady, unshakable. Pulling back, she wiped her face with her sleeve and shook her head.

They'll think I'm ridiculous.

"No, I'm a ruined apple."

"A what?!" Mrs. Romano chuckled. "You are no ruined anything. What man can ruin, God can restore." Edith brought Mrs. Romano a glass jar from the window. Resting on the lip was a wrinkled sweet potato that had been left forgotten.

"*Tesoro*, look at the cut in this sweet potato. Some would say it's damaged, even ruined. But check closely." Tiny green shoots pushed out from the cut. The older woman whispered, "Even when damaged, it reaches toward the light with new growth." Mrs. Romano handed it back to Edith and brushed her weathered hand on Dottie's hair. "When we reach for the Light, there's no ruin. Only new beginnings."

As Dottie tilted into her touch, a verse stirred in her memory, something Pastor Somers had said a few weeks ago. "*In Him we have redemption through His blood, the forgiveness of sins, according to the riches of His grace.*"

The verse drifted through Dottie's mind as she leaned into the head cook's caress... She closed her eyes. She went to finger the cufflink around her neck, remembering she'd left it behind. Its absence felt like freedom from the shackles of shame.

I just need faith.

Her father had been wrong. Maybe, just maybe, Antonio could love her. A blush crept up her neck.

Mae gave Dottie's hand a final squeeze, then turned her sharp gaze on Edith. "Your turn."

Seeing the upper maid's shock, Dottie held in a giggle.

Edith backed up, hands raised in defense. "I think I hear Mrs. Brower calling. She probably needs help with Maria."

"No, she needs no help. We need to have a talk." Mrs. Romano gave Dottie one final squeeze as she went back to the sink, taking the sweet potato with her.

Behind her, Mae somehow beat Edith into submission, and the poor woman had her own teacup.

For a moment, Mae glanced at Dottie and pointed to the forgotten breakfast. "Don't think I've missed you avoiding the food. We need you to eat." She gave a curt nod to Mrs. Romano, who brought her a fresh plate with warmed bacon.

So bossy.

While Dottie took her first bite, she watched Edith clutch her cup until her knuckles turned white. "Listen, we've been over this, Mae. I'm not ready yet."

Mae urged Edith to join them at church. The woman was persistent if anything. But maybe that was her charm. Mae had this undeniable love for others and wanted nothing but good for them.

"How about this. Miss Genevieve and I have a midweek Bible and prayer time every Wednesday night in the library. How about you at least come to that?"

Edith groaned and thudded her forehead on the worn table. "Fine, you win, I'll go to the Wednesday Bible thing." She lifted her head and wagged her finger at Mae. "But no more pushing about Sundays!"

Mae gave a triumphant smile and turned back to her tea. "We'll see." Leaning in, Mae touched Dottie's arm. "I expect you tomorrow night too."

Dottie had been attending church, sitting among a large group of people, hidden, unnoticed. But the idea of being with a small group of people, praying and talking about the Bible felt so vulnerable. She shivered despite the warm room. "Uh, sure. That'll be good." Dottie didn't believe her own words.

It'll be dreadful, she thought as she took another bite of bacon.

❀ ❀ ❀

Antonio refused to enter the manor unless absolutely necessary. And based on what Papà said, it was necessary. Mr. Leland had summoned him for an impromptu meeting in Mr. Frederick's office.

They'll likely be discussing my dismissal.

Deciding it would hurt too much if he saw Dottie, and the breathtaking way she lit up his world, he'd enter through the garden door to the morning room.

Hope no one will be in there today...

So caught up in his thoughts of Dottie, he didn't notice Katie standing at the laundry door until she blocked his way. "I have something to say, but I'm too scared. So here." She shoved a letter into his hand without meeting his eyes. "Don't read it now, I'll be embarrassed. Read it when you're alone."

After how she'd treated Dottie, Antonio wanted nothing more than to toss the letter back at her. Instead, he shoved it in his pocket and kept walking. He didn't bother looking back.

I'm in no mood for more love letters.

Stepping from the terrace through the morning room glass doors, the early sun splashed through the full-length windows, illuminating the entire room. Potted ferns leaned toward the sunlight, and vases of spring blossoms perfumed the space.

Antonio glanced at his dirty boots as he stepped carefully over the cream-colored rugs.

Don't want Mrs. Stratford fussing over dirty rugs.

Mr. Griggs stood at his post in the entryway. "Taking the scenic route today, Mr. Romano?" The old butler dismissed him with an indiscernible nod. Glancing back, Antonio thought the man's shoulders bounced like he was laughing.

He's a strange one.

The detour had cost him time. As the grandfather clock chiming nine, he took the front stairs two at a time, nearly knocking into Mae.

"Whoa, Antonio. You're running like there's smoke at your heels." She adjusted a tray on her hip and placed a reassuring hand on his shoulder. "Breathe. There's no need to rush."

Antonio bent low, hands on his knees, trying to catch his breath. "Sorry, Miss Mae, I have a meeting with Mr. Leland." With his gaze lowered, Antonio gave a self-deprecating laugh. "And don't want to be marked as lazy."

She dipped her head until her gaze met his. "You're not at fault. I probably shouldn't know so much, but trust me, Antonio, Leland is looking for your help, not to punish you."

"Are you sure?"

"Yes, now get going before you're any later."

He almost wished it were Dottie urging him to lift his chin; one glance from her would've steadied him faster than a hundred reassurances. And yet, Antonio's chest felt lighter. Maybe Mae was right, and he wasn't in trouble after all. Taking the stairs again, he called over his shoulder, "Thanks, Miss Mae!"

Approaching Mr. Frederick's study, Antonio quickly brushed off a dusting of dirt from his arms and ran his hand through his hair. The dark mahogany door loomed ahead, shining from a recent polishing. It opened before he could knock.

Mr. Leland's smile should have been a comfort, especially after speaking with Miss Mae, but instead, Antonio's heart raced as he stepped over the threshold.

What if she's mistaken?

Mr. Frederick sat in his leather chair, elbows propped on a simple, yet well-kept oak desk. Soft light filtered through the window, casting a glow around his form. The room felt open and warm. Antonio almost sighed in relief if it wasn't for the estate owner's serious expression.

"Please take a seat, Mr. Romano." Mr. Frederick gestured to the tweed seats before him as Mr. Leland took the other.

"Yes, sir." He wiped his clammy hands across his thighs in a slow rhythm, hoping the motion would calm his nerves.

Mr. Frederick shifted a few papers around before speaking, giving Antonio opportunity to survey the room. An oak bookshelf stood in the corner, each shelf meticulously kept and full of books. A plain clock sat on the top shelf, carefully keeping time with its gentle ticks that gave Antonio a sense of ease.

"Antonio, we brought you here today to discuss the recent incidents in gardens. These are your duties, so we need your assistance in understanding the situation." Mr. Frederick's gaze was warm, but professional.

Mr. Leland opened a notebook and brought it to his lap. "We'll make this simple, going down the line one-by-one, beginning with the boxwoods. Tell us what happened and what you saw."

As Antonio explained the moment he found the boxwoods, he couldn't get the image of Dottie falling into his arms out of his mind. His face warmed. Clearing his throat, he glanced at the two men who waited expectantly. "The boxwoods didn't just fall over, someone shoveled them out. There were fresh gashes at the root balls."

Mr. Frederick's face remained neutral. "Any idea who might have thought that was a good idea? I mean, did the boxwoods do anything wrong?"

Antonio furrowed his brow, contemplating his reply.

Is this man serious?

And then Mr. Frederick's expression cracked with a tilt of his mouth. "Antonio," he chuckled, "I want you to relax. You've sat here for five minutes and still look like you're being held captive. We know these are not your doing and I have no intentions to fire you."

Pushing out a breath, Antonio's shoulders eased, and he huffed a laugh. "I can do that."

"Great, now, let's figure this out." Mr. Leland put his pen to his notebook and started jotting notes, scratching across each page as he wrote.

They discussed misplaced shovels, how glass was smashed from the inside out, the missing fountain bolts, and the strange footsteps in the mornings. "They faded like someone trying to disappear."

Mr. Leland paused in his writing, "Was anyone with you during those times?"

Antonio's ears warmed. He was hesitant to say Dottie's name, because he knew she was innocent. But if he knew Mr. Leland, the truth would be found out, and Antonio wanted to avoid a misunderstanding. "Yes. Dottie showed up after two of the incidents. But so had Papà. Miss Mae was at the boxwood, along with my siblings."

Thumbing the table, Mr. Frederick asked, "Anything else you can remember?"

Before Antonio could respond, there was a light tap at the door. "M-Mr. Stratford?" Katie barely cracked the door open.

Why is she here?

Mr. Frederick waved her in. "How may we help you, Miss Douglas?"

She waited at the door, her hand clutching the knob. "Sir, I wanted to bring you something I found." Katie fumbled through her apron pockets.

Antonio heard the unmistakable sound of clinking metal.

Her hand trembled as she reached past him, placing the fountain bolts in Mr. Leland's hands.

"I—I found them tucked in a drawer in the kitchen. But I don't know how they got there. Looked more like something from outside with the dirt on them."

She kept her head lowered as her body shook fiercely. Not from simple nerves, but from guilt.

Maybe fear.

Antonio couldn't tell which. His body tensed, fighting the urge to stand and confront the girl.

There's no way they were found in the kitchen, Mamma would've known.

Mr. Frederick lifted a brow. "Thank you, Miss Douglas. Is there anything else you'd like to add?"

Slowly backing out the door, the scullery maid shook her head, lips pinched tightly closed.

"You may leave."

With a slight nod, she was gone.

Antonio lifted one of the bolts. "She didn't find this randomly in the kitchen." Letting it fall onto the pile, they scattered across the desk. "So, now we need to figure out how they got into her hands."

Mr. Frederick pushed the bolts to the side. "Someone's looking a bit guilty. Are you certain it wasn't Miss DeGrout?"

Clutching his armrests, Antonio's knuckles turned white. He thought he could trust these men, trust their judgement. Yet, one false accusation from a girl, and they're ready to blame someone innocent. "It's not her, and you know it isn't." He nearly bit out the reply.

Throwing his leg over his knee, Mr. Leland leaned back in his chair. "Then who, Antonio?"

Antonio recounted how Charlie had shadowed him for a few days asking countless questions, as well as his threat against Antonio's job.

After several more inquiries, Mr. Leland glanced at Mr. Frederick. "Looks like we'll be interviewing Charlie Rolston. Let us know if you recall anything else."

With his mind busy mulling over everything, Antonio had completely forgotten the crumpled letter still tucked into his back pocket.

Chapter 13: Wednesday

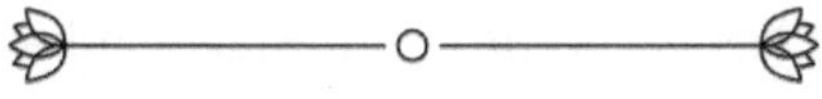

Locking in the last bolt, Antonio stood back to inspect his work. Mrs. Stratford insisted the fountain be replaced immediately, stating, *"No proper spring garden can be without a fountain for a month!"* Thankfully, Papà knew someone in Silkrow who stocked pre-casted iron fountains. The two-tiered statement-piece glittered in the sun as the water flowed to the basin below, restoring a resemblance of order to the garden.

Antonio stretched, his clothes clung uncomfortably to his body as remnants of grime, sweat and water stuck to every surface. A cool breeze picked up, finding every wet spot on his shirt, giving him a shivering chill. "Papà, I think I'll change before getting on with our other tasks." He lifted his arm, watching droplets fall to the ground.

"That'd be wise, *Tonio*. Can't set foot in the main house looking like that! Mamma might take a broom to you!" Papà sent out a peal of laughter and set to cleaning up the tools.

As he walked the path, Antonio caught sight of the kitchen window; and with it a flash of copper hair. It could only belong to one person.

Dottie.

A soft ache settled in his chest. Ever since she pushed him away, he'd avoided the manor, taking his dinners at home. It didn't help though, as every slice of sourdough was a reminder of her. Somehow, she made it better than Mamma's, but he'd never admit it out loud. And through the solitude of being away from her, she was still his only calming presence. When things felt weighed down, one glimpse of her, and Antonio felt he could take on the world.

Lord, I won't press her, but I believe You're telling me it's time. Give me a clear sign telling me when she's ready.

He dug his thumb into a callus in his palm, grounding himself. He wanted to go to her, to make her smile more. Yet fear whispered that his attention would only burden her. He exhaled hard, surrendering his impatience to the Lord, though it left an ache deep in his chest.

Focused on his steps, he didn't notice the footfalls behind him, until goosebumps raised on his arms. On edge, he spun on his heels. "Who—oh, Maria, what are you doing out here?"

The tension in his shoulders eased only a bit until he watched her shift nervously from foot to foot, so unlike her typical self-assurance. "Well, I was..." Scanning the area, she sucked in a breath, and pinned him with a superior look. "I came to find Timothy; Mrs. Stratford is beside herself trying to find missing gloves."

He didn't understand why she'd search the gardens for Timothy, but he could tell by how her eyes shifted that it was a lie, and he didn't have time for her games. "Well, I've not seen him today. Might want to check the main house."

"Right. I'll go check the manor. Thank you." Giving a curt nod, she turned away, but not before checking over the hedges one last time.

Confused by her behavior, Antonio shook his head, sweat dripping from his hair. "Strange." He didn't want to name the feeling that settled in his gut. Cool air wrapped around him, reminding him that he was still drenched.

His steps quickened as he spotted his home. Settled along the wood line, the cottage was dim even on the brightest days. Some might view it as dreary, but for Antonio, it was home. It's where his parents raised him and his siblings, always warm and brimming with love.

The old door groaned as it opened, the floors sagging at the entry.

I'll need to fix this soon.

He'd been putting it off since the manor always took precedence. By the time he arrived home every evening, he was too exhausted for much else except sleep.

The faint scent of cedar and firewood greeted him, pulling him back to winters by the hearth when Mamma sat pouring over new recipes and Papà sang Italian hymns out of tune.

As he changed into fresh pants, a paper dropped from the pocket. "What's this?" The paper crinkled in his fingers as he lifted it up.

Turning it over in his hands, he remembered Katie's letter from the day before, and how nervous she seemed.

Placing it on the nightstand, he dressed quickly, then took the letter into the light. It simply had *Antonio* scrawled across it. The lettering was no light script, instead the lines were deliberate and sharp. Yet something seemed familiar about the handwriting. "Wasn't there another?"

Dashing over to his dresser, Antonio dug out two more letters; one from the shed and Katie's from the day she brought the brownies. "Their taste will haunt me forever." He shuddered, not just from the terrible memory, but as he spread the letters across his bed, each swoop of the letter 'T' was exactly the same. The only difference, the one from the shed was smeared with water stains.

Antonio paced his bedroom floor, the boards creaking under his weight, the thud of his boots creating a perfect tempo.

Why would she have been in the garden shed?

"She only gave me two letters, not three. Who's the other one for?" He scratched his beard. "Should I open them?" As he walked the length of his room, he mumbled to himself. "They're probably all love letters, but something tells me I shouldn't read them alone."

But curiosity stirred. Lifting a letter from his bed, he stared at it in his hand, praying God would take the temptation away. Each crease prodding him to open it.

Maybe just one.

He broke the seal on the one with his name scrawled across it—and knew, the moment he did, he'd made a mistake. A cool shiver prickled the back of his neck. Even the cottage seemed to hush around him as he read the words scrawled on the paper.

Antonio,

I was wrong for pressuring you. I see that now. I just wanted something more than I have, and I'm sorry for it. But you need to be careful. He's angry with you, and if you're not watching your back, there's no telling what he'll do next.

It wasn't signed. No flowery words.

Just a warning.

His hand trembled as he let out a groan, wincing when the tension pulled at his bruise. "Who is *he*? Have they been watching me this whole time? She even knew when I trimmed back the hedges..." The letter crinkled in his clenched fingers.

The smell of mildew wafted up to his nose when his foot hit a pile of clothes needing to be washed. "She even knew I was home when I changed on Sunday, instead of in the gardens..."

Mamma's gossip came to mind. "It's no secret she dislikes Dottie." But the letter never mentioned Dottie. Questions ran wildly through his mind. "Then why all the hostility and destruction in the gardens?"

With one more glance at the pile of laundry, he tucked the carefully folded letters into his back pocket. Taking a breath, he closed his eyes and prayed.

Lord, give me answers.

His spine tingled like he was being watched; every creaking branch and rustle of wind put him on edge.

I'm paranoid. Worrying over the letter is going to drive me to insanity.

As he left, the cottage door slammed behind him, his only focus, going to speak with Mr. Leland.

The kitchen was bustling. Mrs. Romano gave orders to Edith, as the snip of her knife finely chopped carrots for a hearty stew.

Dottie adjusted snacks on a silver tray that would soon head to the terrace. Small cucumber and egg salad sandwiches were carefully stacked. Simple lemon cake squares dotted the edges, small flecks of yellow crumbles scattered on the table while their zesty-sweet scent curled around Dottie as she finished arranging the spongy treats.

The servant stairs creaked with the weight of a man. Glancing up she hoped it was Antonio. She'd missed his reassuring presence. Instead, it was... "Charlie."

Her stomach soured as she frantically sought out Mrs. Romano's protection, but she was nowhere to be seen.

"Did you miss me so much that I took your breath away?" Charlie's clean-shaven face tilted in a smirk, making his ocean eyes sparkle; eyes she used to enjoy glancing her way. Now she just wanted to escape their penetrating stare.

He loomed over the worktable, not giving a care as his shirt pressed into the freshly baked cakes. Dottie tried to slowly pull them away, when his voice brushed her cheek, low and menacing. "So, your little boyfriend thought he'd get me in trouble, didn't he? Got called into the steward's office."

Recoiling, Dottie edged back, hoping to reach the safety of Mrs. Romano's presence. But Edith stepped in first, using herself as a shield between Dottie and Charlie. She leveled him with her most severe look. "I'm certain you're not welcome here, Mr. Rolston. If your business is complete, the door is that way." She flicked her rag toward the exit, spraying small droplets along the floor.

Charlie's lip curled. "I'll leave when I'm ready, and I don't take orders from some nagging maid." He reached behind Edith, shoving her to the side, and snatched Dottie's arm. "We're going to have a little chat." Fixing the upper maid with a glare, he added, "and don't you dare follow, miss, or you might regret it."

Dottie's pulse pounded so loudly she thought he might hear it. Memories of Pastor's message flooded her mind—*God sees you...* She clung to that truth like a lifeline.

As they stepped out of the manor, the sky overhead grayed, matching Dottie's mood.

And she was done.

Done being dragged.

Done being pushed.

Done believing she had no power over her lot in life.

God, I know You love me; give me strength.

A breeze carrying a hint of hyacinth reminded her of Mae's words. She took a stuttering breath as he dragged her, inhaling the sweet fragrance. With an exhale, she released her fears. "Joy after Sorrow."

I can do this.

Dottie dug her feet into the gravel, causing her forward momentum to break. Her heart thudded in her ears as the words fell from her lips with more strength than she knew she had. "Enough, Charlie!" Pain radiated up her arm as she yanked it from his grasp.

Momentarily stunned, Charlie froze, then straightened his shoulders. Everything stilled. Dottie's chest tightened as the air around them simmered. He turned with the rage. "Enough?!" Stepping inches from her, each huff of his anger pushed against her skin.

She hadn't noticed, but they were back by the magnolia tree, blossoms in full bloom. The sweet scent mingled with Charlie's breath, turning her stomach.

He pushed her toward the magnolia, pinning her in place. "Oh, no, Dottie, it's not enough." His clammy hand cupped her cheek, leaving a slimy film on her skin.

Trying to hold in a whimper, her nails bit into her palm. She glanced up to the branches overhead, praying for a solution.

I'm not his and I'll not let him harass me.

She did a doubletake, noticing something odd about one of the branches; it looked almost fully sawed. Fresh sawdust speckled the bark.

It was her out.

Dottie shifted her body away from the branch, just enough to not be under it, her hem catching along the bark.

"Now," Charlie's voice brought her back to the moment, his face just inches away. His thumb lingered on her jaw, as he licked his lips, "I'm done waiting. You've led me on long enough."

She pressed her back into the tree, fingers gripping the jagged bark.

I can be brave.

"Back off Charlie." She used the biggest voice she had, but the quiver near the end gave her bravado away.

He inched closer, his lips hovering above hers.

Sucking in a breath, she held in a gag. Through clenched teeth, she growled. "I said get away from me you foul-breathed pig."

Charlie recoiled like he'd been slapped. Her heart leapt with a small victory, but the celebration was short-lived.

"Foul-breathed pig?!" He barked. "You dare speak to me like that? You're just a lousy maid!" Lifting his hand high in the air, he started toward her. "I would've been sweet to you!"

Just before his fist reached her, Dottie dropped to the ground, his knuckles connecting with the tree trunk with an audible crunch. He bellowed. "Why you—"

The branches above shook. A loud crack echoed through the garden as the sawed limb broke loose and crashed to the ground. The edge snagged his shirt sleeve, causing a small cut on his bicep to bleed.

Little giggles broke out close by. "You can't catch me!" Feet scurried along the gravel path. "Oh, yes, I can! My legs are longer!"

Anna and the twins were playing in the gardens. And though Dottie hoped Mr. Griggs wouldn't catch them, she knew he'd be nearby. He always was. A tear tracked down her cheek.

Please let Mr. Griggs find me.

"Oh!" Anna stopped short. "Dottie, are you ok?" She tilted her head, her small face pinched with worry. "Why're you on the ground?" Rose and Violet ran up behind, pigtails bouncing with the momentum. "Hey, mister, you've got a cut!" "Ro, I'm sure he already knows." "Yes, but he's letting it dribble." Rose squirmed in disgust.

Funny how a girl who catches spiders is afraid of blood.

Tension drained from Dottie's shoulders, knowing she was no longer alone with Charlie. But before Dottie could respond to the girls, footsteps marched up the path, each one with purpose.

Mr. Griggs voice came out in a forceful whisper. "Girls!" Coming around the bend, huffing to catch up, he still somehow looked poised. "Girls, I've told you before, and I'll—Miss DeGrout, are you quite well?"

Slowly scanning the area, the old butler took stock of the situation, and for a brief moment Dottie thought she saw his jaw tick. Quickly, his polished mask returned. "Girls. Please go get your father," turning to Anna, "And soon to be father," he added to the twins. "Immediately." Mr. Griggs' curt tone was one everyone knew to obey.

The girls scampered off to the manor, giggles and hushed conversations passing between them. Dottie wished she could leave with them, but until Mr. Griggs dismissed her from the spot, she was taught to stay in place.

Once they were out of sight, Mr. Griggs came to stand in front of Dottie. She'd been too afraid to rise, her body still quaking with adrenaline. Without a word, he offered his gloved hand to her, his eyes briefly softening.

With a quick peek in Charlie's direction, Dottie inhaled and took the butler's hand. He gave the slightest squeeze, reassuring her. "Miss DeGrout, I believe it's almost tea time, and Mrs. Romano won't take lightly that you're missing."

Fear still pulsed under her skin, yet peace began to take root, small but sure. She wanted to laugh—of all the things he could say, of course it would be about work. She curtsied, grateful that his comment brought her the feeling of normalcy. "Yes, sir."

You did it, Lord. Thank you.

Charlie turned to speak, the anger rolling off him, but Mr. Griggs held up a firm hand. "I'll not allow you, Mr. Rolston, to cause an upheaval on this estate. Miss DeGrout has her orders. And you'll remain here until Mr. West and Mr. Romano arrive, am I understood?"

Grimacing, Charlie gave a tight nod.

As Dottie departed, she could feel his stare piercing her back. She refused to turn around. Not until she was safely in the manor.

Chapter 14: Wednesday Evening

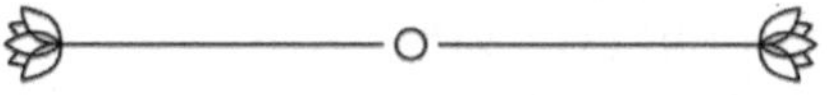

Dottie was told to meet in the library. Walking quietly down the rug-lined corridor, she watched shadows dance along the darkened walls as sconces flickered.

Too dark.

An eerie feeling crawled up her back. The hush of the corridor pressed against her ears. For a fleeting moment she thought she heard footsteps behind her, too soft to be real, too distant to call out. Her heart gave a small stutter.

Still, despite the manor's secrets looming behind her, the double mahogany doors, carved with detailed ornamental flowers, beckoned her to join. Drawing closer, she could hear laughter from inside the room.

For a moment, she hesitated, her hand giving a slight shake on the handle.

Am I allowed to enter as a guest instead of a servant?

She wasn't sure if it was acceptable to enjoy tea, and lounge on soft cushioned seats. This was the life of the privileged, not something for a dingy kitchen maid. Even as a parlor maid, she had been expected to act in a way befitting her role.

Yet, as darkness closed in, a draft stirred the curtains, sending a chill through her bones. Suddenly, the library, with warm light flowing out beneath the door, seemed much more appealing.

Taking a breath, she knocked once and carefully pushed open the door. By the fireplace, surrounded by a multitude of books, sat Mae, Miss Genevieve, Edith, and Mrs. Brower. The east window stood tall, dark against the evening sky. Shelves stretched to the ceiling, crammed with works from various places.

Dottie had seen it before, many times, serving tea to the Stratford family, or straightening the room, but it felt different this night.

On a low mahogany table, settled between a pair of deep brown leather armchairs and a forest green settee, rested a tray of tea and cookies, steam peacefully curling from the platter. The scent of lemon polish and old paper met her like an embrace.

Before she could cross the threshold, Mae stood, arms stretched forward to guide her to a seat. "I'm glad you made it!" Her smile stretched wide. "Edith tried escaping, but we managed to get her here after all."

Next to Mrs. Brower sat a sour-faced Edith, arms crossed over her chest, her apron spotless despite a day in the kitchen. "And I would have succeeded had Mrs. Romano not ratted me out. I mean, the pantry clearly needed reorganizing, why wait another day?"

Mrs. Brower chuckled and settled a hand on Edith's knee. "There's always another day for work. We're called to worship and rest as well."

"Idle hands...." Edith mumbled under her breath while looking warily at the door.

The soft rustle of Miss Genevieve's satin dress filled the pause, a reminder she belonged to another world entirely. Her dress could pay a servant's wages for a year or probably three. Even still, she didn't seem arrogant at all, just delighted to spend time with them. Dottie's back stiffened, she wasn't sure how to relax in the woman's presence.

As if Miss Genevieve perceived her very thought, the heiress patted the cushion beside her. "Come sit."

The moment stretched to a few.

Dottie blinked.

Sit with her?

Miss Genevieve was familiar with Mae, but was she truly at easy that way with everyone? It seemed so foreign. There was supposed to be a clear class divide, one she had once hoped to cross with Mr. Philip. But between the library walls, that line blurred.

Another pat on the spot demanded Dottie begin moving. "Y—yes. Of course, thank you, Miss Van Buren."

"I do hate that name." Miss Genevieve waved her hand in the air with a scowl. "Call me Genevieve when we're here among friends."

Dottie glanced at the other women. No one seemed surprised or concerned. Even Edith, a stickler for rules and formality, seemed untroubled.

"All right?" Dottie raised a brow in question, and Miss Genevieve simply nodded. "Thank you, M–Genevieve."

She released a breath, soft and slow, allowing herself to relax into the cushion, as it molded around her. The green velvet felt soft beneath her fingers. For a heartbeat she let her fingertips trail along the seam, memorizing the texture as if proof she belonged here.

Glancing down, she saw Miss Genevieve's hands folded gracefully in her lap, smooth and delicate. Unlike her own, her nails were uneven and brittle. Dottie tucked them beneath her thigh, embarrassed by her lack of refinement.

Mae gave a short clap. "Now, we wait for Mrs. Carmela." She paused, peaking at Dottie, who shifted under her friend's amused expression. "While we wait, we like to chat about life. Anything new to share?"

Dottie's throat closed tight, and she gripped her apron. She knew Mae wanted to discuss Antonio, but nothing had changed, or maybe it did? Her heart certainly had. But she wasn't ready to say it out loud. Her cheeks heated at the thought of letting him love her.

She picked at the velvet beneath her legs.

Do I tell them about Charlie?

Her heart thudded like a warning. Some wounds felt too fresh to name aloud, like glass that might cut deeper if handled too soon.

Before the silence drew too heavy, the door opened revealing a giddy Mrs. Romano. And she was never giddy. "Dear *bambinas*, I'm here." She held a vase in her hands, full of hyacinth and wild violets.

Same as my vase... so it was, Antonio.

Her heart softened at the idea that Mr. Sal likely had a hand in preparing her flowers as well.

"My Sal brought these to me after work, I couldn't simply rush off!" She smoothed her hair though the wiry frays bounced right back out of place.

Dottie's mouth fell open before a giggle bubbled up.

Mrs. Romano cut her a glance, and with a smirk she added, "Don't laugh, *Tesoro*, you're nearly there."

The comment sobered Dottie with a quiet jolt.

Nearly there? What does she mean by that?

Unbiddenly, the memory of Antonio's tender kiss on her head caused a fluttering in her stomach, and she hoped no one noticed her breath catch.

Mrs. Brower pointed at the flowers. "So glad your husband doted on you, Mrs. Carmela. Are you bringing those to brag or to share?"

Adding the vase to the arrangement on the low table, Mrs. Romano squeezed in next to Dottie. "To share, of course! I thought a little cheer was needed tonight." Her voice grew serious as she peeked down at Dottie, taking her hand and giving it a squeeze. Everyone's attention turned to her.

"What happened?" Mae's brow furrowed with concern.

I can't escape it now.

Dottie sighed and squeezed Mrs. Romano's hand back. "Charlie came back today..."

She didn't want to remember, didn't want to think about it. The memory welled up in her chest, strangling her breath.

"And what happened?" Now Mae leaned forward in her place, drawing her lip between her teeth as her forehead creased with worry.

Dottie sucked in a shuddering breath and dropped her head; she didn't want to rehash the scene. When she thought she would break, Mrs. Romano pulled her into a side-hug. "You don't need to tell us until you're ready. But I will say, Mr. Griggs, grumpy old miser, told my Sal that you were very brave today."

Leaning into the woman's warm embrace, Dottie glanced up.

How could he have known if I was brave? He wasn't even there during the worst of it.

Miss Genevieve hummed and thumbed the pages of a leather-bound book to the very middle, its edges shimmered in the warm light as they passed. "Well, that seems quite fitting for tonight's prayer and Bible time." She took a moment and smiled at each person individually. When she held Dottie's gaze, Dottie felt seen, cared for.

"Psalm 46:1 God is our refuge and strength, a very present help in trouble." Closing the Bible, Miss Genevieve clasped Dottie's hand and Mae's with the other.

Without instruction, everyone joined hands and closed their eyes. Dottie's lids drifted closed as the heiress's prayer lifted through the quiet room.

"Dear Father in Heaven, thank You for always being our refuge and strength when we are in need of You. Help us see You in those moments and put our trust in Your Hands. Amen."

Mae adjusted to look at the group. "Does anyone care to share a time when God saw you through?"

The women waited, no one wanting to speak first. Dottie couldn't help noticing Edith shifting in her seat, trying to hide within the chair's folds. The hyacinths' perfume filled the space with its sweet, green aroma.

Finally, Mrs. Brower piped in quietly. "I'm not sure you all know," she paused and nodded to Edith, "but my time here is getting shortened."

The older woman waited a moment, the fireplace crackling quietly behind them. Her chest rose, voice firming with resolve. "God has sustained me in this role for many years, given me the strength to press on despite daily pain, but it seems He's ready for me to pass it on to another."

Mrs. Brower carefully rubbed the joints in her fingers, and for a moment her eyes misted over. "None of you know, save Edith and Mae, but I have rheumatism in my hands."

Surprisingly, Edith reached over and patted her arm, her cheeks growing red. "Oh, don't worry, I'm not quite ready to retire yet, God's helping me day by day, but soon."

Everyone was silent for a moment.

Skyline Manor without a Mrs. Brower?

It was unthinkable. Blinking back a tear, Dottie could still remember her first day at the manor, walking into the head maid's office, the air thick with the scent of polish and starch.

"Have you any skills? Cooking? Cleaning?" Terrified that the older woman would scold her for her lack of skills, she had kept her head low and slowly shook it. *"Ah, well, we can fix that."* Shocked, a young Dottie's head jerked up, watching the woman's face, hard yet kind, staring back. *"But you'll have to start at the bottom and prove yourself."*

It had been the first time anyone looked at her with expectation instead of doubt. From that moment, she'd promised herself she would be worthy of it.

Dottie wondered if anyone could fill the Mrs. Brower sized space in her heart, but looking around the room, she realized God had already begun to put people in place just for that purpose.

Mae with her warmth, Mrs. Romano with her care, and Edith with her wits.

Yes, it'll be fine even if she leaves.

She looked over at Miss Genevieve and caught sight of a small teardrop dangling from her lashes.

And even Miss Genevieve, for however long her visit lasts.

Dottie drew in a steadying breath and lifted her chin. She could be brave, like Mr. Griggs believed she was. "I'd like to tell my story now, about how God strengthened me." For a moment, her voice went soft, and under the safety of her lashes she checked how the women would respond.

And then she felt it, love wrapping around her heart. Mrs. Romano pressed in with her shoulder, Miss Genevieve placed a hand to her arm, and Mae got up from her spot to sit at Dottie's feet. Even Edith watched with an encouraging, comfortable smile that made the space feel safe.

The women stayed in that room for what seemed like hours, pouring love into one another, until it was time to leave. And for that Dottie was truly grateful.

Quietly, she and Edith made their way back to the servant quarters by way of candlelight, long after the rest of the house had retired.

Edith stopped in the hall before reaching their rooms. "Thank you." Her sigh caused the candle in her hand to flicker. "Thank you for telling your story. I've tried being strong like you. But I haven't quite figured it out yet." She gave a sad little smile before turning to walk toward her room.

But Edith's the strongest woman I've known besides Mae.

Dottie wondered what her story was. Using that same bravery from before, she pulled on Edith's arm. "Then come with us to church on Sunday. I've got a lot to learn, but each day I discover more. Please come with us."

Edith shook her head. "I'm not ready."

"You'll never be ready until you take the first step. I'll drag you there myself, probably with the help of Mae and Clara if I have to." Dottie leaned in. "That one's stronger than she looks!"

With that, Edith giggled, and Dottie was surprised at how lovely it sounded.

"Okay, maybe I'll come, but no dragging," the upper maid half scolded, half whispered. "Now, get to bed, we have an early start tomorrow."

Dottie opened her door, but when she turned, Edith was already down the corridor, her feet quietly shuffling away. "Good night." Dottie's words dissolved into the darkness.

When the door clicked shut, she let out a long breath. The silence felt softer now. Maybe the Lord had been stitching grace through her life all along, tiny threads of kindness she'd been too scared to see.

Chapter 15: Thursday Afternoon

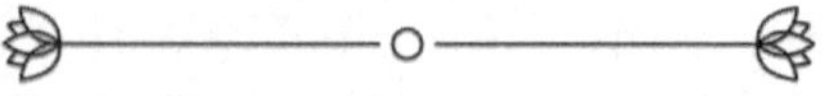

"You mean to tell me none of the pots were washed last night?" Mrs. Romano's voice echoed up the stairs. "What are we going to do?"

Reaching the final step, Dottie watched Mrs. Romano standing over Edith, who equally stood her ground. "How was I supposed to know it'd be left hanging!"

Dottie choked down a laugh and both women shot her a glare. "Ladies, calm down. I'll wash, Edith can dry. And Mrs. Romano, you start up breakfast."

Rolling up her sleeves, she moved quickly to the sink, only pausing to give Mrs. Romano a quick peck on the cheek. What prompted the kiss, Dottie wasn't sure. But it felt like the right thing to do.

Each at their stations, the only sounds between them were the steady drips of water and the sizzling skillet.

By the time lunch was served, Dottie needed a break, with her joints stiff from the constant strain of kneading. They had worked tirelessly since morning. Not only were they cooking the household meals, but they were also preparing for Mae and Mr. Leland's wedding feast.

Extra pans for cake bases, tins full of cookies and treats, rich butter, and lemon mingled with warm sugar. The whole room smelled sweet like a bakery. Flour was found on every surface, and Mrs. Romano's typical banter was restrained. "Go. All work and no pause make for clumsy hands." The woman pointed toward the door, and Dottie didn't have to be told twice.

Stepping out into the bright day was exactly what she needed. Slipping away, warmth prickled at her skin, and the air smelled faintly of lilacs and damp earth. Dottie meandered down the path toward the garden.

I wonder if Antonio's close by.

Her heart quickened at the thought of seeing him. "I still need to apologize for brushing him off the other day," she mused, glancing up at the branches rustling in the breeze. "And thank him for the flowers." Her mouth tugged into a smile.

Mrs. Romano's words from Tuesday echoed in her mind. *"Give* Tonio *the chance to love you. I can see it,* amore'*."*

Dottie nibbled her lip and turned toward the cottages. "But what if Mrs. Romano's wrong and he can't love me past my ruin?"

Her steps slowed as the question lodged in her chest. What if she was too broken for love to mend? For many days she'd begged God to make her new. She paused. The same relief from Sunday in front of the Cross welled up in her chest. What if He already had—and she just hadn't believed it yet.

So caught up in her thoughts, she didn't hear the oncoming footsteps until they were directly behind her, kicking up dust around her hem. Heart pounding, she whirled around and took a step back.

Katie stood there, fists on her hips, taking large breaths. "You're a fast walker, almost wasn't sure I'd catch up to you." She gave a quick smile.

After everything this girl had done, Dottie's stomach clenched; she wasn't sure she could let down her guard. "Not sure whether to take that as a compliment or not. Everything all right, Katie?" She took another step back.

Sliding her eyes closed, Katie sighed. "I've been a fool."

Dottie blinked at her, wondering if she'd misheard the girl. *Katie, of all people, admitting fault?* Her voice hitched. "What?"

Closing the distance between them, Katie took Dottie's hands. The desire to flee welled up in Dottie, but she kept her feet rooted, curious to what Katie would say next.

"I'm sorry." Katie exhaled slowly. "I've let jealousy make me cruel."

All the anxiety that Dottie had bottled up rammed against her chest.

Can I trust her? Or is she plotting again?

Pulling away, Dottie rubbed her palms together, unease prickling at her neck. The garden felt strangely still, the rustle of leaves shifting to a whisper.

"I was so taken by Antonio, his kindness, his smile. I thought if I pushed hard enough, he'd notice me." Katie's voice cracked and then she stared at Dottie. "But he doesn't look at me the way he looks at you."

Could I hope for such a thing?

Dottie dismissively waved the idea away. "Antonio looks at me like he looks at everyone else." She gave a nervous laugh. "He's just a kind man." In her heart, she knew she was lying, but didn't want to admit it to herself nor to the girl standing before her.

"That's not true." Katie huffed through her nose. "I wanted one man to look at me the way they all look at you. You have it so easy!"

If she only knew that easy was full of false hopes.

"I don't have it easy." Dottie's fingers aimlessly brushed across the hedges; a twig pricked at her skin reminding her of all the trouble *easy* had caused.

"I've learned something from all this attention. Most of it's on the surface." Chuckling, she turned to the scullery maid, meeting her eyes. "Most of them never treasured me." Her throat tightened at the thought, as a faint memory pulled her back to Mr. Philip, standing in the dim corridor outside his door. She'd thought he loved her.

Walking quietly to Mr. Philip's room, his letter clutched to her chest, Dottie's pulse quickened. She hadn't been able to talk to him in weeks. And he had finally asked her to return.

Tapping her finger against her thigh, she recalled the secret knock he'd made for her, two quick, pause, then one more. A door in the distance slammed shut.

She had stood before his beautifully ornate door. There was shuffling on the other side, but it hadn't stopped her. Opening the door, Dottie had expected his embrace and a devastatingly handsome smile, but what she found instead was him in the arms of another.

The sting of that night still pricked, even under the beautiful spring sunlight. Blinking back the memory, her heart fractured for a moment. She started reaching for the cufflink around her neck, but quickly remembered tucking it away. After her conversation with Edith the night before, she realized she was ready to take small steps away from the bitter memory and closer to living in peace.

It's all right now.

Full of nervous energy, her feet needed to move. She started back toward the manor but slowed to wait for Katie to catch up.

Perhaps the girl wasn't the only one learning how to let go.

"If what you're looking for is love, slow down, you're still young. The right man, who will completely treasure you will come along." An image of Antonio standing beside her in the chapel on Sunday filled her mind. He had offered her space and a steadying, quiet strength while she took time to heal in the presence of the Father.

Maybe he really is the right man. God, guide my thoughts and words.

Shaking her head, Dottie took Katie's hand in her own. "Don't rush with your whole heart to the first man who pays you mind. Don't give yourself away."

She tried to hold back the tears, thinking about her foolish decisions in the past, things she could never take back. "Wait for the man God sends you."

Katie wiped at her own lids. "It's so hard to wait." Her voice trembled as her gaze drifted down the path toward the gate. "To want love so strongly but be told it's not time yet."

For a fleeting second, her expression darkened, anger clouding them before it vanished as quickly as it came.

Dottie tilted her head, a prickle of unease stirring.

It's almost as if she's been told to wait... not just wants to.

Recalling something Mae had once said, Dottie pressed her hand to her stomach. "Do you know that you already have that all-consuming, nothing-will-ever-tear-it-away Love?"

"There's no man who loves me like that." Katie shook her head, brows drawn low in confusion.

Surprised that she'd be echoing Mae's words from just months ago, Dottie let out a chuckle. "There is. Jesus loves you because He made you, you're one of His precious creations." Letting the truth settle in her bones, Dottie sighed. "And to Him, you are treasured."

Listening to the fountain babbling in the distance, she took in the hush of the garden.

Treasured.

Everything clicked in place.

With a ghost of a frown, Katie followed Dottie back toward the manor. "I still don't quite understand."

Glancing over her shoulder, Dottie's face lit up. "You will. In time, you most certainly will—" Suddenly, Katie's feet stopped walking, yanking on Dottie's arm toward the cottages. "M-maybe we should go this way."

The hairs on her arms lifted, sensing a shift, watching Katie's expression twist in discomfort. "What are—?"

"There you are!"

Letting out an audible groan, Dottie forced a smile.

Of course, leave it to Timothy to arrive at the worst possible moment.

The way his jaw flexed, and his fists clenched at his sides made the hairs on her arms prickle. "Hi, Timothy. Katie and I were just heading back from a break." She kept walking, wanting to get away from the unease billowing in her middle. "So, we'll see you later."

"No, listen." Timothy blocked the path.

When would men learn women don't appreciate being forced into situations.

Dottie eyed him carefully, noticing he held something behind his back.

"I wanted to talk to you."

He glanced at Katie, giving only the smallest nod. Her reaction was so quick, almost natural, as if they'd rehearsed it.

"Oh, oh! I'm sure Helen's looking for me. More linens to be scrubbed."

Before she made it two steps, Dottie's hand closed around her arm, firm, but gentle. "She'll be fine a few more minutes without you," she said, her voice tight. "Stay with me."

Timothy moved forward, presenting a bouquet of flowers. The blossoms were a rainbow of beautiful roses, tulips, and carnations. "Dottie." His chin lifted to the sky, like he was praying for patience. "I planned to discuss it with you privately, but I guess this will have to do." He adjusted his collar, then clasped his hands behind his back, giving him an air of confidence. "I love you!"

When he inched closer, Dottie's grip around Katie's hand tightened. "Y-you do?" Dottie knew better, yet, for a moment, her chest tightened. Two confessions in one week were shocking.

Giving herself a shake, she remembered his adoration was only surface level. "And why do you love me?"

"Well, you're gorgeous. Your hair is like an untamed fire, and eyes like the setting s—" His words were abruptly cut off by Dottie's palm in his face.

Raising her eyes, she looked squarely into his. Knowing God valued her more, she'd no longer fall for empty words. She toyed with the flower petals, hoping the distraction would keep her thoughts focused. "Timothy, while your words are sweet, like these flowers, I cannot accept you."

Timothy opened his mouth to reply but closed it again. The action reminded her of a fish. She held in a chuckle, afraid he might misunderstand, while Katie shifted nervously beside her, fingers growing clammy under the pressure. Dottie quickly released her hand, passing her an apologetic nod.

Regaining his wits, Timothy's brows furrowed. "But I thought you felt the same." He rammed a hand through his hair. "You were always sweet. I've watched you blush and flutter your lashes." His voice shook. "You enjoyed the attention!"

Shaking her head, Dottie placed a hand on his forearm. "I'm sorry Timothy, it was a mistake and wrong of me to mislead you. I love another, so I can't accept these." She handed him the bouquet.

It was true. The instant the words left her lips, she knew she meant them. What she felt for Antonio wasn't heat or a fleeting spark. It was something rooted deep within. She cared for his well-being, his heart, and the quiet strength of his faith. When he stood beside her, all nervous effort to impress faded into the simple comfort of being where she belonged.

Her stomach swooped.

I love him.

Glancing from the flowers to her, Timothy's expression darkened into something deeper than rejection and it had Dottie shrink back.

"You'll regret turning me down for some gardener." He tossed the bouquet at her as he walked away, small petals floated to the ground. His shoes trampled the flowers as he sped up the path, but not before she heard him mutter words that cut at her. "All this time you've been a shameless flirt..."

Dottie wanted to deny the accusations, but she knew she couldn't. She *had* been a shameless flirt. Heat crept up her neck, as all her reckless actions of the past paraded through her mind.

God, please forgive me for my foolishness.

Tears pooled along her rims, threatening to spill over.

I'll believe You now, Lord. When You say You're fighting for me. I see it. I feel it.

With a small inhale, she took Katie's hand. She still had the burden of her past, but Dottie knew she didn't have to continue to carry the shame. Now if her head could simply catch up.

She'd thought Timothy had gone, but somewhere behind the hedge, he hissed. "Not now." There was scuffle, and someone broke out into a soft sob. "Just leave me alone, Maria." A branch cracked, followed by hurried steps retreating toward the manor.

Dottie froze. She couldn't be sure—had he said *Maria*?

Why would Maria be out here?

A chill ran up her spine. She peeked at Katie, who quickly paled. Dottie realized then.

This is a lover's quarrel.

He had set his sights on three different women.

The gall of him to cast stones at me when he's doing the same thing.

Letting out a nervous huff, she brushed a petal from her skirt and shook off the tension. A sparrow *chirruped* in a nearby tree, earning a chuckle from Dottie.

I'll cheer up, little bird, once all this drama is behind me.

"Well, I guess we should get going before they send out a search party?"

Pleased that pruning hedges was ticked off his list, Antonio headed toward the shed. He heard muffled sounds further up the path, barely noticeable above the fountain's babbling, and the sound of his boots against the gravel.

He stopped, straining to listen to the conversation. Mrs. Stratford wasn't due in the gardens until later that afternoon. His palm itched remembering all his other tasks that still needed to be accomplished.

Unless she's come for a surprise inspection!

His steps quickened toward the visitors, hoping to postpone the inevitable. Mrs. Stratford seemed to always find more fault with him. And then he heard her voice.

Dottie.

"Y-you do?"

Antonio's chest lifted at the thought of her being so nearby. But the mix of shock and hope in her voice made him wonder whom she was speaking to. He moved off the path closer to the bushes.

Mamma would beat me with a spatula if she knew I was eavesdropping.

But he didn't care—

"And why do you love me?"

Antonio lifted his head just above the hedge to see which of her admirers were professing their love this time. Standing next to her was a nervous Katie.

Dottie's grip tightened around the girl's hand as if steadying herself.

Odd.

Of all people, why was Dottie seeking her support? After everything that had happened, Antonio didn't trust the girl was as innocent as she appeared.

But who is she talking to?

He angled his head to catch a glimpse of the person just out of sight. His chest tightened with jealousy.

Would they love her like the treasure she is? Adore her? Protect her?

"It'd better not be Charlie." He mumbled quietly, catching a petal from the cherry blossoms above. The breeze lifted the delicate bloom from his open palm. He prayed his love for her wouldn't be whisked away just as quickly.

"I'm sorry Timothy, it was a mistake and wrong of me. I love someone else..."

A smile tugged slowly as Antonio's lips and his pulse thrummed.

Could it be me?

His joy was quickly wilted when Timothy's clipped voice cut through. "You'll regret turning me down for some gardener."

And then there was silence. Antonio's heart hammered as he slid down to the ground. Leaning his arms on his knees, he fiddled with a piece of grass, twirling it between his fingers. The ridges rubbed smooth against his pads. "She didn't deny it..." He chuckled softly and peered up to the sky. "Thank You, Lord."

He stayed there a while, the grass cool beneath his palms, the echo of her voice lingering. For all the storms that had swept through their lives, maybe this was the clearing. Still, a faint unease tugged at him, not everyone would be glad for their happiness. He brushed it aside for now, content to let hope bloom.

Chapter 16: Thursday Evening

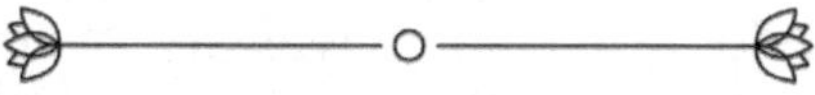

"*Papà*. I need your help." Antonio stood in the shed doorway, clutching his shears as he shuffled from foot to foot. Dust lazily floated through streams of light coming through the window. He barely registered the sour scent of oil, that had become so commonplace.

The old man looked up from his toolbox, squinting at the light hitting his eyes. "What's wrong, *Tonio*?" The crease in his wrinkled brow deepened.

Rocking back on his heels, Antonio cleared his throat and distracted himself with organizing tools on a shelf. The wood had worn smooth from years of use, full of nicks and dents, just like him. Yet, it held strong against the toughest jobs.

"Well, are you going to keep me waiting like a groom waiting on his bride?" Papà stood, his knees popping with age. Waving away a buzzing fly, he came alongside his son, and stilled Antonio's fidgeting.

Antonio's ears heated at the thought of Dottie, walking towards him in her bridal gown, her radiant smile on display, hair pinned with wisps framing her face. "Well, I want to show Dottie what she means to me." His palm rubbed at his neck. "But I," he huffed a breath, "I don't know how."

She's worth the work to figure this out.

"Ah, *ragazzo*, you've come to the right person." Papà clapped his son's back, knocking him off kilter. Antonio often wondered how the old man had such strength. "I've been known to be quite the wooer in my day."

Raising a skeptical brow at Papà's weathered face, Antonio smirked. "Truly, have you seen yourself?" He poked the old man's stomach.

"*Si'*, if it wasn't for wooing, do you think I'd be with *Mamma*? She would have taken one look at my ugly mug and tossed me back!" He chuckled. "I had to win her heart before she'd set her sights on me."

Antonio shook his head. "Fine, if you think you can help me, I'll willingly listen." Pointing the shears at the old man, he smiled. "But no serenades, I've heard you sing! You'd scare the birds from their nests!"

With a wide grin, Papà walked over to the door. "We might have to employ Mr. Leland on some of this, too." He winked, tossing his hat on with a flourish. "He has the means to make something magical happen."

"*Papà*, I don't need magic, just something... nice." Antonio hung the shears on their hook, closed the newly replaced door behind him, and ensured it was locked.

"That's where you're wrong, Antonio. The right type of wooing always needs a bit of magic." The old man called over his shoulder. "Now let's hurry, there's no time to waste when it comes to *amore*!"

Antonio's heart leapt in his chest.

Love! I need to show her she's worthy of love.

Watching the magnolia branches wave in the breeze, he never could understand why Dottie thought she was worthless, but if she'd let him, he'd spend his whole life showing her just how treasured she was. The corners of his mouth tugged, his legs moving to catch up. "*Papà*, wait up!"

The kitchen was finally silent, save for a few dishes clinking in the sink. The oven was turned low, holding a steady *whoom*, while the stovetop had been given a rest. Even Edith deserted the remaining tasks to catch up on other duties with Mrs. Brower.

As Dottie placed the last boiled potato on a serving dish for the Stratford family dinner, Mrs. Romano sidled up beside her.

"So, *Tesoro,* I heard you've jilted three men in one week!" Her eyes twinkled with mischief. "You've been rather busy."

Dottie puffed out her cheeks. Exhaling slowly, she lifted her head in defiance. "I've jilted just two men, not three." She nudged her shoulder into the older woman's.

With a chuckle, Mrs. Romano adjusted garnishes on a tray. The roasted chicken's aroma filled the space with savory richness, kissed with lemon. "Hmm, well then, who haven't you jilted?"

Heat ran up Dottie's neck to the tips of her ears.

I can't say it's her son.

"Oh, you know, just someone, somewhere..." Her words drifted as she glanced at Mrs. Romano's bright smile.

"Would that someone happen to be a certain gardener who's dear to this old cook's heart?"

If Dottie wasn't red before, she was now. She stared back at the older, perceptive woman with widened eyes. She didn't want to confirm it, but the woman already knew. A squeak rose, tickling the back of her throat before she could stop it.

Mrs. Romano gave a satisfied smirk and bumped the girl with her hip. "Well, that's all I needed to hear." She walked over to the counter and brought over a lantern. Then handing Dottie the lantern and a burlap bag of cut apples, she gently pushed her towards the back door. "Take these to the stable. I heard the horses have been whining for something other than oats!"

"I don't understand." Dottie peered out the door, the sky had turned to light pinks and oranges. "Why the lantern? It's still light out."

"Trust me, *Tesoro,* take the lantern and bag of apples." The woman paused, tugging a wool shawl from a hook by the door. "Don't forget this! April evenings cool quickly. You need your health!"

Before Dottie could protest, she was herded out the door. It knocked her in the back as it firmly closed. For a moment, Dottie just stood there taking in the slowly changing sky. Pinks, oranges, and crimson painted the heavens. The sky held a promise of a perfect evening. Something special, even exciting.

She inhaled. "So beautiful."

As she took the path to the stables, Dottie was sure she knew exactly who she'd be meeting. Birds flitted around for their last meal of the day while squirrels chittered at the wood's edge. In the distance she could hear the braying of the horses.

The building rose above the back gardens, with a carriage house attached at one end. Its massive beams holding up a roof that spoke of years of snow and sun. The whole building seemed like it could rival the main house in size. Dottie thought it had to be older than the manor itself.

As she neared, golden sunlight poured through the stable's opening, and standing there, watching the changing sky was Antonio. His whole body was relaxed as if he, too, marveled at the beautiful painting above.

The crunching of her shoes alerted him of her presence. For a moment, he stared, unfocused. As she stepped closer, his mouth broke into a shy smile, his hand aimlessly rubbing the back of his neck. "How long were you watching me?"

Dottie's stomach fluttered at the sight. She tried keeping her expression neutral, but her lips tugged up without permission. "Good evening, Antonio. Not long..."

Long enough to find you adorable.

She refused to finish her thought, affection swelled in her chest, full and a little ridiculous.

Mrs. Romano was plotting this whole time.

For as much as Dottie wanted to be frustrated with the interfering woman, her heart wouldn't allow it. The cook knew more than Dottie had ever wanted to confess. And yet she still supported love between her son and a disgraced maid. Awestruck by the trust the woman was giving her, a tear clung to Dottie's lash.

Antonio stood before her, taking the bag from her hands. It gave a small thud as it landed on the dusty ground. "Good evening." His smile faltered for a moment; brows drawn low. "Are you all right?" He hesitated, but then cupped her jaw, his thumb unhurriedly brushing away the tear.

Dottie leaned into his touch, relishing the feeling. "I'm fine. Just very happy."

With his smile returning, he stepped closer, lifting her chin. Everything slowed. The breeze around them, every breath she took, the very beat of her heart.

"I'm glad you're happy." His voice had deepened, his breath feathered across her temple.

Her chest tugged toward him. Then with her eyes dancing in amusement, she corrected him. "No. I said, '*Very* happy.'"

His rough thumbs skimmed across her freckled cheek, as if memorizing the pattern, leaving ripples of warmth in their wake. "My apologies, *Tesoro.* Very happy."

There it was. His wish in a faintest whisper.

In that instant she heard it and equally longed for the same hope, to be loved just as she was.

His dark-chocolate orbs beckoned her to trust him. Having been gullible for so long, the thought of trusting another made her nervous.

Can I really entrust my heart to Antonio?

Deep down in her core she believed she could. But then she remembered her secret and backed away from his touch, fear overriding her longing.

For a moment it seemed he was going to reach for her again when a horse whinnied, saving her from having to explain her retreat. "So, I guess we should go spoil the horses?" Dottie's voice hitched. While shifting to lift the bag of apples, she saw the ache in Antonio's eyes.

"Antonio." His name a whisper on her lips, she took his hand and led him toward the stables. "Let's get these apples to the horses."

The air had changed around them, stilted, careful, but just beneath, Dottie could still feel the simmering need to stay close to him.

Though the stable was well swept, dust hovered in the air, each step stirring up more. Leads hung lazily along the wall; hay stacked tightly into a corner. A bag of oats laid open beside a bench, with tiny grains littering the ground around it.

Dottie jumped when an orange tom cat came bounding through chasing a mouse. Antonio let out a soft chuckle as a horse snorted at the disturbance.

They approached a gray and white mare whose eyes seemed to tell a story. Her tail swished in a carefree beat and the scent of hay filled the space.

Antonio took the bag, handing an apple to Dottie. With the apple clutched in her fingers, she held it toward the creature, but Antonio caught her arm, pulling it back.

"*Tesoro.* You'll get bit that way. Let me show you." His fingers gently wrapped around hers, loosening her grasp. He turned her palm upward so the apple could rest in the middle. But he didn't let go, simply guided her hand toward the horse's muzzle, calmly tracing circles on her wrist with his thumb.

We're alone. But never once have I ever felt safer.

His chest brushed against her back, and it took everything in her to not lean into him. His breath danced across the nape of her neck as he whispered. "Easy now." The world around them disappeared, until it was just them.

And then something prickled her skin. Everything came back into focus as the horse's warm breath brushed her arm, whiskers tickling her outstretched palm as it nibbled the treat.

"See," Antonio spoke lowly in her ear, making her want to melt into his hold, "she can't get your fingers that way."

Dottie allowed him to lead her toward the rest of the horses until the bag was empty and the horses satisfied. Their hooves quietly beat the ground as they settled for the night. A breeze blew through, whispering that the peace wouldn't last. Securing the shawl around her shoulders, she refused to allow any dread to creep in. She'd cling to the moment for as long as she could.

Lord, please let nothing, including myself, ruin this.

Antonio had been so sure this would work. When Dottie had said she was very happy, his heart felt like it could soar, only to come crashing down when she pulled away earlier.

Yet, he could feel it, she wasn't rejecting him.

No, something else held her back. Father, let her heart remain open.

He watched Dottie ball up the empty bag and take the lantern as she turned toward the doorway. "That was such fun. Thank you for letting me try something new." She fidgeted with the lantern handle signaling that she wasn't ready to leave quite yet. And that was perfect because he had one more surprise.

"Actually, I have something else arranged, if you're up for it?" He lifted a picnic basket that he had hidden behind a barrel and smiled at her wide-eyed surprise.

When a brief flicker of doubt flitted crossed her face, Antonio knew he'd need to persuade her before she found an excuse to flee. "We haven't had supper yet, so why not a picnic?"

There was a gentle quirk of her lips and Antonio knew he'd chosen well. Coming closer, he offered his arm, leading her out the stable and down the path. Manicured lawns gave way to drifting wildflowers as they stepped out of the garden.

The sky had shifted to of purples and indigo, while spring peepers played their evening songs. Antonio caught the slightest gasp from Dottie when they drew closer to the willow tree that hung over the pond. Small lily pads hovered silently on the water. The glimmer of small candles danced in mason jars, encircling a simple blanket.

Dottie's feet slowed. "You did all this?" Her voice was barely above a whisper as she spun to look at their surroundings. Her fingers lightly brushed the velvety cattails at the water's edge. Antonio watched a delightful blush grace her cheeks.

He gestured toward her, pride blooming in his chest at her response. "I did, just for you, *Tesoro.*" Placing the basket down, he took her hands and led her to rest against the tree. Dottie relaxed her shoulders with a small hum from her lips, crossing her legs at her ankles.

As much as he knew he should keep his distance for propriety's sake, Antonio settled next to her, bringing the basket between them. Bread, cheese, and a jar of jam filled the basket, along with a helping of canned peaches.

Antonio wasn't sure what to say next, he was never confident holding conversations, and hoped his gesture was enough to show her how special she was.

A soft sigh escaped her lips. "Thank you." That was all she said, nothing more, as she looked over the pond.

He gazed at her profile, mesmerized. Night blanketed them, yet the full moon still illuminated her pale skin, giving it a radiant glow. But more than that, her peaceful expression pulled him in.

"*Tesoro.*"

She turned and looked at him. Searching. Questioning. "Antonio, why do you and your Mamma always call me treasure?" Her lips drew into a frown.

Antonio thought carefully before answering; he knew no ordinary answer would do. "From the moment I met you—"

"When I was fourteen?" She paused mid-bite, peachy syrup slowly dripped down her fingers. The sight distracted Antonio.

So kissable.

Gathering himself, he held up his hand to halt her interruption any further. "When I first met you, you had just been abandoned by your mother. Yet, through all that pain, you pushed forward, not letting grief hold you back." He fidgeted with the blanket, soft between his fingers.

"I wanted to protect you from any more pain. Show you what God saw in you, His child. But I realize I'm not enough. Just a lowly Italian gardener." He looked out over the pond, wrapping Dottie's slender fingers in his, warmth blooming between their intertwined fingers. "You're God's treasured child, Dottie."

They sat in silence, save for the chorus of spring peepers, simply being together. A cool breeze carried across the pond, gently lifting Dottie's hair, and her body trembled, the shawl doing very little to ward off the evening chill.

Without a word, Antonio shrugged off his coat and settled it over her shoulders.

"You *are* enough, Antonio." Dottie turned away, shaking her head. "But I'm not."

Not enough?

Antonio wanted to yell, pull her into his arms and prove to her exactly how enough she was. But he wouldn't. He'd hold back. He'd wait until she was ready to fully see it.

Instead, he lifted her hand and pressed a kiss across the back of it. "I'll just have to keep showing you, *Tesoro.*"

Chapter 17: Friday Morning

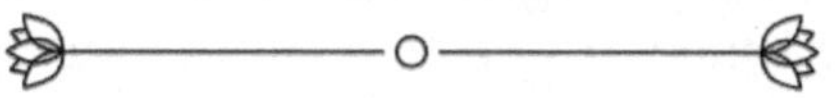

Despite the radiator malfunctioning, Maria's snide remarks, and the uncomfortable glances from Timothy, it was the hundredth time Dottie's lips curved into a smile that morning. It felt strange, this joy. Not the kind that slipped away with disappointment, but something rooted deeper, as if it came from somewhere beyond herself. She couldn't hide the fluttering in her stomach when she thought back to the picnic by the pond.

Everything had been perfect. *Then the moment he kissed her hand...* she clapped a hand over her mouth to hold in a squeal. Never before had a man stopped short of pressing for more. Yet, every minute the evening before, Antonio remained a gentleman. He didn't need to kiss her to show her how much he truly cared.

Closing her eyes, she relived the moment he stood and reached his hand to her.

"Tesoro, would you like to dance?" Glancing around the pond, afraid someone would see, she had hesitated, but he simply waited. She huffed a laugh. "I'm not sure how well we'll dance without music." His returning smile sent her nerves singing, and she realized they needed no music. Tentatively she had placed her hand in his, and he pulled her up without effort, tugging her close. A sharp breath of air escaped her lips.

Antonio had guided her in a small circle, his touch on her waist was so careful, so gentle. Entwining their fingers, he held them close to his heart while his thumb rhythmically rubbed the back of her hand. She could still feel the warmth of his breath when he had bent low toward her ear, and his deep voice reverberated through her core as he sang. "O love of God, how rich and pure! How measureless and strong! It shall forevermore endure..."

Air swept past her ankles. Blinking, Dottie realized Mrs. Romano paced from one end of the kitchen to another, checking on meals in various stages and directing tasks. Katie was back in the kitchen to assist with extra work from Mae's wedding.

Dottie's gaze flicked to the girl. Things felt better, but it was hard to fully forgive her after months of bullying. Mrs. Romano touched her arm, interrupting her worries. "*Tesoro,* distractions are nice, but not while you're holding a sharp object." Dottie didn't miss the smile that played on her lips. "I need the bread sliced and plated in the next minute. Trays are already taken to be served!"

"Yes, Mrs. Romano. Be done in a jiffy!" She shook her head, swiftly working her task. But with the bread's warmth below her fingers, her attention returned again to Antonio, how warm their interlaced fingers had been, and her hand stilled.

Antonio made her feel safe. Her heart gave a quiet, helpless flip. All the men in her life had made her feel desired, but never had they made her feel protected.

Only Antonio.

"Excuse me." Katie walked by, bumping into Dottie's back. The momentum knocked her into the worktable. Dropping the knife, she braced her stomach's impact with her hand. The table's edge biting into her palm. The metallic clanging of the steel blade sliced through the noisy kitchen the same way it would fresh baked bread, quick and smooth, and everything quieted.

For a heartbeat, Dottie wondered if it had been on purpose, all the old hurts rushing back. Her fingers tightened in the rough weave of her apron, holding in the panic welling up within her.

"Oh, my goodness. Dottie, are you good?" Katie peered up at her, worry etched across her brow.

Not the expression she used to wear when making threats.

It made Dottie pause. Shoulders strained, she took a slow breath in. "Yes, I'm good. Are you?"

Reaching for the knife, Katie's words were low. A pained smile stretched across her face. "I, um, I've had better days." Her eyes flicked toward the hallway door and back to the blade. "I'm so very sorry. I'll be more careful next time."

Dottie brushed off the incident. "No harm done. I need to get back to slicing." Taking the knife, she winked at the girl. "Or Mrs. Romano will come hollering." Katie gave a small laugh, but Dottie noticed her hand trembling.

What has her so afraid?

Distracting her, Mrs. Romano placed a small paper bag on the table before her. The roast beef and rye bread coming from the bag had Dottie's mouth water. "*Tesoro*, please deliver this to my Sal and Antonio. I forgot their lunch this morning."

Shaking her head, Mrs. Romano's dark, speckled hair tumbled free from her bun. "Forgetful me. They'd starve without me."

Dottie doubted that Mr. Sal would ever starve but kept the thought to herself.

The cook's eyes twinkled with mischief. "You'll find them in the greenhouse." As Dottie took the bag, Mrs. Romano slid the basket of break toward Mae, who'd just entered the kitchen. "Hurry, we've still a lot of work to do!"

Dottie didn't have to be told twice. Grabbing onto Mrs. Romano's hand, she leaned in, and spoke just above a whisper. "Thank you." She gave the cook a tender kiss on the cheek as she turned to leave.

The older woman chuckled. "You should be saving that for your sweetheart! Not some old woman."

Leaving her apron on the hook by the door, Dottie waved to the two busybodies. She could see them whispering. About her no doubt. She rushed to greet the morning sun. Tulips and daffodils danced in the breeze, their perfume swirling around her as she strode to the greenhouse, her hem swishing with each purposeful step. Feathery ferns laid low along the path.

"Mae never did pick a greenery for her bouquet. Why didn't I think of these before!" Dottie imagined the bold, white magnolia blooms and carefully placed pink hyacinths, surrounded by lush green ferns. "Beautiful."

She closed her eyes, briefly imagining herself holding such an arrangement while friends and family watched on. Standing before her was Antonio. His gaze sparking a want she didn't know she was allowed to have anymore.

To be truly loved.

Almost brushing the idea away, she let it linger instead. A warmth rose from her chest while she fought the urge to break into a run.

I love Antonio.

❀ ❀ ❀

Though the greenhouse was well-heated for the moment, the morning soil and water still held a bite. Antonio had been preparing marigolds for transplanting all morning, leaving his fingers with a deep ache. He looked over the rows of plants under his care, their delicate, green sprouts sparkling under the morning sun that cascaded the wall of glass.

The radiator let out a disgruntled groan. It had been more temperamental in recent days. On more than one occasion, Antonio found frost-tipped leaves on his young sprouts. Watching Charlie hunched over the machine had Antonio wanting to let out a groan of his own.

Antonio despised the man, yet there was no other qualified person in Valebrook to fix it. He had to tolerate Charlie's presence if he wanted to save the work he had poured into all winter and spring. "Do you think you'll have it fixed today? Or should I wait for summer to come to have some heat?"

Charlie muttered something that would've had Mamma reaching for her broom. He knew he shouldn't provoke the man, but his anger over how Charlie had treated Dottie left him little room for civility.

I should probably leave before I say something I'll regret and he pummels me.

Walking into the storage room, it took a moment for his eyes to adjust, with its dim lighting a contrast from the bright greenhouse. A small desk sat in the corner; receipts piled from recent purchases lay across it. Beside the desk sat a fresh bag of fertilizer. Empty seed pans were stacked neatly on a shelf on the adjacent wall. The smell of his lunch tempted him to eat sooner than planned, but he needed to finish preparing the transplants.

Antonio fumbled with the kerosene lantern on the desk so he could find the gloves he'd tucked in a drawer when he heard the scrambling of feet.

The door swung open, bathing the room in light. Dottie stood in the doorway, hair ablaze like a sunset. Her breaths came in short bursts as she held her chest.

"Did you run all the way here, *Tesoro?*" He wanted to chuckle, but the thought of her rushing to him had made hope blooming in his chest.

Is she ready to let me love her?

Stepping toward her, he ached to pull her into a hug, but was stopped by her outstretched arm holding something that smelled like Mamma's cooking.

"I came to bring you this." Each word was punctuated with a breath. "Mrs. Romano said Mr. Sal forgot it this morning."

Glancing back at his lunch, he grinned; the woman always enjoyed playing matchmaker.

Taking the bag from her, Antonio couldn't resist briefly clasping her fingers beneath his own, pulling her closer. Dottie's small gasp at the touch had Antonio's heart leap. "Thank you." He placed the bag on the table, then turned back, eager to speak to the woman before him. "I—"

Placing a palm on his forearm, Dottie silenced his words. "Actually, I have something to say." Her lashes lowered while she shuffled her feet nervously. He froze when her eyes lifted to his, and for a suspended heartbeat, the world stilled.

Antonio wasn't sure who moved first, but the distance between them reduced to mere inches. A perfume of bread, spices and flowers swirled around Dottie, making her feel like home.

He gingerly brushed her copper strands from her face, silky against his skin. When his touch grazed her ear, a shiver ran through her. With his thumb resting at her jawline, he lifted her chin, and his gaze caught hers with an unexpected intensity.

Everything surged within him to close the space between them with a kiss.

But now's not the time. Not yet.

Instead, he placed a soft kiss to her nose, earning a giggle that lit his heart.

It's all too much.

His chest burned.

"*Tesoro...*" Tilting her chin higher, he left a lingering kiss along her jaw, warm against his lips. Her fingers curled into his shirt, pulling him closer.

"*Tesoro*..." As he whispered against her ear, Dottie's grip tightened. Lifting his head to watch her, their breaths mingled and her lashes fluttering closed.

Then realization hit like a punch to the stomach. He longed to show her exactly how he felt, with a kiss to her hopeful lips. His heart constricting under the weight of waiting.

I promised to treasure her.

Antonio squeezed his eyes shut.

How could I let myself get carried away when I promised to protect her?

With a sigh, he opened his eyes. His fingers traced the edge of her jaw, watching each aching breath she took.

I love her. And I'll continue to protect her heart.

Warmth spread through his veins, knowing he was making the right decision. He'd prayed for strength to protect her, and now he prayed it wouldn't break him to hold back.

"*Tesoro*..." Antonio placed a final, tender kiss to her temple, breathing in the moment.

Stepping closer, Dottie rested her forehead against his chest, fitting perfectly beneath his chin. Antonio's palm settled at the small of her back, steady and protective, while the other tangled softly in her hair, drawing her tighter to himself.

"I love you, *Tesoro*..." He hadn't meant to say it, but Antonio knew the words were true. And he wouldn't apologize, nor would he pretend it was accidental.

As silence stretched between them, he feared she didn't feel the same. Doubt flooded his mind.

Maybe I shouldn't have said it. But I won't give up now.

Resting his cheek on the crown of her head, he took in the lingering scent of bread in her hair.

"Do you believe me?"

She responded with a nod against his chest, soft sobs echoed through the small room.

"Well, isn't this a beautiful sight?"

His back stiffened. Timothy waltzed into the room, as if it belonged to him. "I'm toiling away, looking for Mrs. Stratford's lost glove, and here you two are all lovey-dovey in the greenhouse?"

Antonio could feel Dottie stiffen in his arms, but he'd not let her go. Glaring at the intruder over her head, Antonio whispered, "It'll be ok, I'm here."

"Who's being lovey-dovey?" Antonio held in his groan and glanced over his shoulder to see Charlie walk in, covered in grease and wearing a smug smile. "Oh, well, well, Dottie sure does make her rounds." Disdain dripped from his lips as he walked across the room. "This makes for quite the scene."

The two men circled them like vultures, chuckling like they'd found their latest meal. Antonio wanted, more than anything, a way to keep Dottie from more pain.

Dear Lord, we need you. I'll fight if I must.

And for her, he knew it wasn't an empty promise.

"I'm sure I told you to keep away from her, immigrant." Charlie growled in his ear, his clothes reeking of sweat and something bitter. Antonio held in a gag, but he wouldn't abandon the trembling woman in his arms.

Timothy rounded the other side. "Dottie, Dottie, Dottie. You should've aimed higher." Each step shuffled across the floorboards, as if he was struggling to stand.

Has he been drinking? Mr. Griggs would never allow it.

Suddenly, Antonio's arm was yanked away from Dottie. "I'm talking to you, half-white." Charlie encroached into his personal space, leaving no room for retreat.

Taking slow, calm steps, Antonio backed away toward the desk, carefully pushing Dottie behind him to block the men's view of her. He began rolling up his sleeves, knowing things were going to get physical.

"Gentlemen, I suggest we take this elsewhere. If the Stratford's catch wind there's fighting in their prized greenhouse, they won't hesitate to run us all right out of New Jersey."

"I'd like nothing more than to see you go jobless, Romano." The vein in Charlie's neck throbbed, and Antonio knew they'd not get out without a scuffle.

Too focused on Charlie, he missed how Timothy had gotten closer. With fisted hands, the man lunged toward them. Antonio just managed to pull Dottie along as he dodged out of the way.

Something shattered. For a single heartbeat, he knew something had gone dreadfully wrong. Before he had the chance to realize the danger, flames shot up from the fertilizer bag. The air immediately soured with the sharp reek of ammonia and scorched hay, mingled with something meaty and foul.

The blaze quickly spread to the desk, and up the shed wall, licking the roof above. Charlie and Timothy ran for the door, but the flames skittered across the path, leaving them trapped. Glancing out, Antonio noticed Katie standing there, mouth open, stunned still.

Coughing over the stinging in his throat, he yelled out. "Get. Help. Now!" He prayed she'd listen, and his prayers worked. She shook out of her stupor and ran as fast as she could toward the manor.

The beams above creaked and groaned. Dottie clung to Antonio's arm, shaking. "I'm scared! How will we get out?"

"We'll figure it out. God's got us." He pressed a kiss to her temple, trying to reassure her. But as he looked around the room, options were running out. Ash stung at his eyes. He blinked hard, unable to wipe them clear.

Suddenly, there was a snap above their heads. A beam screeched, piercing Antonio's ears, as it came crashing down. Dottie's guttural scream pitched above the roaring fire. "Please, the baby!"

Baby...

Instinctively, he grabbed her and sandwiched her between the floor and himself. Propping himself on his elbows, he left just a small gap between them. The wood smashed into his back. Pain radiated down his legs and into his skull. It took all the strength in him to remain upright.

God in Heaven, hear me. Help us.

Sweat streaked down his brow, falling onto Dottie's tear-stained cheeks. Her trembling hand reached up to wipe away tears of his own he hadn't realized he shed.

"I'm sorry." Her voice was strained against the smoke. He couldn't hear it, but the words on her lips were undeniable. "I love you, too."

Antonio could do this, he could get them out, even with the heat swirling around them. Even with the pain coursing through his body, he'd protect her.

Growling, he pressed up, shifting the beam off his back. It landed on the floor with a thud, just missing his hand. Pulling her up to stand, he made the decision. "We're going to jump. Do you think you can do that?"

Dottie laid a protective hand over her stomach, as if shielding something precious. His eyes followed the movement.

She said, "baby." She's with child...

Antonio had questions, and he probably already knew the answers, but right now, they needed to escape.

Smoke clawed at his lungs, but he managed to speak. "See that opening?" He pointed toward the greenhouse door, where a few bricks had fallen in the door frame. "We can get out with just a small jump."

As they dodged around pockets of fire, Antonio hastily checked the shed to see if Charlie and Timothy had made it to safety. He saw movement out the door. They huddled on the ground with blankets around their shoulders.

The greenhouse door was just steps away, but a trail of flames blocked their path. Squeezing Dottie's hand, Antonio leaned down. "One big jump and we're out."

"All right." Her chin was set with determination, staring down the obstacle like she was ready to wage war.

Antonio intertwined their fingers, kissing the back of her hand. "One. Two. Three. Jump!" The blaze lapped at his heels, and a small kindle caught Dottie's hem. Stepping over the bricks, Antonio quickly bent down to snuff out the flame. "Let's get out of here."

They ran down the aisle, past the plants Antonio had dedicated his time to.

Hopefully they'll contain the blaze before it gets past the brick wall.

Crossing the greenhouse opening, they both gulped clean air. Dottie bowled over, coughing for a moment until her breathing slowed to a steady rhythm.

Smoke still curled from the greenhouse behind them, but sunlight spilled across the grass, promising hope that Antonio hadn't felt in a while.

With soot, sweat and tears marring her face, Dottie never looked more beautiful. He didn't care that she was carrying someone else's baby. Deep down, he had a feeling he'd already known. There had been talk amongst the servants, and looking back, things his Mamma said made more sense now. But he didn't care, he loved her too much, treasured her too much for her past to matter.

"Dottie." He tugged her hand that still held his, but she refused to look his way, curling her shoulders like a shield. "*Tesoro*, look at me."

"I'm afraid to, Antonio." She tried pulling her hand away. "I'm afraid I'll see in your face what I've always seen in others."

He wrapped an arm around her shoulder, drawing her in, pain still radiating through his body. "*Tesoro.* You'll not find it in me." With dirty fingers, he tried brushing strands of tousled hair from her face. Her amber eyes glowed in the bright sun, drawing him in.

Lifting her chin, Antonio waited for her permission. "I need you to hear me, *Tesoro.* I loved you a year ago, despite myself. And no matter your past, you're not the person you were then, and I still love you."

Dottie let out a soft whimper as fresh tears flowed, erasing soot as they traced a path down her cheeks.

"There's a lot we need to discuss. I have many questions that need answers."

She nodded into his palm.

"But for now, I'm going to kiss you, ash and all, if you'll have me." Antonio gave a tilted grin. Maybe he shouldn't. Maybe this was all just the adrenaline after the fire. They'd have a lot to overcome, but Antonio was willing to do whatever it was to keep Dottie by his side.

A small giggle bubbled up from the woman he loved, just as he hoped. "Alright."

As Antonio leaned down, watching every fleck of light in her eyes, his lips hovered a breath away.

"Tonio! *Tesoro!* Where are you?!" Mamma's frantic yells pulled them from the moment.

Resting his forehead against Dottie's, Antonio chuckled. "We'll have to try this again later."

"I can wait." Stretching up, she gave the tiniest brush of her lips on his and stepped away just as Mamma turned the corner, rushing the whole way. Her usual sway traded for a hurried waddle, face flushed with exertion.

Through the haze of smoke, Antonio thought he saw a shadow slip around the greenhouse corner.

Maria?

But when he blinked, the space was empty. She was sweet on Timothy or had been. But the footman was on the other side of the greenhouse. So why was she there? Antonio's jaw ticked.

Maybe she wanted to see how Dottie faired.

"I'm so glad you're safe!" Mamma wrapped her arms around Dottie so tightly, Antonio thought she was wringing water out of a blanket. "Let's get you inside."

He brushed off the thought of Maria, wanting to instead focus on Dottie's brief kiss. He longed for her attention again, her nearness.

Wrapped in a blanket, Dottie was guided away by an attentive Mamma. "By the way, the fire's nearly out. They've called Dr. Winston. He'll check over you," the older woman called over her shoulder.

Antonio waited for his Mamma to notice him standing there too. But when she made no effort to hug him, he cleared his throat. "Um, *Mamma*, I'm not well, I got a bit hurt in there."

The woman turned to him, smiling. "You're standin', aren't you? And had a beautiful woman in your arms? You'll be just fine."

Antonio shook his head in disbelief. Heat ran up his neck, not from the fire or pain, but from the thought of Dottie's lips against his. It wasn't enough, but he'd waited this long, and now she realized she loved him. Nothing else mattered—not the ruined greenhouse, not the men who wanted him gone, not even the weight of her past. Only this truth mattered. She loved him back.

Chapter 18: Friday Afternoon

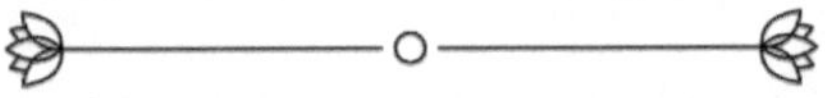

Exhaustion hit before Dottie had time to get washed up. Yet, somehow, with Mae and Edith's help, she'd been quickly bathed and dressed in fresh clothes.

Lying in her bed felt like a welcomed relief as her body unfolded from the strain. The faint scent of lavender soap still clung to her skin, mixing with the lingering trace of smoke she couldn't quite scrub away.

Dainty flowers covered her new dress, the cotton soft against her skin.

I'll ruin this in just one hour down in the kitchen.

She was too tired to ask where the dress came from, but more than grateful to be out of the smoke-stained work dress.

Dr. Winston had released her back to work as long as she wasn't coughing. With her chest still tight, and breathing labored, she was ordered to rest in her room for an hour as a precautionary measure. But an hour alone meant time to contemplate her tangled thoughts.

Heat rose to her cheeks as the moments replayed: the crash of the beam, her blurted confession, and finally Timothy and Charlie's shocked expressions.

They'll surely stay away.

She could laugh about it now, but at the time their appalled faces stung.

A light breeze floated through the room, giving her lungs a small reprieve. With her laughter fading, her lips parted with a small breath.

I kissed Antonio.

She was so sure he would've turned her away with disgust knowing her secret. But he hadn't. Dottie tilted her head to watch the curtains fluttering, casting a soft shadow on her floor.

Even knowing the truth, how could Antonio still accept me?

She could still feel the sensation of his lips against hers, the pressure of his hand on her chin. Her fingertips brushed her lips, as warmth pooled low in her stomach.

For all the chaos of the fire, that moment glowed brighter than the flames.

Fiddling with her dress, she wondered how the rest of the house would treat her. The smooth fabric slid through her fingers. Certainly, Timothy would tell the whole lot, and she could imagine the hateful remarks and sneers from the other staff. The thought made her stomach twist.

"You're God's treasured child..." The words glided on the breeze. Breathing them in, Dottie's lashes trembled.

"Lord, I might say the wrong thing; never one for praying. But thank You for protecting Antonio, me, and the baby. Thank You for treasuring me, even when I'm a wretched mess."

Tears pushed at her lids as she finished her prayer. For a heartbeat, something, soft and unseen, wrapped around her, like the echo of an embrace. Then came a knock.

"*Tesoro*, may I come in?" Mrs. Romano called through her door. Not one for formalities, she didn't wait for an invitation and plowed through the door. Dottie smiled at how familiar the old cook treated her.

Like family.

"I've fixed you something nourishing to eat!" She placed a bowl of fresh stew on the chair beside Dottie's bed, then started straightening things on the dresser. The aroma of chicken, broth and carrots filled the room.

Lifting the bowl, Dottie carefully took a sip. "Thank you, Mrs. Romano." The meat was tender on her tongue, and the spices blended perfectly. Warmth slid down her throat, easing tension she didn't know she still held within.

Mrs. Romano picked up the silver comb, inspecting it in the afternoon light. "Ah, *Tesoro,* I think you've earned the right to call me Mrs. Carmela." There was a twinkle in her eye, one full of mischief and love.

Dottie sputtered for a moment, droplets landing on her new dress. She quickly brushed the spot, hoping it wouldn't leave a mark. "I wouldn't dare call you that! I'm not allowed!" Worry etched on her brow, trying to decide if this was Mrs. Romano's way of teasing or a test.

"I should think I'm the one who decides what you're allowed to call me, *cara.*" The older woman placed her fists on her hips. "And I know I just told you to call me Mrs. Carmela!"

Shaking her head, Dottie opened her mouth to argue, but Mrs. Carmela's plump body nudged her over on the bed, so that they sat side by side. Dottie's body was practically squished against the wall.

"*Tesoro*, I already know what you're going to say. You've said it ever since you've entered my kitchen." She moved the bowl back to the chair and took Dottie's hand. Her cracked, thick fingers, worn from years of work, were warm around Dottie's. "Things like, 'I'm ruined' or 'I'm not worthy'."

Mrs. Carmela took Dottie's cheek in her other hand. "But Dottie, who makes that decision whether you're worthy or not?" She gave a brief chuckle. "I'll tell you right now, it's not you who makes that choice."

"I just don't understand it all" Dottie exhaled softly. "I hear you, I hear Mae, but it just doesn't make sense."

"That's the fun part, *Tesoro.* We don't have to understand someone's love to accept it. You're worthy because God created you. He says in the book of Psalm, 'I praise Thee, for I am fearfully and wonderfully made. Marvelous are Thy works; and that my soul knoweth right well.'" Mrs. Carmela groaned as she stood. "Don't forget, *cara.* The Lord Himself fashioned you wonderfully. His works never lose their worth, even when the world tries to mar them."

She carefully touched the comb again. "Eat your stew, and when you're ready, come downstairs. Dinner's waiting and the cook seems to be missing!"

As the door closed behind Mrs. Carmela, Dottie thought again about what she said. "Lord, I know You keep sending people to remind me over and over. It's just difficult to see past my sin and pain. Help me view myself the way You do."

Sunlight spilled across the floor, soft like a promise. Gentle tears rolled down her cheeks. Each one felt like a painful memory being released. Dottie gave a stuttering breath. As peace settled into her heart, a grin tugged at her lips. "I'll try harder, Lord."

After Dr. Winston bandaged the bruising on his back, Antonio was summoned to discuss the fire with Mr. Leland.

Pacing in front of the door, each step thudded against the old floorboards, jarring his aching muscles. The clock in the hall ticked a quiet reminder that his time was limited. He quickly brushed his damp palms against his thighs.

The faded door squeaked open, revealing a simple office and modest desk, as sunlight filtered through the window.

"Antonio, please come in." Mr. Leland watched with amusement while Antonio brushed off his coat and took a deep breath.

Gesturing to a pot of coffee, the estate manager sat in his seat behind the desk, while Antonio took the wooden chair facing the man who would seal his fate. "Some coffee? It might calm your nerves a bit. Not everyone's a fan, but I quite enjoy it."

Looking up, Antonio wondered what angle the estate manager was getting at. Friendly or interrogating? He wasn't quite sure.

"I'm all right, sir. Maybe another time." The steady beating of his heart matched the bouncing of his leg, anticipating what would come next.

"Antonio. I need you to relax. I've said it before and I'll say it again, you're not in trouble here." Mr. Leland looked over the rim of his mug and grinned. "Well, you might be if we can't get this settled before tomorrow morning. Mae won't appreciate it if I miss my own wedding."

Letting out a chuckle, Antonio allowed his shoulders to relax. Mr. Leland would keep his word. "Everything's been a mess since winter. If it's not one thing, it's another. I'm always on edge that the next problem will cost me this job."

He leaned over, resting his elbows on his knees, staring directly at Mr. Leland. "You and Mr. Frederick have been far too gracious with me all these months."

"While I agree we've been gracious, we've known you're not involved. Mr. Frederick and I have worked together for years in Silkrow, watching over Stratford & Co for problems." Flipping open a book on his desk the man continued, "So we recognize when someone's guilty or being set up."

Rotating the book around, Mr. Leland pointed to the list of every incident from January to April. "And you, Antonio, are being set up."

The muscles in Antonio's hands tightened as he gripped the chair. "That's worse than just being random accidents. Wh-why would someone do that?" Anxiety rose in his chest, heart racing.

"To find that answer, we need to ask who did it." Mr. Leland raised an eyebrow so high up, Antonio thought it might get caught in his hairline. He held back a smile.

Dragging his hands over his face, his mind raced until he remembered. "We never read the letters. Do you still have them?"

"Good call. Our meeting was cut short when the twins came to get me after the magnolia incident with Mr. Rolston." Pulling the three letters from a folder, Mr. Leland laid them in a row.

Habits die hard for an ex-detective.

But the humor left as quick as it came as his jaw ticked recalling the magnolia accident and the smug look of satisfaction that Charlie gave. *"Just a little accident during our rendezvous, no need to look concerned."*

A hand waved in front of his face. "Antonio, where'd you go?" Mr. Leland reached across the desk, tapping his finger on the letters. "Let's read these."

A faint musty smell rose up as he pulled open the envelopes, the pages crinkling under his fingers. The first two were love letters; Katie professing her affections and devotion. But something caught Antonio's attention.

"Read this. Katie says, 'Thank you for the beautiful silver comb. I've never had something so precious! It'll be a reminder of our devotion.'" Antonio handed the letter to Mr. Leland. "I never gave her a silver comb."

Mr. Leland scanned the sheet, taking slow sips of his coffee as he read, the sharp scent of roasted beans carrying across the desk. "There's no name on the top, just 'Sweetheart'. Was this the one found in the shed?"

Antonio nodded. "Yes, the day I found the shattered glass." Every nerve was on edge, Katie had another man while pursuing him.

Was the other man targeting me?

He shook off the shiver that raced down his back.

Opening the final envelope addressed 'Antonio' Mr. Leland slowly perused the contents. Antonio looked on, shifting in his seat uncomfortably, causing the chair to creak beneath him.

Minutes ticked by until Mr. Leland finally glanced up. "Well, that was interesting." He handed the papers over to Antonio. "She half confessed to everything."

Turning the letter over, everything was in there. The boxwoods, the glass, even the fountain. But something didn't sit right. "She didn't say she did them, but she knew about all of them? And then she apologized?" He didn't understand.

"Exactly. So, someone else is pulling the strings. But maybe they had her help?" Mr. Leland took back the papers and placed them inside the book. "Now we just need to figure out who."

"Think it could be Charlie or Timothy?" Antonio's mind whirled. "I mean, Charlie's been lurking around a lot. Nearly every day he has some excuse to show up." His jaw tightened at the thought of the man. "And Timothy's had plenty of opportunities. Though I'm not sure why he'd do such a thing."

"It's hard to say; both have motives. Both claim to like Dottie. Charlie despises you. Not sure about Timothy yet." Mr. Leland rubbed his chin in thought. "Anyone else?"

Antonio straightened in his chair. "You know, Maria's been acting off lately... Came looking for Timothy in the gardens the other day. Seemed nervous. She even made some excuse about looking for Mrs. Stratford's gloves. They're always claiming to be looking for her gloves."

"Odd." Then, checking his watch, Mr. Leland stood. "I hate to cut this short, but Mae told me, under no circumstances, was I to miss checking over the feast the kitchen has prepared." He leaned in with a conspiratorial whisper. "I've got my eye on some fruit cake Mrs. Romano's whipped up, hoping to get a sample before tomorrow's festivities."

Leaving the office, the two men walked side by side down the halls. "Listen, Antonio, about Dottie."

Antonio raised his hand. "Sir, I respect you, and I'm sure you already know everything there is to know about Dottie, given you're with Mae."

Mr. Leland nodded his head, but kept silent, waiting for Antonio to finish.

"I don't care about her past. She's not that same girl anymore. I can see it here." He held a hand to his heart. "And that's all that matters."

He watched for a reaction. He'd come to respect Mr. Leland as a mentor, and still valued his opinion, but wouldn't be swayed on this. "Some might even say I'm reckless to love someone in her situation, but—" Antonio hesitated, trying to find the best words while they walked the silent hall. "But my love for her is steadfast."

Antonio stepped in front of Mr. Leland, making him stop mid-step. He met Mr. Leland with determination. "So, if you're going to try to dissuade me, you can stop now. I'll not abandon her."

Mr. Leland chuckled and clapped his hand on Antonio's shoulder. "I'm so relieved to hear you say that."

Blinking, Antonio stepped back. "You are?"

"Antonio, I'd never push my opinions on you, or anyone else here. But I've always been under the mindset that we should treat others as God would treat us." Tugging at his collar, he added, "He sees our sins, but He still loves us and pursues us despite them."

Busy chatter from the kitchen drifted up the stairs, interrupting his speech. "Before we go down, let me finish with this. Dottie needs that kind of love. Mae's been pouring it into her. I've even seen Mrs. Romano do the same." Glancing down the stairs to make sure no one was coming; Mr. Leland spoke in a hushed voice. "And aside from God's all-encompassing love, I imagine yours will be an amazing love story."

The estate manager hurried down the stairs with a grin on his face. Antonio stood there, letting those words settle into his heart.

Amazing love story.

He took a breath.

"Yes, that's exactly what I want."

Chapter 19: Friday Evening

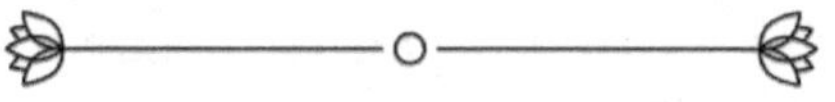

Dottie descended the servant stairs into a kitchen full of people, laughter, and food. A smile spread across her face, as a mixture of aromas invaded her senses, from freshly baked bread and stew to sweet cookies and warm cinnamon.

There were trays, tins, and cooking utensils on every counter. Glancing at the stove, she saw Mrs. Carmela stirring something with vigor while calling over her shoulder to Edith.

In the middle of the room, three delightful girls ran around the worktable. Rose wielded a spatula, while Anna waved a dishcloth like a cape. Violet held back, peeking into the different tins.

Likely planning out her choices for tomorrow.

As Dottie surveyed the kitchen, she watched as Mae's eyes narrowed at Mr. Leland. "Well, I never thought I'd catch anyone daring to sample the wedding sweets before the vows."

He froze, fork mid-air. "I just wanted to see if the cake was...worthy."

"Worthy?" Mae snatched the fork. "You'll find out soon enough, but until then, hands off—or I'll find a way to make *you* part of the centerpiece."

Dottie giggled. Her friend might sound like she was scolding her betrothed, but the twinkle in her eyes told another story. This was the lightheartedness she'd longed for in a home all her life—and at last, it was hers to share. A quiet ache swelled beneath her ribs. She'd never thought joy could feel so gentle, so personal.

She caught sight of Antonio watching her, and her cheeks heated. When his mouth tilted into a smile that felt like it was only for her, her heart fluttered wildly. Despite everything, he still looked at her as someone of worth.

Lord, is that the way You see me too? Completely smitten?

"Ah, *Tesoro*, I need you!"

Blinking, she looked away to find Mrs. Carmela pressing a bowl of frosting into her hands. "Go frost the cookies." Before Dottie could reply, the cook bustled back toward the oven, throwing words over her shoulder without looking. "*Tonio*, you're needed at the cookie counter, holding trays steady."

Antonio's gaze found Dottie again and didn't waver. "Yes, *Mamma.*"

Oh my, will I be able to get any work done with him looking at me that way?

She clutched the bowl against her body, trying to quell the butterflies in her stomach. Her fingers trembled, but not from fear. It was strange, how safety could feel just as overwhelming as danger once did.

Stepping forward, Antonio removed the bowl from her grasp, his palm engulfing her hand. When he moved closer, his shoe tapped the side of hers and everything stilled, until it was just them. No noise, no kitchen, just them.

That is, until Anna ran by, knocking Dottie straight into Antonio's chest. He managed to move the bowl just in time, saving her from being covered in sticky frosting.

With her nose buried in his shirt, he smelled of fresh earth and the warmth radiating from him threatened to draw her in. The cotton fabric was surprisingly soft against her skin. It felt so right. The thought made her heart skip, but she restrained herself from snuggling into his chest.

"Sorry!" Anna giggled as she ran toward the pantry, Rose following close behind.

In a low, deep voice that lit Dottie's heart, Antonio talked quietly, his breath skimming against her ear. "I don't believe she's sorry at all."

Dottie's nerves pulsed as the space between them simmered. She could feel his fingers barely graze her arm and the closeness made her skin sizzle.

Someone behind them cleared their throat. Antonio stepped away first, rubbing the back of his neck. "Uh, let's get these cookies finished."

But despite his cool reply, Dottie noticed his ears reddening and couldn't help but find the look absolutely captivating.

At the counter sat two trays of cookies waiting to be frosted. Their sweet lemony scent greeted her nose as she lifted the chilled bowl in her hand. They worked together in tandem; Dottie spooned out the soft, creamy frosting and Antonio rotated the tray.

She was grateful for the comfortable silence because she could feel the rest of the room staring. Occasionally, she'd glance over her shoulder, and everyone promptly turned away, focusing their attention elsewhere.

Such a meddlesome bunch.

The thought made her laugh. She might not have any family of her own, but these people had taken her in, bruised and broken, and loved her through it. Love had crept in quietly, the kind that didn't demand perfection or repayment.

As Antonio adjusted the tray, their shoulders rubbed, a fleeting contact that neither one pulled away from. Every touch sent Dottie's pulse leaping wildly and she felt the need to inch closer. Not because she wanted to flirt, that desire had long since disappeared. She paused, spoon in the air, frosting slowly dripping off.

I don't need it anymore.

Her lips tugged into a smile. Dottie knew now she didn't need man's carnal attention because she had God's love all along.

"*Tesoro*, are you all right?" Antonio peered at her, concern etched across his brow.

Looking up, she smiled. "I'm fine; just had a moment. But we need to finish these cookies." She playfully bumped his shoulder and pointed the spoon his way. "And if we don't, your Mamma will scold us."

Antonio's deep laugh radiated through Dottie's core, and the pull toward him hummed. "All right, *Tesoro*." But before she could scoop the next serving, he swiped a small drop of frosting off the counter, and with a quick bop, placed it on her nose.

Eyes wide, Dottie stared at him in disbelief. As her lips parted to reprimand him, she felt his hand brush against the small of her back, pressing in. Her stomach quivered and breath caught. Leaning in, mouth inches from hers, Antonio whispered. "You have something on your nose, *Tesoro*." His breath fanned across her skin, and her lashes fluttered closed.

Dottie's chest rose and fell, each breath straining for her to tilt her head up just so. And then, with the briefest kiss to her nose, Antonio shifted back, but not far enough away for the tension to ease. "Mamma's watching." When his thumb wiped away the remaining frosting, his fingers lightly grazed her cheek. She watched as he licked the frosting from his thumb.

I want to kiss him. How can he make something so simple feel absolutely extraordinary?

Every fiber in her wanted to squeal and stamp her feet with delight. Only her wits kept her from doing just that.

Her bliss was promptly shattered when the hallway door burst open, and a voice she didn't want to hear echoed across the room. "Mrs. Romano. Mrs. Stratford is waiting on her dessert." Maria walked in, hands on her hips, flanked by Timothy. His expression was almost unreadable, save for the smallest downward twitch of his mouth.

Maria seems pleased and back to her old self. They must have reconciled.

Antonio's hand on her back tensed. Peeking up she watched his jaw tick while he stared past her shoulder. The small cakes were set within Dottie's reach, she'd have to deliver them to the parlor maid, but her feet felt fused to the floor.

I don't want to hear her insults today.

But Maria had already spotted the tray of lemon cake squares. "Oh, Dottie, would you mind bringing them over?" Her voice dripped with superiority.

With trembling fingers, Dottie set down the spoon and reached for the tray, but Antonio stilled her hand. His closeness made her skin heat. "Don't let her words tear down what the Lord has built up. Only His opinion matters."

And His opinion says I'm treasured.

The word lingered in her mind—*treasured.*

Not pitied.

Not tolerated.

Chosen.

Her body relaxed slightly, and with the smallest of nods, she raised her chin. "Okay." The tray handle dug into her palms as she tried keeping her hands steady. Each step toward the worktable felt like a mission. And for her faith, her family and most of all, for herself, she'd succeed in not letting their words matter. "Here's Mrs. Stratford's cakes. Make sure to take the tartlets with you as well, they are Mr. Stratford's favorite."

Timothy scoffed. "Of course, you'd pick tarts. Bet they're Antonio's favorites, too."

Heat crept up her neck, but Dottie wouldn't let the dig affect her.

Maria grabbed the tray, letting a snigger escape her throat. With one last glance, Timothy sneered before leaving the room.

She hadn't realized her lungs had caught until the door swung closed, resulting in a stuttering breath.

He'll likely be bitter for a while, and he will have to figure that out himself.

The jabs didn't sting nearly as painful as she expected. Turning, she found everyone waiting, as if she might break down at any moment. But the shame didn't take root like it had in the past, instead her heart felt light, her mouth lifting into a smile.

Thank you, Lord, for giving me peace.

Mae walked briskly over and wrapped a hug around her. "It'll get easier, I promise. And we're all here." She waved her arm around the room.

Following Mae's gesture, Dottie's gaze met Antonio's and held. His chest lifted with what looked like admiration, and a thrill ran through her. "Yes, I agree. It will get easier." As she surveyed the room, finding comfort in the faces of her Skyline family, she said, "I think we have some work to do. Yes?"

Everyone called their agreement and set back to work. Dottie and Antonio stayed side by side, sneaking glances at each other any moment they could. She'd never felt support like this. This no-questions-asked, no expectations support. The people that filled that small space simply loved her and wanted what was best for her.

By evening's end, the pies, cookies, and sandwiches were ready for the morning. On tired feet, Mrs. Carmela called her good night and headed for the back door, wrapped in her shawl. Anna laid sleepily against Mr. Sal's shoulder as he hummed an old Italian lullaby in her ear. Mae and Mr. Leland had retired an hour before with their own sleepy girls.

There was something comforting in the stillness after a busy day. Simply knowing she had a home in this small space protected by people who'd become her family. The room had quieted while Edith and Katie took to washing down surfaces and rinsing dishes.

Dottie was tasked to cover all the trays and plates to keep the food from spoiling overnight. As she laid the final cloth over the sliced bread, still soft and yielding, Antonio propped his hand against the counter, blocking her in. The air shifted. He wasn't touching her, but his nearness felt like a tender caress. Her breath caught as his calloused fingers skimmed against her neck.

He's so close.

When he swept her hair from her shoulder, Dottie's body unbiddenly leaned into the solid warmth of his chest. His breath stirred the loose wisps framing her jaw as his cheek rested against hers, his beard softly scratching against her skin.

"You're no tart, *Tesoro*. To me, you're honey; golden, pure, and worth keeping. And I'm privileged to be allowed to love you." Antonio's lips grazed her jaw as he spoke, heat blooming beneath, warm and tender; the intimacy carried sweetness she never knew she could have.

She remained there, suspended, allowing the moment to linger and his words to flood her heart. Antonio brushed a soft kiss on her cheek. "I love you."

Dottie's skin tingled and she almost turned into his words, the thinnest pause kept them apart as she recalled the two other women in the room. "I love you, too." Her gaze lifted to his dark chocolate eyes, which slowly traced her face down to her parted lips.

Lord, if Your love is so much more than this man's, I can hardly contain it.

A light giggle pulled Dottie's attention toward the sink, breaking the intensity of the moment. Antonio edged away, clasping his hands behind his neck, while trying to find his words. "Well..." His ears bore the same blush from earlier that Dottie was beginning to enjoy and looked forward to seeing again. "I should be going."

"All right. I'll see you in the morning?" Her hand rested on her chest to calm the fluttering. For the first time, she didn't feel like an outsider watching joy happen, she was part of it.

"Yes, *Tesoro.*" Antonio lifted her chin and stole a kiss to her temple. "In the morning."

Chapter 20: Saturday Morning

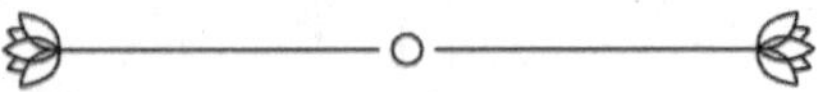

Rushing to beat the grandfather clock's morning chime, Dottie descended the servant stairs, almost slipping on the last step. She hadn't intended to be so late, but as she readied herself in her new work dress, she realized her silver comb was missing. Her search proved fruitless, not a single prong or glint of silver could be found.

Why would someone take an old comb?

The comb wasn't worth a penny, yet its absence left her with a strange unease she couldn't quite name. She shivered, thinking Charlie might have snuck in.

He wouldn't. Entering an unwed mother's room unsupervised? He'd be foolish.

Mrs. Carmela stood over the stove, skillet sizzling, the scent of warm eggs and sausage filled the room. Katie busied herself stacking tins and trays for the wedding meal. But as Dottie watched, she noticed the girl's usual boldness seemed snuffed out.

With the amount of work they had, there was no time to talk. Spotting a pile of fruit and a knife already set on the worktable, she realized she'd have to speak with Katie later. While tying on her apron, she called out to the busy cook. "G'morning! Where do you need me, Mrs. R-, I mean, Mrs. Carmela?"

The older woman beamed as she embraced Dottie. "Good morning, *Tesoro*! I need you exactly where you are!" Hustling back to the stove, she said, "And once breakfast is complete, finishing touches on the wedding feast!"

She couldn't remove the image of the scullery maid from her mind. Glancing back, Dottie wondered why her shoulders slumped. She remembered her old self—how alike the two of them were. False confidence to cover up the consuming heartbreak within. Anything to distract from the sorrow.

Maybe that was why Katie's emptiness pricked something deep in her chest. She knew too well the ache of pretending. It was a heavy kind of loneliness—the kind that only grace could ease.

With each slice of the apples, her worry deepened.

Maybe she's just jealous of me and Antonio?

But her thoughts were interrupted by the morning meeting letting out. Whispers floated through the room. "Did you hear..." "Could it be true?" As people left, sideways glances slid Dottie's way. "She always was a flirt...." Of course, Maria's whispers were loudest of all.

Timothy wouldn't look at her, his focus was solidly on the space in front of him. Exhaling, Dottie was grateful nothing further was said. Whispers she could endure, but not hostility or unwanted conversations.

Clara walked over, hands clasped behind her back. "I just wanted to check on you. I had no idea, and if I had, I would, I don't know... I would have stuck up for you more." Her foot shuffled across the tiles, but her eyes lifted with the same determination they had a week ago. "Please, next time, tell me, I don't know much, but I do know a family takes care of each other."

Family.

Dottie smiled. "Thank you, Clara. I'll remember that." Dottie glanced up and noticed Henry staying at the hallway door. His eyes kept peeking up toward Clara, as if he was waiting just for her. With a tilt of her lips, Dottie chuckled. "You'd best go, or both of you will be late." She gestured with her chin toward the young footman.

Clara's cheeks bloomed with a light pink tinge. "Mr. Kelly'll be fine. He's been trailing me for weeks without a word; one more heartbeat won't unravel him."

When Clara left, Henry held the door for her. As she had predicted, he didn't say a word, but a blush tinged his ears. Dottie suppressed a giggle as she went back to chopping fruit.

Mrs. Carmela slid a block of cheese in front of her to begin slicing. Behind them, pots crashed to the floor and Katie groaned. The girl knelt on the floor clearing the pots, her hands trembling with each dish dropping into the sink.

This will not do.

Dottie brushed her hands on her apron and called Katie over. "Katie, I could use your help. Can you come here please?"

It wasn't lost on Dottie that Mrs. Carmela back stiffened, listening in on the conversation, as if anticipating a conflict.

"Coming." Katie sighed as she put down a pan and dragged herself over to the worktable. Katie kept her eyes downcast. "How can I help you?"

With her brows furrowed, Dottie fiddled with the knife, the blade smooth under her fingers.

Lord, lead my words. I trust You in this.

For so long, her prayers had been timid, uncertain, offered from a heart that feared rejection. But this time, she spoke with quiet assurance. Even if she stumbled over the words, He heard her. He always had.

"I'll be down in the pantry. Forgot a few ingredients." Mrs. Carmela called from across the room.

Once the woman was out of sight, Dottie laid the knife to the side and took Katie's hand. "Something's wrong, isn't it?"

She didn't want to ask, but the concern would nibble at her mind until she understood. "Are you..." She huffed.

Just ask.

"Are you still jealous?"

The girl chuckled, but there was no joy in it, just sadness. "No, not jealous about you and Antonio. Well, not in *that* way at least."

"What do you mean?"

Katie's lips parted, but no words came out. And then a tiny tear dotted her lashes. "I can't say." Her voice was so small, Dottie almost thought she imagined it.

"You can't say?" Dottie felt like a parrot as the girl wrung her apron in her fingers. "What can't you say?"

Shaking her head, Katie kept her gaze low. "I just know too much. And I was told if I said anything, anything at all, I'd be sorry."

Dottie searched the young maid's face, trying to decide if she was playing a trick, or if the girl was really scared. But as the tears trailed down Katie's cheeks, and her face flushed red, Dottie knew she wasn't faking.

Pulling Katie into her arms, Dottie patted her back tenderly. The girl's hot tears seared Dottie's skin. "Shh, it's ok. I won't press further. But know, if you need to talk, I'm here." Katie nodded slowly into Dottie's shoulder.

What is she so afraid of? Lord, something doesn't feel right. Whatever shadows are silencing her, bring them to light. Comfort her.

The kitchen door flew open, and Katie stiffened at the sound. Quickly stepping back, she kept her head turned away as she wiped her face with her sleeve.

"Dear Dottie! You're exactly who I'm looking for." Mae radiated the type of joy a woman in love should. And though Dottie wanted to be just as excited, concern for Katie dampened her enthusiasm.

"You're positively glowing." Dottie tried forcing happiness into her voice, but it didn't quite land.

Mae's brows furrowed, asking with her eyes what was wrong. She had become more like a sister to Dottie these past few months. And they no longer needed words to communicate.

Dottie gave the slightest nod toward Katie. Taking up the knife to finish her task, she pointedly stared at her friend. "So, what brings you to the kitchen so early? You have today off."

"You're exactly right! I'm not here for work, I'm here for you!" Mae came over and took away the knife. But before Dottie could protest, Mae was behind her, untying her apron.

"Mae, I don't know what exactly you're planning, but I need to help Mrs. Carmela with finishing breakfast and getting the wedding meal set." Dottie tried tying her apron back, but Mae snatched it.

There was a swishing behind her. Dottie turned to see Mrs. Carmela scurrying over. "Don't try getting out of this, *Tesoro*. I've got Katie, and Edith. Plus, plenty of others to help! Go with Mae." She shooed Dottie toward the back door.

She gave a quick glance at Katie. For some reason she didn't feel comfortable leaving the girl alone. But Katie shrugged a shoulder and turned away, plunging her hands into the sink full of suds.

With a knowing nod, Mrs. Carmela leaned in and whispered, "I'll keep watch over her. Now go."

As Mae pulled her along, Dottie huffed a laugh.

Why am I always being shooed?

"Mrs. Carmela, one day you're going to shoo me away, and I might get my feelings hurt!"

"Ah, then I'll kiss both cheeks like my mamma did, and you'll forget all about it." The older woman waved her hand at the girls and shut the door.

Mae led Dottie down the path toward Mrs. Brower's cottage. Digging her heels in, Dottie caused her friend to stumble with the stopped momentum. "Truly, Mae, what on earth are you doing? Shouldn't you be getting ready for your wedding?"

"I am, but to do that, I need you! Now come or Mrs. Brower and Genevieve will reprimand me!" Laughing, Mae's eyes twinkled, and she went back to guiding Dottie.

Reaching the modest home, Dottie could see a bustle of activity inside. The twins' laughter echoed from an open window.

The home was bright, every window open, curtains billowing with the breeze. A small table sat in the middle of the room, strewn with cloth, flowers and ribbon. Flowers adorned the counter and side table, filling the space with a sweet aroma.

"You're finally here!" Mrs. Brower clapped her hands, slightly trembling with her rheumatoid. "Now we can get started." She held up the loveliest dress. Ivory rayon caught the spring light, giving the smallest shimmer. When Mae was dressed, the fabric danced delicately across her collarbone, hugging her frame perfectly, as it flowed gently to the floor.

Dottie's breath caught. "You look stunning, Mae. Just beautiful!" The bride-to-be glowed, gliding her hand across the fabric. "Thank you."

She watched Violet and Rose arrange Mae's tresses. "Mama, your hair is going to be gorgeous!" "We need to add another flower to this side." Their chatter was catching, full of excitement and joy. And Dottie found herself smiling at the intimate scene.

Mae turned, her lips tilted in her usual mischievous way. "Now, it's your turn."

"Mine? I'm—I don't understand." Dottie edged toward the door, her only means of escape.

Why would they need to fix my hair?

It was just as it always was, braided and covered. As a guest, she had no need for her hair to be fixed.

Rose and Violet pulled her arms and effectively moved her off the couch. Rose pointed to a chair. "Sit. And don't get up 'til we're done."

To refuse such adorable girls would have been a mistake. Obediently, Dottie sat as a giggle bubbled up in her chest. The chair creaked under her weight. Before her laid a rainbow of ribbons and flowers.

"Girls, that needs to wait." Miss Genevieve carried a dress of blue rayon blend in arms. "Dottie still needs to dress before her hair is done." Holding the dress out, she added, "This is my gift to you."

"Wait." Dottie stood quickly, knocking over the chair. "I can't wear that!" She pointed at the dress like it had offended her.

It's too beautiful for someone like me.

Walking over, Mae placed a palm on her shoulder. "Look at me. I wanted you to be a part of this from the moment you let me in." Cupping Dottie's cheeks, her friend moved closer. "Leland agreed. And everyone," she gestured to the room. "Everyone here supports my decision."

Dottie shook her head and stepped back. Her hand trembled as it held her barely rounded stomach. "You don't understand, I can't stand up there, next to you, who's so good. And next to her." Dottie pointed to Miss Genevieve. "She's—she's one of them. And I'm just a kitchen maid." She flung out her hands, tears welling up.

Don't they understand how questionable this will appear?

"It's simply not done!"

Miss Genevieve approached her. "Stop." At her order, the room quieted, even the breeze stilled.

Crossing her arms against her stomach, Dottie looked down, finding her shoes more interesting than the commanding woman.

"You're going to stop. First, this is Mae's wedding and what she says goes. Second, are you really going to waste Helen's skills by not wearing this beautiful dress?" Her voice softened. "And third, have you learned nothing?"

This woman would make a fine mistress to any estate. The definition of grace mixed with authority.

Dottie's fingers clenched, humbled by the lady's words. She hesitantly peeked at the women around her, a little ashamed that she fell back into thinking she was unworthy.

Mae's eyes shimmered. "You are so loved, Dottie, more than you could ever imagine." She clasped Dottie's hands, drawing her closer. "You're wanted here."

Quickly brushing away a tear, Mae straightened her shoulders. "Now, start listening. Put on that dress, and let the girls fix your hair. No more arguments."

Dottie held her tongue. She had learned about how God saw her, felt it in her core, His amazing love for her. But to see it in others still baffled her.

Why do they so blindly love me?

Obediently, she took the offered dress. In the privacy of Mrs. Brower's room, she slipped it on; the fabric was soft and cool on her skin. It had panels on the side, with laces, just as her other dress did. It felt delicate against her skin and fit like it was made specifically for her.

Stepping into the living room, she heard a gasp. Mrs. Brower's expression softened. Mae held a hand out to Dottie, pulling her close. "You are lovely."

I feel lovely.

She wasn't ready to say those words out loud, but she felt them deep down.

Sitting carefully, Dottie allowed the girls to unbraid her hair, twisting her strands into a simple plait. Rose leaned over to Violet and spoke in hushed tones. "Don't forget the comb."

Glancing over, Dottie saw Violet holding her missing silver comb. "We thought it would be the perfect addition to your hair. Don't be cross! We had Mrs. Carmela slip it out." "We just wanted to surprise you! Were you surprised?"

With a laugh, Dottie peered at the two wide-eyed girls. "Very surprised. Thank you."

Miss Genevieve brought over a simple hand mirror. "See the incredible person you are, Dottie."

Her breath slowed as she watched the reflection staring back at her. It was an amber-eyed girl whom she didn't recognize.

Copper hair blazing brightly in the morning sun, framing her freckled cheeks perfectly. The dress's country blue hue contrasted her fair skin flawlessly.

Could this really be me?

Her heart thudded in her chest.

Gone was the abandoned child, the flirt, the damaged girl. Instead, an extraordinary child of God gazed back, a daughter redeemed, seen through the eyes of her Maker.

Maybe this is what grace looks like.

Beauty freely given.

Chapter 21: Saturday Morning II

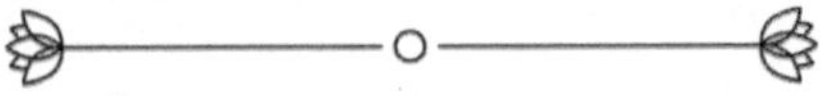

As the latch gate to the wooded path creaked closed behind Antonio, something caused the hairs on his arms to prickle. When he glanced toward the manor, there was the unmistakable sense of being watched. A branch cracked in the distance, soft but sharp, setting his nerves on edge.

He scanned the grounds and saw nothing unusual. But still the unease lingered.

"*Tonio*, you coming?"

"Yes, *Papà*, just checking something." He called back, all the while keeping his eyes on the yard. With one final sweep of the area, Antonio thought he noticed a shadow lingering near a tree, but it was gone before he could recognize it.

Probably nothing but my imagination running wild.

But something inside told him it was no illusion. Someone was watching.

Forcing his attention to the path, Antonio rolled the tension from his shoulders. He'd not let his anxiety rule the day, for just ahead was the woman he loved.

The walk to the church was full of all things beautiful. Wild violets and bluebonnets clustered along the path. Dogwood blooms bowed low with the girls trying to jump and reach a few. Black-capped chickadees and sparrows sang welcoming songs to entertain.

And most beautiful of all is Dottie.

He'd always noticed how light followed her, even the shadows seemed gentler when she was near. Just a few feet ahead of Antonio, his eyes barely left her, except when his Papà demanded attention.

Dottie's face glowed as she spoke with Miss Mae and Miss Genevieve. Her red tendrils perfectly braided and laid across her shoulder, a silver comb catching the light. Whenever she'd peek back, their gazes held, and Antonio's heart hammered. He loved watching her cheeks bloom red whenever she saw him.

The rest of the walk to church was almost a blur while his thoughts whirled around her. Mamma prattled on

about how everyone wore their Sunday best. Mr. Leland looked dashing in his suit, but what took Antonio by surprise
was how the man's eyes would soften anytime he spied his betrothed.

Mrs. Brower walked alongside Edith, speaking in hushed tones, while Mamma had Katie by the hand. After all the trouble the girl brought, the dear woman still took time to care for her. He'd never be as generous, but he was grateful she took time to show others the Lord's love.

Antonio's attention turned as Dottie giggled, earning him an entertaining scene when Mr. Frederick's shoulder briefly brushed against Miss Genevieve's. What was more fascinating was Mr. Frederick's face, which had blushed a brilliant red.

The anticipation of the wedding teetered on reverence as the chapel came into view over the slope, everyone's voices one by one quieted. Even Anna and the twins' laughter died down.

Aside from birds chirping in the trees, and a light rustling through the branches as a breeze passed through, the only sound to accompany them were the crunching of shoes along the path.

Antonio's only desire was to stay near Dottie throughout the festivities, but she felt just out of reach.

As she stood at the church doors, waiting for the procession to begin, Dottie could still feel the warmth of Antonio's gaze. She had wished to walk beside him, possibly even hold his hand, but custom called for her to remain with the wedding party. And now she drew in a steadying breath, ready to take her place at the door. The morning air cooled her warmed cheeks.

People filed into the old chapel; pews creaked as they filled. A low chatter rippled through the room as Miss Betsy began the prelude.

Dottie shuffled nervously; worried what whispered words might be heard as she walked down the aisle alongside Miss Genevieve. Her grip tightened around the small bouquet she held, but she knew those who mattered most held no prejudice against her.

Staring down at the bouquet, she smiled. Mae had added the ferns as she suggested. The feathery greenery tickled her cheek as she sniffed the magnolia and hyacinth blooms.

When the music swelled, Dottie felt a nudge in her back. Miss Genevieve leaned over. "It's time to go. One step at a time." In front of her was an enthusiastic Anna, spreading flower petals between the pews, not elegantly, but with all the intensity of a small puppy. As the girl edged closer to her Mamma's narrowed stare, she instantly settled into the proper flower girl she was expected to be. The room filled with soft laughs.

Mrs. Brower swiftly moved an errant hair from Dottie's brow while Dottie drew in a fortifying breath. With her chin held high, she took her first step into the chapel. Expecting gasps, whispers, and looks of disgust, she briefly peeked around the room, yet the faces before her held only kindness, not judgment. Her eyes widened in surprise, realizing she was surrounded by people who love exactly like Mae loves.

They don't despise me.

The sweet scent of candles mingled with magnolia and hyacinth pulled Dottie from her musings. Beeswax. She hadn't breathed that aroma since before the Crash.

But how could a rural church like this afford it?

A glance at the altar, where Mr. Frederick stood beside an enamored Mr. Leland, reminded her that the Stratfords could afford such luxury.

With each step, Dottie's tension loosened, until she felt the air around her thicken. And then she saw him, Antonio's eyes locked onto hers, unwavering and full of admiration. Her cheeks flushed under his earnest gaze, and the room faded until she reached the altar.

Though she should have been focused on her friend gliding down the aisle, with her adorable daughters giggling as they escorted her to the altar, Dottie's body was acutely aware of the man in the second row. She shot Antonio a sideways glance, a silent warning, hoping he would look away. But instead, his attention only intensified, leaving Dottie's heart galloping.

Pastor Somers called the room to attention when Mae came to stand before Mr. Leland. Their quiet "I love you's" could be heard through the room. The question was asked, "Do you promise to love her, comfort her, honor and keep her, in sickness and in health, and, forsaking all others, keep yourself only unto her, so long as you both shall live?"

Dottie involuntarily turned toward Antonio. His gaze answered with a resounding '*yes*' that sent a shiver of longing up her spine.

Yes, yes, Lord, do I.

Realizing how much she loved this man, her knees went weak.

How had I missed him all this time? Loving me without me realizing it?

As she pressed her heel into the floor to steady herself, a throat quietly cleared beside her, and she turned to see Miss Genevieve give a knowing smirk.

Pointing toward the doors, the heiress added. "It's time to go, Dear."

"Ah, yes. Sorry." Dottie's neck heated, having been caught in her momentarily distracted. With a final glimpse at Antonio, he rewarded her with the briefest wink and kissable tilt of his lips.

This man is going to be the end of me.

The rear garden pergola was wrapped in ivy with small flowers dotting the vines. Nearby, the brook babbled, adding to the delightful sounds of children laughing. A light breeze blew through the trees and rippled the wildflowers along the forest edge. Picnic blankets were dispersed across the back lawn. Platters and tins with neatly stacked treats were a welcomed feast for all.

Dottie sat carefully in her new dress, enjoying a few cookies, with sticky crumbs gathering on her fingers. With the sun filtering through the trees, warming her back, she took in the details of their small, shared life. Mae and Mr. Leland converse in hushed tones, their heads nearly touching. No one else existed to the newlyweds, except for when Rose or Violet interrupted to share one of their desserts.

Henry brought his fiddle; a hidden talent Dottie never knew he had. His fingers glided with practiced ease along the strings as he bowed out a sprightly jig. Clara watched on from a nearby blanket, her foot tapping to the melody, a small smile playing on her lips.

Mr. Frederick and Miss Genevieve sat nearby having quiet conversations. They exchanged a brief glance, both taking in the gentle chaos of the garden, a silent acknowledgment of the surrounding joy that contrasted with their usual formal world.

Pastor Somers talked animatedly with Mr. Sal while his son, Joseph, ran along with the other children. Dottie couldn't help but notice Edith taking quick glances his way. It was odd behavior for a woman who always held herself so professionally. Dottie giggled.

She must like something she sees.

But as she took in the moment, she noticed Katie sitting alone at the edge of the garden, her plate of treats had barely been touched. The scullery maid jumped at almost every sound or movement around her. Suddenly, she met Dottie's gaze and just as quickly turned away. Katie's face twisted in anger as she absentmindedly touched her braid.

Lord, I'm still so confused on how to help her.

Taking a sip from her lemonade, the sharp sweetness mingling with fresh-cut grass, Dottie wondered, *Maybe I should go speak to her.*

The thought was broken as the air around her brimmed with a delightful tension. A flutter of warmth spread through her chest, knowing Antonio was nearby.

"*Tesoro*, may I sit with you?" Antonio's voice rumbled deep, causing her insides to tip off-balance.

He might have asked, but he didn't wait for her response as he settled down beside her.

Just like his mamma, making himself at home with no mind to others.

It didn't bother her, instead his presence made her feel at home. His thigh brushed against hers with a jolt ran up her leg, the warmth between them to seep through the cotton of her dress. But she didn't move, content to finally remain close to him, to have permission to lean into his shoulder.

Brushing the crumbs off the blanket, Dottie gave a satisfied sigh when she looked over the garden. "It's lovely, isn't it?"

"Yes, you are lovely, *Tesoro.*"

She could hear the smile play in his voice. Dottie's eyes met Antonio's as he leaned in to brush a whisper against her ear. "You were radiant this morning."

Her hand itched to touch him. Reaching up, she rubbed his beard, soft against her palm, and rested her forehead against his. "Thank you."

There was a rustling behind them. Startled, Dottie turned to see Anna run up, and dramatically lay, limbs spread wide, on the edge of the blanket. One hand rested on her stomach. "*Tonio,*" she gasped, chest heaving. "I ate a lot too much."

Dottie's eyes crinkled as she laughed. "Don't you mean you ate a little bit too much?"

Leaning back onto her elbows, Anna smiled impishly. "No, because if I said a *little* too much, that'd be a lie."

Glancing at Antonio, Dottie tried to hold in the giggle, but it burst forth, leaving them all in a laughing mess. And as fast as she arrived, Anna was off again, running with her friends.

Wiping tears from her lashes, Dottie once again sought Antonio's gaze. The garden might have been lively, but silence settled heavily around them. Her finger mindlessly fidgeted with the edge of the blanket, the weave grounding her, as they both leaned in.

Dottie caught her lip between her teeth, then let it slip free. Antonio's eyes flicked to her mouth and held there.

He's going to kiss me.

Every nerve in Dottie's body hummed.

He snapped his eyes back to hers, like he just realized they were in public view. "I'm sorry, *Tesoro.*" His nose grazed hers, the softest nuzzle that made her breath falter.

Another rustling caught their attention and Antonio huffed a sigh. "Anna, if you've come—" He stopped short as he looked up. Dottie watched his jaw tense.

As she turned her attention toward the wood line, her brows furrowed. "What's wrong, Antonio?"

"I get the feeling we're being watched, but no one's there." His eyes searched the forest edge slowly. Placing a protective arm around Dottie's waist, he gently pulled her closer, angling her away from the trees. Her pulse tripped, not from Antonio's nearness this time, but from something unseen in the trees.

Clutching Antonio's arm, Dottie tried to lighten the mood. "Maybe it's Anna and the twins playing hide and seek?" Her voice wavered as she glanced toward the woods, and goosebumps erupted across her skin.

Antonio tenderly rubbed his palms up and down her arms to brush away the chills, and she fought the need to lean against his strong chest. "No. They'd never have the ability to be *that* quiet. Anna's like a bull in a china shop."

Her next question came out hushed, afraid to voice what her heart was afraid of. "Do you think it might be Charlie?"

"I don't know, *Tesoro.*" Pulling her nearer still, Antonio rested his chin on her shoulder, overlooking the party. His earthy scent wrapped around her, easing the anxiety rushing through her veins. "But what I do know is that I'll never let him near you again."

Henry's voice could be heard over the group. "Come join in for one more love song." He sent a coy glance toward Clara. "And then we clean up! Mr. Frederick here doesn't want his servants lazing about all day."

That earned a laugh from the crowd and a mock-glare from Mr. Frederick.

Dottie refused to let the afternoon end with unwarranted worry, she'd had enough of that in her life. But the niggling feeling wouldn't leave.

Something's not right.

Shuffling to a stand, she pulled Antonio to an empty spot on the lawn. "Let's dance."

The tilted smile he gave nearly undid her as his fingers intertwined with hers, bringing her close.

As Henry started bowing the ballad's first few notes, Antonio's hand hovered above the small of Dottie's back, hesitating just long enough for heat to coil in her stomach. The fiddle's notes drifted through the air.

Finally, his hand firmly pressed her closer, drawing her into his hold. They stood so close that Dottie could feel his heart thud in her chest. She curled her fingers into the soft wool of his jacket, anchoring herself to him.

Dear Lord, thank You for opening my eyes to this man who loves me like You do.

Her prayer was interrupted by Antonio's resonant voice brushing against her ear as they slowly danced. "I love you truly, truly dear..."

Dottie gave off a faint hum, letting the words wash over her heart.

Life with its sorrow, life with its tears; Fades into dreams when I feel you are near; For I love you truly, truly dear...

Chapter 22: Saturday Afternoon

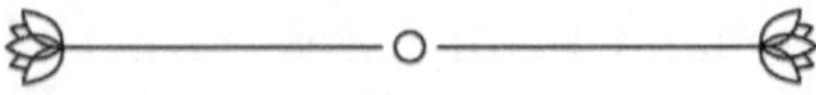

The newlyweds had set off for a short overnight honeymoon as the sun dipped past the treeline. The afternoon chill settled in the back gardens. Energetic children had spent every ounce of energy where laughter slowly transformed into yawns. Mrs. Brower herded them back to the cottages like little chicks to the roost.

A few servants lingered clearing blankets and chatting with Mr. Frederick. Dottie had taken up with Mamma cleaning up the meal and dishes.

Antonio took the opportunity to watch the two work in tandem. It was important that whomever he chose as a bride could seamlessly blend with his family. And Dottie did just that. Watching her now, her faith blooming, he could wholeheartedly pursue her. Antonio rubbed the back of his neck, full of nervous anticipation over their future.

Carrying a crate of vases with flowers, Antonio made his way toward the manor. He didn't want to leave her, still worried over the unsettled feeling from earlier, but his tasks awaited him. His steps faltered as he spotted the one man he feared had been lurking on the property.

Charlie stood at the back door, tossing an air valve in his hand, the steady toss-catch creating a tense tempo. Surely Mr. Leland wasn't interrogating him on the day of his wedding, but one never knew with the estate manager.

"Ah, just the man I wanted to see." He pitched the air valve at Antonio, causing the crate to slip, glass shattering around his feet. Charlie tsked. "Better be careful, Mr. Romano. Mrs. Stratford won't take kindly to you breaking her things."

Recognizing the bluff, Antonio wouldn't allow this man to rile him. "Why are you giving this to me, Mr. Rolston?"

Chuckling, Charlie stepped closer. "I know you're more than capable of fixing that radiator. Plus, I'd rather not be tainted by stepping foot in that wicked little thing's room."

Antonio's pulse thudded at his throat. Never one for violence, it took everything in him to not retaliate. He threw on a tense smile as a few people walked by, carrying supplies into the manor. "That won't be any trouble, Mr. Rolston, a radiator's an easy fix."

Once the passersby were out of earshot, Antonio moved closer into the man's face, his voice was low and threatening. "Don't speak about Dottie like that again."

Antonio had seen the way Dottie grew under God's love, found grace over shame. She didn't need more shadows dragged into the light—she'd carried enough of them already. God had redeemed her, nothing else mattered.

Charlie paced back, hands held up in defense. "You don't need to worry about me, she's *all* yours, and all her mess too." But the smirk on his face said he was more amused than frightened.

"Excuse me." Maria brushed by, carrying a tea tray toward the formal gardens.

Must be Mrs. Stratford, best I avoid dealing with her today.

"Why, hello beautiful." Charlie's voice dripped with a charm that made Antonio want to gag, while trailing behind the unsuspecting parlor maid.

I should probably warn Maria about him.

While Antonio bent over to clean the shattered glass, Dottie walked past carrying an armful of trays, followed by a solemn Katie. "Oh, goodness, Antonio. Let me set these inside and fetch the broom and bin." The back door groaned as she scurried by.

Though he'd only been away from Dottie for a little while since the wedding, for him it had felt like hours, and he was intent on savoring the time while he could.

He quickly searched the area. The infuriating repair man took a path on the other side of the expansive grounds. He didn't want Charlie, or anyone, interrupting the short moment he'd have with Dottie.

Antonio's attention caught as the back door creaked open again. Dottie carried a broom across her shoulder. Taking it from her, his fingers briefly grazed her shoulder, the contact sparking under his touch. For a heartbeat, they stood, fondly smiling at one another, until Katie came through the door, nearly knocking Dottie over.

"I'm so sorry, Dottie!" She glanced back toward the kitchen, as if looking for an escape. The expression she gave was almost like a signal or warning, with exaggerated widened eyes that quickly settled into a dull stare. Her fingers twisted nervously in her apron.

Brushing off her apron, Dottie turned. "It's fine, I was a bit distracted and had blocked the entrance." With a small smile, she cut a quick glance to Antonio. He wanted to return her affection, but something about Katie made him pause. His nerves once again ratcheted up, wondering about the girl's odd behavior. Why did he feel like something terrible is going to happen? *What's she not saying?*

Dottie's expression faltered, and Antonio could have kicked himself for making her worry about his affection. He immediately held her wrist, drawing circles on the soft space under her sleeve. A quick shiver run up Dottie's arm. He was rewarded with her cheeks blooming an endearing pink hue.

Clara slipped around Katie. "Well, are we all just standing here? Or are we going to help clean up the back gardens?"

With her normal timidness gone, she pulled Katie's sleeve, encouraging her to follow. "Right. Yes." Katie hesitated a moment, and then went down the path with Clara. Antonio could have sworn the chambermaid winked at Dottie.

I thought the girl was bashful, but clearly she's gotten close with Dottie.

"Hey Dottie," Antonio pulled her close. "Was anyone else in the kitchen a moment ago?"

Tilting her head, Dottie thought for a moment. "No, just Katie, Clara, and me. Why?"

Something didn't feel right, but Antonio wasn't sure what. "Nothing. Let's gather the broken glass."

Once every scrap of glass was off the ground, Antonio gave Dottie a brief kiss to the temple, reluctant to let her go. With a flushed face, she headed off to help Mamma.

I'll get to see her later. It's fine.

The bucket of glass clinked against his leg as he walked toward the shed. Not far off he could hear Mrs. Stratford and Charlie sharing unimportant gossip with Mrs. Van Buren. The man's voice carried like he was making some important announcement, leaving the older women twittering with laughter.

Antonio had every intention of ignoring the chatter, but curiosity won out as he peeked over the hedge.

Their table was set beneath a pergola. Its posts were crafted with the finest stone, holding up weathered pine beams tangled with ivy and climbing roses, whose blossoms nodded in the breeze. Bits of white paint faded along the aged pines.

Another task to add to the list.

A robin had built its nest on one of the beams, and Antonio couldn't help but think it would be quite the scene if the bird made a mess of Mrs. Stratford's fine tea service.

His daydream was interrupted by footsteps, light and small behind him. Stopping mid-step, he waited.

"Antonio," Katie's voice hissed. The girl had ducked down so her head was below the bushes. "You need to go back." Her voice shook as she spoke.

Bending down to her hiding spot, Antonio noticed the sweat gathering along her temple. "Katie, shouldn't you be in the back gardens helping?"

"Shhh. They'll hear us." She grabbed his arm and squeezed, nails digging into his skin.

Fear of getting caught in a compromising position had Antonio taking a step back. "Katie, what's going on?"

And then he heard a creaking just beyond the hedge.

The pergola.

"I've got to go." His footsteps swiftly carried him toward the noise, ignoring Katie's pleads as she staggered behind him.

When he rounded the bend, the pergola shifted above Mrs. Stratford's head. The pillar groaned under the weight of the beams. Katie grabbed hold of his arm. "We gotta leave here!"

With determination to reach the pergola before it fell, yanked his arm away. He paused, spotting Timothy next to a pillar, holding something that fit the palm of his hand.

The shim.

The foolish footman had pulled out the shim that held everything up.

Spotting Antonio, Mrs. Stratford shrilled, "How dare you barge in during my tea time!" Her shouting startled

Timothy and he panicked, hastily throwing the shim into the shrubs.

Overhead, a loud shuddering could be heard. The ground shook, robins scattering from their perch. For a second, the footman's grin froze, not from guilt, perhaps, but from the sudden knowledge of how badly things could have gone.

"Everyone out, now! It's going to fall!" Antonio drew Mrs. Stratford up by her arm, while Charlie whisked Mrs. Van Buren out of the way. Maria gawked, staring at the leaning beams. "Maria, run!" He snatched her wrist just before the first stone from the compromised pillar fell.

The air split with a sharp crack, the scent of dust and crushed pine filling his lungs. Ivy tore from its lattice with a hiss like paper ripping.

Antonio twisted around in search of Timothy, but the man had disappeared with the floating dust.

"Tesoro," Mrs. Carmela called while carrying three empty tins, the aroma of delicious lemon cookies still rising from them. "Where is Katie? She's run off again!" The chef jostled the tins, trying to arrange them in a comfortable position. "Please, go find her."

The space had quieted since the festivities died down as everyone went back to their posts. A small peace settled through the back gardens. Dottie glanced up, searching the lawn. A gray work dress swished just out of sight, past the hedge, toward the formal gardens. "I think I see where she went. I'll go fetch her."

"Thank you, dear." Mrs. Carmela ambled up the path, tins rattling with each sway of her hips.

Turning toward the formal gardens, Dottie let out a sigh. "When will she stop running off?"

But something shifted. The air brimmed in anticipation. Birds quieted and the branches stilled. Her legs pushed her faster toward the hedge, she wasn't sure why, but she could feel trouble stirring.

And then Dottie heard it. Something heavy rumbled in the direction Katie had gone. Rushing faster toward the sound, she prayed, "*Lord, please let it not be Antonio." He's been through so much, let him be safe.*

Rounding the corner, her feet tripped over a lump, landing her in a patch of gravel, bruising her knee.

Well, I suppose I'll be scrubbing tonight.

Huddled against a bush sat Timothy. He held the side of his temple, a small trickle of blood leaking through his fingers. Before she could ask what happened, Antonio's voice yelled out, tense and in charge. "Everyone out, now! It's going to fall!"

Her knees ached as she rose from the ground. Standing on her tiptoes, Dottie peered over the boxwood to find the pergola shifting dangerously as Antonio and Charlie pulled people from beneath. "Oh, my goodness." Just as Antonio moved Maria out of the way, the pillar and beams collapsed in a dusty mess. Glancing over, she noticed Mrs. Stratford fanning herself as if on the verge of fainting.

Antonio whirled frantically around. Dottie watched in confusion. "What's he looking for?"

"Me."

Timothy growled in her ear. His voice was cold and menacing enough to shake her.

"You?" Dottie turned, eyes wide, to find Timothy's hands raised above his head, holding a small prybar. She tried backing away, forgetting the hedge had her blocked in. The branches bit into her back and snagged her hair.

He's going to hit me.

Her lips trembled at the thought, but there was no way to dodge the blow.

"Excuse me. I'll be taking that." Mr. Frederick's tall form loomed over Timothy, snatching the metal from his hands. "While I appreciate zealous employees, I don't take kindly to my staff harming others." Handing Dottie the prybar, Mr. Frederick snatched Timothy's hands behind his back.

The cold tool felt heavy in Dottie's hand. She wasn't quite sure what she was supposed to do with it, except wait for Mr. Frederick to request it back.

"Miss DeGrout, are you all right?" Mr. Frederick gave her a leveled stare.

With all that happened, she decided it was best to fake her well-being, not wanting to distract from the troubling situation at hand. She slowly set the prybar on the ground. "Yes, quite fine. Just concerned about that." She pointed toward the now destroyed pergola.

"Tesoro!" Antonio ran up, pulling her into an embrace. His mouth found her cheek as he whispered into her ear. "Why are you here? It's not safe." For the briefest moment, his hand grazed her stomach, protective and warm. It fluttered wildly at the intimate touch. The solace she found in his hold brought her immediate relief.

He's worried about the baby.

Her heart thundered behind her ribs. It wasn't even his child, yet he cared just the same.

Wanting to show him she was fine, she put on a brave face. She hoped to distract him from the blazing heat in her cheeks. Dottie pressed her hands against his chest and smiled. "I'm fine. We're fine." Nodding toward Mr. Frederick, who still held Timothy prisoner, she added, "Help came at the perfect time."

Trying to free his hands, Timothy mumbled to himself, "A little too perfect if you ask me."

By now a crowd had gathered around them, speaking in hushed tones. Even Mrs. Stratford seemed to recover, looking quite flushed.

"You're right, Timothy." Mr. Frederick gave a stilted laugh. "Mr. West and I have been watching you, waiting for the moment you'd slip up."

Everyone turned to him with surprise. "You see, Mr. Brooks, a little birdie let slip that you were causing trouble. Actually, it was one of her letters, where she described stunning blue eyes and asked that you release her from assisting with the mischief you were causing." He shook his head, glancing toward the crowd.

Dottie's eyes followed his stare as Katie let out a small squeak, trying to tuck herself behind the group. It was all too much as Dottie tried keeping up with the unfolding information.

Jutting his chin toward Katie, Timothy growled. "It was her idea! Said since Antonio didn't like her, she wanted to get even!"

Antonio's arms tightened around Dottie's waist, as if anticipating an attack.

"What!?" Katie came stalking out from the midst of the group. "Me?!" She shoved her finger in his chest. "You're the one who claimed Antonio wasn't deserving of all that praise he got, and if I didn't help, you'd tell everyone about—about.... my secret." Her voice softened at the last words.

Dottie was baffled.

What secret could she possibly have that was worse than being unwed and pregnant?

Timothy's laugh was chilling, more from grief than anger. "You mean the fact that you're married and your gullible husband out there maintaining tracks has been sending you money thinking you're due any day?" He scoffed. "And then you've been over here flirting with every man who has a pulse." He pushed his shoulder toward Dottie, wincing as Mr. Frederick held him tight. "You're as bad as she is!"

Everyone quieted, watching the quarrel brew. Dottie slowly pieced the details together.

No wonder she had those new clothes.

"You imbecile! You promised you'd not say a word if I helped you, and I did, didn't I?" She started pacing. "I got you the tools. Hid your evidence. And what do I get? You blabbing to everyone!"

Timothy glared at the girl. "And you promised me that I was the only man for you! I gave you so many gifts!"

Katie sobered and glanced at Dottie. Understanding flooded her mind as she reached her hand to the ornament in her hair.

He took my silver comb and gifted it to Katie. No wonder she looked upset.

Maria let out a sob, rushing off toward the manor without a second gland. Dottie felt that pain before. Someone was always searching for love, only for it to be crushed beneath callous feet. It seemed like heartache was a part of Skyline Manor.

But I found love in You, Jesus. And in Antonio.

"I think we've heard quite enough, don't you?" Miss Genevieve moved to the middle of the group. "Frederick, while this is all quite entertaining, maybe we could conclude this performance? The sun is beginning to set, and it seems we'll have quite the week sorting things out."

Mr. Frederick let out a muted huff. His attempt to appear stern gave way to a tilted grin, as if he secretly enjoyed the spectacle. "Miss Genevieve, thank you. Everyone, you're dismissed."

As the last murmurs faded, the gardens seemed to exhale. Dust drifted through a shaft of late sunlight, settling on overturned tea things and broken blossoms. A strange peace hovered where fear had been moments before. Dottie's gaze swept the wreckage, aching not only for what had fallen, but for what God might rebuild.

Letting out a slow breath, chest still fluttering, she was grateful the danger had passed. Or it could have been for the man beside her, still holding her.

Peeking up, she watched him carefully. As everyone departed, his eyes remained closed, slipping his arm tighter around her waist. She watched as his lips moved silently with reverence.

Realizing she was intruding on his prayers, Dottie attempted to slide away, but Antonio's grip tightened as he ended with a whisper. "Amen."

She tilted her head to the side. "What did you pray for?"

Letting out a sigh, he pulled her closer still. "I thanked the Lord for keeping you, and everyone, safe. Then for Katie and Maria's hearts." He moved a strand of hair from her cheek. "And then for Timothy. He's going to have a long, hard road, and I pray he finds God's light one day."

Her heart leapt. His care for others despite their failings was spectacular—and humbling. Lifting onto her toes, she placed a kiss on his cheek. "Thank you."

This man. This fine, stunning man.

Chapter 23: Sunday

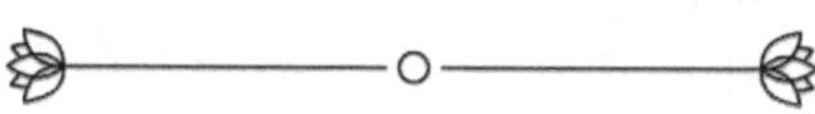

The cufflink sat beside Dottie's vase of flowers; she hadn't worn it in days. Fingering the sparkling keepsake, she realized she could finally let go of the memory of a man who never loved her. No, she found love in a much stronger way. In a man who cared for and pursued her, a family who loved her even at her lowest, and a God who treasured her.

Dottie's lips curved upward. No longer in frayed clothes, no longer living in shame. Putting on her shoes, she thought back to the night before.

It was a strange quiet in the halls. No pattering of shoes or creaking floorboards. The maids had ceased their whispering gossip and even the grandfather clock's ticks seemed distant. Katie had been sent to pack her things. And though Mr. Frederick was a merciful employer, he had no patience for servants who would aid in harming others.

Dottie knocked, but after a moment of silence, she gently pushed open the door. Katie sat on her bed, tears streaming down, her red-rimmed eyes clinging onto Dottie's. "I'm so, so sorry." Burying her face into her hands, she sobbed like a girl broken. "I didn't mean for it to go that far!" The scene tugged somewhere deep in Dottie's heart.

Adjusting her blanket on her bed, she remembered a similar night, not so long ago, when she'd sat, broken in the same manner, drowning in shame, when Mae had reached across the valley with mercy instead of judgment.

Finding a spot next to the girl, Dottie laid an arm around her shoulders. "Look at me. Do you think I meant for all my mistakes to get out of hand?" Shaking her head, she laughed. "We're human. We sin. We make mistakes. The question is, what's next?"

Dottie strolled down the corridor. Never in her life did she think she'd be discipling another person, yet there was doing just that.

She pulled Katie's hands from her face. "You can choose to wallow in this self-pity, or you can see yourself as God sees you, ask for His forgiveness, and follow His call on your life."

"I-I don't know..." Katie's shoulders slumped. "I doubt my husband will be so forgiving."

"Only one way to find out, Katie dear. Be brave, be honest, and do better."

Dottie drew the girl into an embrace. "Do you want help packing?" Katie's arms had wrapped tightly around Dottie like an anchor. Her voice was soft. "Yes, please."

The memory broke away to light laughter from the kitchen. As always, the bottom step groaned in protest.

Edith stood, wearing a deep emerald dress Dottie had never seen before. It made Edith's green eyes pop and honey blonde hair stand out. The dress was made of simple cotton, but the bodice was fitted, and the cut looked elegant. Her spine was straight with her chin lifted high, as Clara tittered in the corner.

It struck Dottie how, though Edith still came off stiff and guarded, something was softening in the woman, and she couldn't wait to watch her flourish!

"Miss Edith, you look stunning. What's the occasion?" Dottie walked over, while eyeing the dress.

Edith's ears pinked but she didn't respond, until Clara came up beside them, grabbing Dottie's hands, softly whispering, "She's coming to church with us! Isn't that wonderful?" Clara's enthusiasm was infectious, and Dottie's beamed.

"It is! But Mae might feel slighted if she missed this grand event!" She passed a mischievous smile at Edith. "You were trying to avoid her nagging on your first visit, weren't you?"

Edith swallowed, her throat bobbing. With a cough, she finally found her voice. "And don't you dare go gossiping about me either. Let's just get going before the Romano's think we've left without them." She rushed to the door, throwing her shawl across her shoulders.

Sunbeams streamed through white clouds, dappling through the tree branches. Everything budded with bright green leaves that swayed in the breeze.

The three maids walked toward the cottages, happy to meet with the rest of the family.

My family.

Dottie's smile widened as she watched Rose and Violet dart out their door, while Mrs. Brower called after them. Mrs. Carmela snuggled close to her husband. Vincent dramatically rolled his eyes as the girls darted around the group.

And then there was Antonio, standing off to the side. He beheld her as if she were something precious, tender, and beyond description.

"Good morning, *Tesoro*."

Just as Dottie reached for his offered arm, Antonio surprised her by entwining their fingers and guiding her into an embrace, earning the lightest laugh from her lips. "I've missed you."

Lavender drifted from Mrs. Carmela's porch, mixing with his earthy scent of tilled soil. The world itself seemed to breathe again.

Tilting back to view him better, Dottie grinned. "You saw me only yesterday."

"*Si*', but that was still far too long." He traced his finger along the ridge of her nose. Despite the rough pad of his finger, it felt gentle across her skin.

Her eyes drifted shut for a moment, sinking into the sensation of a man who adored her.

Thank you, Lord, for opening my eyes to what real love is.

She felt his lips glide over her brow. As his thumb lifted her chin, his breath swept across her cheek. Savoring the moment, she kept her lids closed.

"I love you, *Tesoro*."

Lifting on her toes, Dottie wrapped her arms around Antonio's neck, pulling him closer. She could feel his breath hovering just above her lips, his beard scratching lightly at her chin. Everything hummed and her chest fluttered. Just as he closed in with the lightest of kisses, someone *tsk*ed.

"If you two don't come on, we'll be late!" Mrs. Carmela called out, a warm laugh lifting her voice. "No point lingering, Antonio. The Lord's patient, but I'm not!"

Antonio let out a chuckle against her lips, causing her mouth to draw into a wide smile. Dottie tugged his sleeve, turning to follow the group. "We should probably go."

Taking the path, hands interlaced, she no longer carried the weight of the past. Antonio's love, a caring family, and a God who called her beloved. This was enough.

Valebrook Baptist Church rose over the hill. It's chipped paint gleaming in the early sun. As the bell tolled that service was soon to begin, birds flew from the belfry, their startled chirps filling the air.

Small forsythia bushes blazed with little yellow flowers, welcoming those who graced the old, wooden steps. As the doors opened, the scent of flowers and candles lingered from the day before.

Neighbors greeted each other, children ran about, and little old ladies sat in the corner solving all the world's problems.

The Skyline Estate family filled their pew, the old wood groaning under their weight. Antonio smiled down at Dottie, happily tucked by his side.

They were squeezed in so tightly, that his leg pressed against hers. Opening his hand, he waited for Dottie to place hers in his. When she accepted, tingles traveled up to his heart.

Miss Betsy started the first hymn, and Antonio worshiped with his whole self. He never realized how special it would feel to stand with the one he loved while praising God. It was a delight to hear Dottie's voice mingle with his. In the harmony, Antonio heard the sound of promises kept.

Pastor Somers stepped up to the pulpit. "Beloved, we do not need to live in fear of what tomorrow may bring. The Lord has planted each of us where we are, and He does not abandon His children. Scripture tells us, 'For I know the thoughts that I think toward you, saith the LORD, thoughts of peace, and not of evil, to give you an expected end.' Let us rest in that promise. Whatever trials may come, God has already gone before us, and He will hold us fast."

The words sank deeper than Antonio expected. He'd faced men's lies, fire, even death's shadow, and through it all, the unseen hand of God had steadied him. Even when things pressed in, he had no reason to doubt the Lord's plans.

Peeking down, he saw a tear glisten on Dottie's lash.

Thank You, Lord, for letting me be a part of her hope.

Reaching over to brush away the drop, Antonio bent close, his nose nuzzling above her ear. "You're my future, *Tesoro*. You and the *bambino*."

Dottie's chest caught. As she turned, her temple brushed against his. And he could feel her breath feather across his beard.

And then an elbow landed in his ribs. His Papà's voice was quiet but firm. "You keep that up, and we'll have to switch this from worship to wedding."

Antonio chuckled as Dottie's eyes widened.

"No need to rush... we've only just begun. But soon, *Tesoro*, soon."

She gave the slightest nod, meeting his gaze, and answered with a whispered, "Yes."

He knew that *yes* was her answer to his unspoken proposal. One day soon, before God and family, he'd claim that *yes* with a vow, and a kiss she'd never have to question.

Your plans, Lord; I'll trust them.

The story continues...
Keep an eye out for the next novel in the Secrets of Skyline collection.

Join my newsletter to be the first to hear when it releases.

Secrets of Skyline

Book 1: Where Warmth Waits: Mae
Book 2: Where Grace Grows: Dottie
Book 3: Coming Summer 2026

Mrs. Carmela's Sausage Frittatas

Ingredients (serves 4–6)
6 large eggs
½ cup milk
½–¾ cup cooked breakfast sausage, crumbled
1 small onion, finely chopped
¼ cup green pepper or celery, chopped
½ cup shredded cheddar cheese
Salt & pepper
1–2 tbsp butter

Instructions

- Preheat oven to **350°F**.
- Cook sausage in a skillet and set aside.
- In the same skillet, melt butter and sauté onion and pepper until soft.
- Beat eggs with milk, salt, and pepper. Stir in cheese, sausage, and vegetables.
- Pour into a greased oven-safe skillet or baking dish.
- Bake for **20–25 minutes**, until set and slightly golden.

Taylor Ham, Egg & Cheese — the NJ Classic

Ingredients
3–4 slices Taylor Ham (pork roll)
1 egg (fried or scrambled)
1–2 slices American cheese
1 hard roll (Kaiser roll), sliced
Butter (optional)

Instructions

- Score the Taylor Ham **slices** (3–4 small slits around edge) so they cook flat. *(Otherwise, they roll-up)*
- Cook the slices in a skillet until browned on both sides. Fry the egg to your preference.
- Layer Taylor Ham, egg, and cheese on the roll. Add butter if desired, assemble, and serve warm.

About the Author

A wife and mom trying her best, with God's help. Terri Rosa Fox is a self-proclaimed "jack-of-all-trades" who finds joy in art, photography, crafting, and storytelling. From children's tales to historical romance, her work is grounded in a love for God's creation and the quiet strength of everyday moments.

Find more of my titles at:

www.amazon.com/author/terrirosafox

terrifoxcreatives.com

www.ingramcontent.com/pod-product-compliance
Lightning Source LLC
LaVergne TN
LVHW090513110826
845146LV00003B/841

* 9 7 9 8 9 9 3 5 3 4 8 1 7 *